Praise for The *Oddling Prince*

A *Publishers Weekly* Top-Ten Spring Science Fiction, Fantasy and Horror Pick

"In *The Oddling Prince*, Nancy Springer has written a small, perfect epic, three words I did not think could ever live well together. And yet here it is: romantic, heroic, moving, satisfying—and not an overblown farrago of words. Read it—and believe."
—Jane Yolen, author of *The Emerald Circus* and *The Devil's Arithmetic*

"*The Oddling Prince* is Nancy Springer at her very best. If you don't know her work—which seems most unlikely—*The Oddling Prince* is the perfect place to start!"
—Peter S. Beagle, author of *Summerlong*

"In *The Oddling Prince*, Nancy Springer juggles the tropes of fantasy and folklore with skill and wit, exploring kingship, brotherhood, friendship and heroism of many kinds while telling a story that kept me up far too late finding out what was going to happen next to characters I really cared about."
—Delia Sherman, author of *Changeling*

"Lyrical and lovely, *The Oddling Prince* feels both fresh and like a classic ballad that's been part of the English canon for centuries."
—Sarah Beth Durst, author of the Queens of Renthia series

"This very well could end up being my favorite book of the year. 5/5 stars."
—*Way Too Fantasy*

"What a thrilling yarn! Fast-moving, full of surprises, and yet infinitely satisfying. Every time you think you know what's

going to happen Springer pulls a new but perfect rabbit out of the hat. *The Oddling Prince* is one of those great books that'll be reread over and over again."
—Brenda W. Clough, author of *How Like A God* and *A Most Dangerous Woman*

"*The Oddling Prince* is fantasy at its best. Lyrical prose, memorable characters, and a haunting story bring to life the never-were worlds of Calidon and Otherland. Filled with magic, fabulous horses, swordplay, and treachery—at its core, *The Oddling Prince* is about the power of love. This skillfully wrought novel reminds readers of why Nancy Springer is one of our top fantasy writers. A must-read book!"
—Vonnie Winslow Crist, author of *The Enchanted Dagger*

"I loved this so much. It felt a bit like Juliet Marillier's stories with the peaceful pacing, fae elements, vibrant medieval Celtic setting, and very little violence. 5/5 stars."
—*A Page with a View*

Praise for Nancy Springer

"Ms. Springer's work is outstanding in the field."
—Andre Norton

"[Nancy Springer is] someone special in the fantasy field."
—Anne McCaffrey

"Nancy Springer writes like a dream."
—*St. Louis Post-Dispatch*

"Nancy Springer is a treasure."
—Ellen Kushner, author of *Swordspoint*

"Nancy Springer's kind of writing is the kind that makes you

want to run out, grab people on the street, and tell them to go find her book immediately and read them, all of them."
—*The Salem News*

On *Fair Peril*

"An exuberant and funny feminist fairy tale."
—*Lambda Book Report*

"Moving, eloquent . . . *Fair Peril* is modern/timeless storytelling at its best, both enchanting and very down-to-earth."
—*Locus*

On *Larque On The Wing*

"Satisfying and illuminating . . . an off-the-wall contemporary fantasy that refuses to fit any of the normal boxes."
—*Asimov's Science Fiction*

"Irresistible . . . a winning, precisely rendered foray into magic realism."
—*Kirkus*

On *Chains of Gold*

"Fantasy as its finest."
—*Romantic Times*

On *I Am Morgan le Fay*

"Nancy Springer has created a world of beauty and terror, of hard reality and dazzling magic."
—Lloyd Alexander, author of *The Book of Three*

Selected Books by Nancy Springer

Series

Book of the Isle
The White Hart (1979)
The Book of Suns (1977;
expanded as *The Silver Sun*,
1980)
The Sable Moon (1981)
The Black Beast (1982)
The Golden Swan (1983)

Sea King
Madbond (1987)
Mindbond (1987)
Godbond (1988)

Tales from Camelot
I Am Mordred (1998)
I Am Morgan le Fay (2001)

Tales of Rowan Hood
*Rowan Hood: Outlaw Girl of
Sherwood Forest* (2001)
Lionclaw (2002)
*Outlaw Princess of
Sherwood* (2003)
Wild Boy (2004)
Rowan Hood Returns (2005)

The Enola Holmes Mysteries
*The Case of the Missing
Marquess* (2006)
*The Case of the Left-Handed
Lady* (2007)
*The Case of the Bizarre
Bouquets* (2008)
*The Case of the Peculiar Pink
Fan* (2008)
*The Case of the Cryptic
Crinoline* (2009)
*The Case of the Gypsy Good-
bye* (2010)

Standalone novels
Wings of Flame (1985)
Chains of Gold (1986)
A Horse to Love (1987)
The Hex Witch of Seldom (1988)
Not on a White Horse (1988)
Apocalypse (1989)
*They're All Named
Wildfire* (1989)
Red Wizard (1990)
Colt (1991)
Damnbanna (1992)
The Friendship Song (1992)
The Great Pony Hassle (1993)
The Boy on a Black Horse (1994)
Larque on the Wing (1994)

Metal Angel (1994)
Toughing It (1994)
Fair Peril (1996)
Looking for Jamie Bridger (1996)
Secret Star (1997)
Sky Rider (1999)
Plumage (2000)
Needy Creek (2001)
Separate Sisters (2001)
Blood Trail (2003)
Lionclaw (2004)
Dusssie (2007)
Somebody (2009)
Possessing Jessie (2010)
Dark Lie (2012)
My Sister's Stalker (2012)
Drawn into Darkness (2013)

Short Fiction
Chance and Other Gestures of the Hand of Fate (1987)
Stardark Songs (1993)

As editor
Prom Night (1999)
Ribbiting Tales (2000)

THE
Oddling
Prince

NANCY
SPRINGER

TACHYON | SAN FRANCISCO

Cover art "Warrior Heart" Copyright © 2011 by Brian Giberson
Cover and interior design by Elizabeth Story

Tachyon Publications LLC
1459 18th Street #139
San Francisco, CA 94107
www.tachyonpublications.com
tachyon@tachyonpublications.com

Series Editor: Jacob Weisman
Project Editor: Jill Roberts

Print ISBN: 978-1-61696-289-0

Digital ISBN: 978-1-61696-290-6

Printed in the United States by Worzalla

First Edition: 2018
9 8 7 6 5 4 3 2 1

To Oddlings Everywhere.

CHAPTER THE FIRST

S PIRITS COAXED AND CALLED, sang and sighed in the wind outside the benighted tower where I sat beside my dying father, the king. The *king*! Six feet tall, golden bearded, and strong as a bear, but struck down in his prime by—by a visible mystery. On the third finger of his left hand glowed the uncanny thing, the ring, its own fey light enough to show me my mother's still, white-clad form on the other side of the bed.

How the ring had come on to my father's hand, no one could fathom. Only a month ago, on a fair spring day when the furze bloomed yellow and the thistles raised their crimson heads, we had gone a-hawking, he and I and our retainers, to the hills high above the sea. The hawks had flown well, so that we each carried a brace of grouse or hare slung from our saddles. But that afternoon as we rode homeward down ferny glens, the king, my father, had noticed the ring shining, no color, all colors, on his hand. We had all halted to gaze upon it and exclaim over it and wonder at it, for when he tried to slip it off to show it to us, it would not heed his touch or obey his will. It stayed where it was like a scar. And how it had come to be there, on the finger nearest his heart, he knew not, nor did any of us.

How or why it had sickened him, no one knew either. But since that day, he had not been able to eat, or sleep, and fever burned him away from within, until now, four short weeks later, he lay gaunt and senseless. Many men, strong and wise, had tried to remove the ring, with unguents, with spells, by main force, but it would not stir from his finger. To cut the finger off, to mutilate the personage of the king, would have doomed some portion of Calidon, his kingdom, to be hacked away, destroyed by the barbaric Tartan tribes ever threatening from the Craglands. This could not be. Yet for some reason no one knew, the ring had doomed the king.

My father. How could he lie dying?

Wait!

I sprang to my feet, snatching up a candle for better light, and yes! For the first time in many a day, my father had opened his eyes. And he looked straight at me. But those were not the brave bright eyes I knew; their blue was like shadows on snow.

"Bard?" Mother called to him by her pet name for him.

His dim gaze shifted to her. "My true love," he said in a voice that seemed to echo from a great distance, "it is time. Only let me touch once more your face."

She pushed her white head drapery back over her shoulder, knelt beside him, and lifted his hand—for he had no strength to do it himself—she lifted his right hand to her face, and kissed it, and laid it against the flowing seal-brown hair at her temple.

Then I understood that this was the lucid interval sometimes granted to great men before their—death. . . .

Such a rebel storm surged within me that it thundered in my ears. I snatched up my father's hand lying inert outside the bedclothes that swaddled him to his neck. With both hands, I seized the ring and pulled. I could feel the ring's glowering heat and its sullen, mocking defiance as I tugged, tugged, without moving it an iota. Cursing it, I strained against it to the utmost, and it flickered like small lightning, stinging my fingers as if in warning of what it could do to me if I persisted. I gasped, yet gripped all the harder—

"Aric, no!" my father's faraway voice commanded. "Will it help us if the freakish thing takes you too?"

I ceased the struggle yet still held his hand. "But this cannot be," I cried. "You cannot leave! Your throne, your people, we need you!"

Many folk adored him, but none so much as I. Perhaps a few minds within the castle were sufficiently scheming to think that I, his only son—indeed, his only living child—had somehow done this thing, so that I, a mere youth seventeen years of age, could take his throne in his stead. But if they thought such evil, they were sorely wrong. I knew myself unready to succeed him. A prince I was, yes, but in looks no more than passable—no comelier or taller than most men— and in prowess, no better with sword or lance or horses or—or anything. I had quested nowhere, had wooed no true love, I was—I felt myself nothing compared to my father. I loved him. I would have given anything, anything, my own fingers cut off, to make him well and strong again.

"Aric," he bespoke me gently, "you are my beloved son and my living pride. It is hard, but you will do—"

Do what, I never knew, for even louder than the keening of the wind around the tower rose cries from the courtyard below, the shouts of guards and, worse, the screams of men in terror, warriors who would face battle-axes without a whimper now shrieking fit to tear their throats out.

"It's Death come in," moaned one of my mother's hand-women from the shadows at the back of the room.

"Hush," my mother told her.

"Invaders," Father muttered. "Bastard Domberk can't wait till I die. Aric—"

I gripped his hand hard, dropped it, and ran out of the room, for lacking the king's leadership, all the castle was my responsibility. At breakneck speed I leapt down the tower steps, through the great hall and out toward the courtyard's torch-lit darkness.

But I halted on the wide stone steps of the keep, struck dumb by the sight before me.

A rider. On horseback.

Only one single rider and horse.

But they were such a rider and such a horse as no mortal had ever seen.

In the middle of the courtyard, the rider and his horse stood like a great alabaster statue surrounded by a multitude of pale ovals, the frightened faces of guards and soldiers with their swords out, or their pikes raised, or their bows with arrows nocked to the drawn strings. Yet he, the horseback rider, sat at ease among them as if on a coracle floating amid water lilies.

A slim youth. Perhaps no older than I.

He drew no weapon.

His hands stirred not from the reins.

He gazed straight ahead of him as if in a dream.

He and his milk-white steed, both horse and rider far too

beautiful to belong to this mortal world, shone in the night. They glimmered head to foot as if they carried moonlight within them.

My neck hairs prickled at the sight. My heart halted like my feet, like my staring face, and for a moment I felt as if it might stop entirely. But I could not weaken; a king's son is not permitted to weaken, ever. With all the force of my father's authority, I shouted at the guards and soldiers. "Hold! Fall back!" I commanded. "Would you attack one who offers you no harm?" For the honor of my father's hospitality was at stake, be the visitor mortal or—or otherwise.

Only too willing to fall back, still the men-at-arms did not lower their weapons. And they continued to cry out, "It's fey!" "Uncanny!" ". . . across the moat treading on top of the water, through the iron of the portcullis and the wood of the gate . . ." "It's not of this world. Belike it's Death!"

If it were death, then fair was the face of death. When I took command, the stranger shifted his gaze to me, and I could have fallen to my knees, for I looked into the face of a god, an angel, I was terrified—yet in the depths of his brilliant eyes, I thought I saw something of need, even of yearning.

I, Aric son of Bardaric, I must be strong. Forcing myself to hold my head high, I stepped forward onto the circle of cobbles that had opened around the visitant, I walked to him, I stood by the shoulder of his lambent, swan-necked steed. "If you come in peace, then welcome, stranger, whoever you may be," I told him, looking up into his—handsome is too weak a word—into his glorious face. "Welcome to Dun Caltor. I am Aric of Caltor."

"And I am called Albaric. Prince Aric," he replied, his voice low yet so surpassingly resonant that it silenced the shrieking of the onlookers and even of the wind, "I would speak with King Bardaric, your father, if I may."

"The king lies dying." Somehow I said these words steadily, watching the fey rider's luminous face.

He swallowed hard, stroking his steed's thick white mane as if for comfort; although calm, he seemed much moved. "I thought so, yet I hoped not," he said when he could speak. "I must go to him at once. If I alight, will you take me to him?"

"Perhaps, provided you mean him no harm."

"I intend for him all good. Will you take me to him at once? Before I alight, I need your promise."

I gazed into his eyes for a moment, and even though my heart still quivered in terror—no, in awe—I sensed greatest honor there. I judged, decided, and nodded. "I will take you to him. You have my promise."

At the moment I said it, the great white steed snorted, pawed the cobbles so that sparks flew, and reared straight up, giving forth such a blaze of light that shouts and screams alarmed the night once more, my eyes winced, I stepped back, and when I looked again, the horse was gone as if it had never been, leaving behind yet greater hubbub in the courtyard.

And Albaric.

For Albaric remained. Glowing all over with a whisper of white light, he stood on the cobbles, levelly facing me; we were of the same height. He wore a plain, unadorned tunic, leggings and boots, yet stood like a lord of Othergates, even while something in his gaze implored me as if he were a waif.

I could barely find my voice. "Come with me," I whispered, beckoning, and with awareness of his presence prickling in the skin of my back, I led him up the wide stone steps into the keep.

chapter the second

"**D**OES FATHER YET LIVE?" I demanded, entering the tower room where the king lay, where in the dark rafters hung the shadow of death.

"Yes. But he has closed his eyes." My mother spoke with quiet dignity even as she sat with her white head-linen trailing and held Father's right hand, the one without the ring. In the bed, his face wasted to the bone and nearly as white as my mother's linen, my father seemed lifeless to me, like a carving of stone. My mother's handwomen huddled in the back of the room. All were so silent that I could hear my father gasp for each shallow, struggling breath.

Or they were silent until I walked in, Albaric a step behind me. But at their first sight of him, they shrieked and cowered, pressing their backs to the wall, the whites of their eyes like hollow moons, their faces contorted—I could see them, for Albaric's fey glow lit the dim room like a sconce of candles. And in that white light, the black death hanging overhead showed too plainly, a bat-winged, faceless enormity far larger than the tower, oozing through the stonework.

But my mother did not scream, and she moved only to turn her head, looking at me and at the strange visitor I had brought with me.

Albaric did not seem to hear the whimpering women or see my mother, nor did he cower under the canopy of death. His gaze had sped straight to my father's wan face. One stride, and he folded to his knees at the bedside, grasping the king's doomed, ringed hand in one of his own; with the other, he snatched something out of his tunic. Some sort of strand or thread; one could barely glimpse it in the weird light, but by his motions, it was plain to see what he did. He tied the filament around my father's finger between the ring and my father's heart. And then he began to wind it around my father's finger in the same place, again and again and again ringing my father's finger with this invisible thread behind the ring, and as if his motions had set a trance on those who watched, all the room grew silent, a silence as of bated breath.

Gradually the thread must have built until it began to force the ring from my father's hand, for the ring fought back furiously, blazing blood red and as bright as fire, striking out with swords of light. But it could not sting Albaric as it had done me, for he never touched it; he only wound and wound and wound the thread behind it—the filament so fine I could not see it—the uncanny strand that seemingly the ring could neither burn nor resist, for slowly, flaring blue darts of fury, so slowly that at first I could not be certain—perhaps I was only wishing it—no, truly the ring began to move.

I gasped, blinked, continued to gaze, and yes, yes! The ring—surely it moved.

And the thread with which Albaric forced it to move, that strand of wonder seemed never to cease, for he brought it forth, circling, circling, circling behind the ring to make it lose its clutch and creep, a frightening lambent thing slower than any snail, away from the flickering remnants of my father's life. The ring's smooth encircling band turned all ice-blue fire, then poison green, then a horrible black light I cannot begin to describe or explain. It was, I think, in extremis at that point, for Albaric lifted my father's hand and the ring fell off. We all saw it fall. We all heard it clatter to the planking of the floor somewhere.

Albaric sank back on his heels and spoke for the first time, sounding exhausted. "Let no one touch it." And in that moment, as the ring fell, his light went out. Moon glory silvered him no more. He crouched in the shadow beside the bed, still fairer than any mortal youth had ever been, but otherwise ordinary now, a tired stripling in a woolen tunic and leggings.

But the darkest shadow, the faceless black shadow overhead, had withdrawn.

And my father took a deep breath, stirred in what had been his deathbed, and opened his eyes—this time fully. Eyes that sparkled like bonny blue skies. I think everyone cried out. I know I did. My father looked quizzically into my mother's face as she bent over him, clutching both of his hands.

"What in bloody blazes is going on?" he asked.

And he sounded so much like himself, like the king before any dire thing had happened, that everyone in the room burst out laughing or crying or (speaking for myself at least) both. And Father *looked* like himself again also, the flesh lost to fever and starvation returned to him, his face firm and healthy again, his grip strong. "A wonder!" "A marvel!" "White magic!" "The most marvelous of wonders!" cried

Mother's handwomen, all astonishment and joy. Snatching up candles, they ran forth, crowding the door, jostling one another to be the first to spread the glad tidings throughout Dun Caltor.

Meanwhile, Mother answered her true love placidly, "You were sick, dear."

Only a shadow among shadows—for the room had gone very dim in the light of a few oil lamps, and quiet, the wind no longer troubling the tower—without a word Albaric crouched rewinding his thread, gathering it in until it parted from my father's finger with a tweak that made the king startle and look about him. "What was that?"

"I, Sire." Tucking the thread into his tunic, Albaric stood so that the king could see him—but why was he afraid? Unmistakably I saw him trembling like a peasant, although he stood like a lord, head high.

Father looked at him, frowning, but only because he was puzzled.

"This is he who gave you back your life," my mother said with her heart in her soft voice.

"Sire." Albaric's voice quivered like his limbs as he addressed the king. "Sire, do you not know me?"

Father gazed at him, thinking deeply, unblinking. "Such a fair youth I should remember from anywhere in this world," he said, "but I am all bewilderment. Who are you? Why have you—"

But Albaric turned away, choosing that moment to bend and search the floor, perhaps to hide his face.

There were many things I could have said, including his name. I felt for him, so I said nothing.

"It matters not." Albaric straightened, as steady as the earth now, with the fateful ring cupped in one hand. Like a living thing, it sulked in the hollow of his palm, dark and faintly glaring its own green-black glow.

At first sight of it, my father stiffened, eyebrows alarmed. "Whence came *that*?"

By way of answer, Albaric only said in a low, somber voice, "Sire, its power is great, and greatly dangerous, for it is a trickster. Command it, and it may obey you, but only as it chooses. To risk putting it onto your finger, or the finger of another, is to risk mortal peril." Lifting the ring by grasping the outside of its circle, Albaric leaned across the bed to give it to the king.

But Bardaric of Calidon did not at first accept it. Looking much shaken, he protested, "But how—why—"

"It is yours," Albaric told him. "You are the king."

Silently, Father let Albaric place the uncanny ring into his hand.

Mother started to address Albaric. "Fair youth, we owe you more than any boon can ever repay. If—"

She would have asked what we could give him, do for him, how best to bless his life. But she was interrupted as a great cackle of servant folk bustled into the tower room, bringing ale, fresh-baked oat bread, platters of mackerel, mutton, stewed herring, dried apples, and even expensively imported dried peaches—they came bearing every sort of delicate food, exuberant as if for a high feast. Laying the ring aside, the king sat up in his bed, at which there was great rejoicing, and for a while no one thought of anything other than serving the daintiest of food and drink to the king who had lain so near to death.

CHAPTER THE THIRD

S CANT MOMENTS LATER, I looked around to offer Albaric something to eat or drink, but he was gone.

I bolted up from my seat at the foot of the bed. "Where did Albaric go?"

Many eyes fastened on me, and my father was not the only one to ask, "Who?"

"The—the visitant, the oddling! Where has he gone?"

Folk looked at one another. An old manservant suggested in jest, "Perhaps he has disappeared in a burst of white fire, like his horse."

"What?" my father exclaimed. "What is this you say?"

An odd hush followed, for no one cares to speak of the uncanny. But then the old man, commanded by the king's gaze, began with stumbling speech to tell of what he spoke. Meanwhile I ran from the room and down the stairs, demanding of every servant I met whether they had seen the stranger. None had. I left the keep, crossed the courtyard, and spoke with the guards at the gate. No one had gone out, and certainly not the fey youth who had so recently come in without being admitted, who had ridden his magnificent white mount through metal and solid wood.

"He could have flown away like a nighthawk, that one," said one of the guards, "and we none the wiser."

But I remembered how he had required my promise before he alighted to the earth, and I sensed that without his eerie horse, he could not depart so readily.

"If I may say it, you showed great courage, my Prince, facing him," said one of the men in a diffident tone that was new to me. "At the sight of him, I could barely stand on my feet."

I felt only small pleasure, for my thoughts were on Albaric, and it seemed to me that it was he who had showed courage, coming here where weapons upraised had greeted him. I sensed great courage in him, remembering how he had trembled as he said to my father, "Sire, do you not know me?"

But the king had known him not.

Why had he thought my father should know him?

It seemed he had come here solely for that, to save my father.

At what cost to himself?

What was he?

I began to see him in my mind like a reflection in water, mystery in its depths, and as the image formed, I began to sense where he might have gone.

Back into the keep I ran, and back up the stairs of the King's Tower. I glanced in at the door, meaning only to reassure myself that my father was well, but despite the servants standing in the way, he and my mother saw me immediately. "Aric!" Mother summoned, and my father demanded, "Aric, who was that youth?"

"He is called Albaric. Whether he be born of woman or fallen from the sky, I know not. I must find him, Sire. Excuse me." Again I bolted from the room, but this time I ran not down the stairs but up.

Almost as if on level ground, I sprinted to the top of the tower and out into the night without a torch to light my way. But then, perforce, I stopped where I stood, so utterly in darkness that I fancied myself standing within the belly of black-wing death. I could see nothing, and a misstep might take me over the low, crenellated wall around the platform and send me plummeting to the crags and the cold fierce water far, far below—for, of course, the castle of the King of Calidon was set atop the rocky shore's highest cliff, which jutted into the northern sea, defended on three sides by stormy waves. The King's Tower, atop which I stood, was the tallest and most inaccessible, so impregnable that the king's chamber was allowed the luxury of a wide, unbarred window of precious glass, a vista of boundless restless sky and water.

Standing atop that tower, I hearkened but could hear only the roar and crash of breakers against rock as the sea wind made a mane of my hair, blowing fit to send the stars overhead sailing on their midnight ocean of sky—but I could not see the stars.

Nor could I see Albaric, or hear him, yet I sensed he was up here with me. How, in the darkness? The same way I had known earlier that there were voices of spirits in the wind. One knows not with mind but with gut and spine.

"Albaric?" I called.

He did not reply. But my breath passed through me in a long, shaky sigh of relief and pain.

Relief that he had not gone away.

But pain—the pain I felt was *his.*

"Albaric." Quite sure of each step, I walked toward him, hands outstretched, until my fingers just grazed the unearthly fabric of his tunic. Then I stopped. I did not dare touch him further. With my other hand, I groped about and found stone. Yes, we stood directly at the wall, which terrified me, for what I sensed in him almost made me weep. His suffering was not simple but a vast and fearsome tangle of many hurtful thorns.

"Listen, Albaric," I blurted as if to a child, "it will be better, somehow. I promise you."

Silence. I heard his breath catch. Then he spoke, his melodic voice wavering between wonder and mockery. "Have you always been able to see in the dark, Prince Aric? Or can you hear this mortal thing, eye-water falling?"

"Neither. But I know your light is gone. Have you ever before stood so benighted, Albaric?"

Longer silence, as his pride surrendered to my touch and my hand settled to lie upon his shoulder.

"No, never before in my—in my life," he said quietly. "It is a weighty and frightful thing to have human life, to feel time passing. Aric, if I were to throw this body of flesh and bone off this tower, if it were to break on the rocks below, would *I* then be gone?"

His words pierced me like a dirk between my ribs. If he questioned whether the soul survived after death, I failed to answer and knew no answer. Yet already I knew a deeper truth. With difficulty, I said, "Please do not, or I would go with you."

My hand slipped off his shoulder as he turned, his back now to the wall, facing me even though we were but shadows in the darkness.

I asked him, "What are you, Albaric, that I feel your suffering as if you were my second self?"

I think he could not speak, but I felt some of his anguish turn to wonder.

Greatly I feared the sea, yet I told him, "I would leap into the sea for you." Simplest truth.

He whispered, "But—why?"

"I know not. It is a weighty and frightful thing," I said in sober jest, "to be willing to die for a stranger." All the more fearsome to me because I had never—how had I known he was on top of the tower? How had I walked to him surely in the dark? How did I sense with certainty what he was suffering? No such powers had been mine until now.

Nor had I ever before felt such compassion.

"Prince Aric, I am all amazed," he whispered, "for I thought perhaps you would be my enemy."

"How so, when you have saved my father's life?"

"You are a true son of King Bardaric."

"Yet he would have died as I watched. Bah." The reason I could dimly see Albaric's form, I realized, was because the utter darkness had at last lifted away, and truly it had been Death a-waiting. Looking up at myriad stars, I shivered with something more than cold. "Inside, come inside," I coaxed. "Come downstairs and have something to eat, some warm milk to drink."

"Mortal comforts," said Albaric with gentle irony, but he came with me.

Hearing our footsteps descending, I suppose, my mother awaited us at the king's doorway with a candle in her hand and many questions in her eyes—but in her eyes only. She would not be so indelicate as to speak them.

She, Queen Evalin, would have been far more fit than I

to rule had father died. A tall and beautiful noblewoman who did not depend on her beauty for anyone's regard but measured everything in her mind, she should have been far more than wife or even queen; she was unfortunate to have been born female.

Mindful of Albaric's discomfort, I asked Mother, "Have you sent away the servants?"

"Yes, and your father sleeps peacefully at last." After a month of restless fever. "You came just in time," Mother said humbly to Albaric. "A little longer and I would have been a widow."

Deep in Albaric's throat sounded a sort of moan, and he turned his face away.

"Time distresses him, I think," I told my mother, "for he has known only a timeless place. Albaric, am I right?"

Still facing away, he nodded.

"And a body of flesh weighs heavily upon him and bewilders him with its wants."

My mother's lips parted but she did not speak, staring at me.

"Now you have perhaps weariness, a need for sleep?" I asked Albaric.

He turned to me like a child. "Is that what it is, this wanting to lie down? I have never felt it in—in forever."

"And the heartache—is it because, now that your horse departed and your feet touch the earth, you cannot go back to—to forever?"

"No, it's. . . ." He hesitated before he spoke on, his tuneful voice very low. "It's not that. I knew when I left that I could not return. Perhaps I delayed longer than I. . . ." With lowered head, he faced my mother. "Queen Evalin, for what—time— has King Bardaric been ill?"

"For a month."

"Is that a large time?"

"You mean long? It only seemed so," said Mother.

"It is not so very long," I told Albaric. "There are twelve months in a year. I am seventeen years old. You seem to be about the same."

"Yes, I—he—" But whatever our guest from Othergates was trying to say, bewilderment stopped him.

The concern in my mother's eyes may well have matched that in my own.

"Won't you have a cup of mulled cider?" she offered Albaric. "Something to eat?"

But he needed sleep worse than food. Taking a torch from a sconce in the wall, I led him downstairs, then along a passageway—the servants who saw us shrieked and fled, confound them—to my own chamber, where I guided him to my bed. I knelt to pull the boots off his feet. Never had I seen such boots, of leather so thin and soft it could have been skinned from flowers.

"Prince Aric, no, please. I'll do it. . . ." But he was too exhausted; he needed my help. I gave him my bearskin for covering; pulled the curtains of the canopied bed; set aside my own boots, belt, and sword; then laid myself down beside him with my clothes on, for I felt he was not ready to be left alone.

"Do you mortals customarily sleep two to a bed?" he murmured.

"Sometimes three or four." There is not much room in a castle keep, so when I had been a lad, my bookmaster, my weaponmaster, and my manservant had all slept with me, each scratching his lice and fleas—a thought I pushed hastily aside, wishing I could keep such things from the newcomer forever. "Do you know how to sleep, Albaric?"

He nodded. "We did it sometimes as a diversion, for the sake of the dreams. . . ." His voice faded.

"Sweet dreams, then."

He actually laughed, albeit weakly. "I doubt it," he murmured but then lapsed into sudden slumber, as if he had been stunned or had fainted.

I lay wide awake and shivering from the sheer strangeness of it all, not from cold. Mine was a trembling like that which comes after the battle, from the surpassing joy of victory—my father lived!—but also from my own uncanny passions and the nearness of death, its motionless black wings far too close over my head as I had stood atop the tower.

CHAPTER THE FOURTH

I DOZED PERHAPS A FEW HOURS around dawn and woke as if to a dream, seeing Albaric in daylight for the first time, gazing upon his face in amazement. How such a being could have come to my home, how his features could be so exquisite yet unmistakably male, how to describe—the seashell bones beneath the eggshell skin, the perfection—and yet breathing, warm, not merely breakable but somehow wounded within—I could scarcely comprehend the wonder of him.

I got up quietly, bathed from cold water in a bowl, changed my clothes, and ate some of the oat scones and cheese and venison my manservant had brought me. But I did not then leave the bedchamber; I sat by the hearth waiting for Albaric to awaken, for who else would take care of him?

And care was needed. He awoke with a jerk and a gasp, sitting bolt upright, half panicked until I stood at his side. Then he fixed upon me a long gaze, studying my face, I suppose, much as I had studied him when he was sleeping, and he seemed to calm, to gather his wits. "Is it what they call morning, Prince Aric?"

"It is."

"Then I wish you good morning. Prince Aric," he added, still intent on me, "you will grow to look verily like your father."

Hand to chin and head bowed, I pretended to mull over his words. "I suppose that is not a bad thing," I murmured finally.

"Of course not! King Bardaric is—" But he broke off, giving me a different sort of look as I smiled. "Bah, you befool me! Mischief, already?"

"I cannot seem to help it."

"Rascal." He almost answered my smile. "What now? I suppose I should wash."

"Eat first. You must be famished." I brought him the tray of food, but he shook his head.

"I cannot eat yet."

"But aren't you *hungry*?"

"There is some pain, yes, but this new belly seems not yet to accept me." Sloughing off the clothing he had ridden in and slept in for time beyond knowing, he headed toward the washstand where clean water awaited him.

Once he had bathed, I offered him a tunic woven of lamb's wool dyed the color of heather, with a braided leather belt and soft fur breeches from my wardrobe.

He shook his head. "I cannot wear your clothing."

"Why not? We are the same size."

"But you are a prince."

"And so are you, unless I am much mistaken."

With a sharp intake of breath, he stared at me. Then he slowly exhaled and asked me, "How do you know so much of me?"

"I know not how I know. But is it not the truth? Wear the finest raiment I can offer you."

He pondered me a long moment, then said, "Before I can do anything else, I need to have something over with."

"What, must you jump off the tower after all?" I could not believe my own boldness, jesting of his despair.

But it was all right. He smiled, a small wry smile that struck me to the heart. "Not if you stand by me, Aric. Have you heard, how is our—" He lost his smile. "How is the king today?"

"Almost as well as he ever was. Why?"

"I need to speak with him."

"To 'have something over with'?"

He nodded.

Once more all servants fled at the sight of Albaric, and the men-at-arms faced him not much better, but my stern command made them stay long enough to tell me where I might find the king.

"In the garden."

"Of course." How better to spend such a fine, sunny morning as was rare in Calidon? And this was no ordinary garden, but the high-walled garden of a royal castle, a private place of fragrance and flowers, arbors and bowers.

"With her Highness, your mother, my lord Prince."

Except for its caretakers, the garden was forbidden to anyone but the royal family. Something in the guardsman's tone warned me that Mother and Father had gone there like a pair of young lovers recently reunited. So I called from the gate and waited until Father called back a welcome.

Walking in with me upon the flagstone path, Albaric lifted

his gaze to the trellises of roses arching overhead, the pear and apple trees in the full sweet leaf of early summer, the grape arbor and bower of fragrant juniper, the hawthorn hedges and walls garlanded with ivy. "Pleasant," he murmured, "but why is everything growing in straight lines?"

Having no ready answer, I led him toward where I heard the strumming of harp strings, to the pavilion, aromatic with the scent of violets clustered all around it. There my mother and father sat on one of the benches, the king plucking a love song. But as they caught sight of Albaric, they sobered. Father set his hand harp, no larger than a lyre, aside. "Come in," he said.

As we did so, ascending the low wooden steps, Mother said to Albaric, "Fair youth, we owe you all thanks—"

"Pray be seated," said my father at the same time, although Albaric had made no move to kneel or even bow before him.

And Mother, "Are you well? If there is anything—"

"There is," Albaric said quietly, seating himself on another bench to face them. "Sire, Queen Evalin, I must speak with you."

I asked, "Shall I leave?"

"No, Aric, stay with me!" For a moment, he looked as if he would spring to his feet to detain me. But as I sat on the bench beside him, he calmed. "It is a long and sad tale," he explained, "and I would far rather tell it just once, to all three of you."

"Tell on, fair youth," said my father.

"Albaric," I said, realizing that neither of them could remember his name. "Prince Albaric of—for want of a better word, of Elfland."

My father looked astonished, my mother awed, but Albaric

spared them the embarrassment of having lost control of their royal countenances, for he faced me. "It is a word of which I have need," he said. "Thank you." Then he clasped his hands and spoke.

"It began when the most comely of kings, his royal son, and his retainers rode to go a-hawking," he said. "I imagine they rode happily and flew their falcons with joy, until they reached the hill where a spring flows and they let their horses drink, where the oaks grow tallest and the most deeply green, and there they encountered my—they saw the Queen of Elfland riding with her retinue."

"I remember no such thing!" I exclaimed before I could stop myself.

Albaric gave me a glance both quizzical and quelling. "Aric, please. This is difficult enough." Then a thought seemed to strike him. He turned to the king and asked, "Sire, might I borrow the harp?"

"Of course." Father passed him the instrument. Cradling it in his arms, Albaric plucked its strings, and they gave forth notes of such ethereal beauty that I sat openmouthed.

In a voice to rival that of angels he sang,

> Her dress was of the grass green silk,
> Her mantle of the velvet fine.
> From every braid of her horse's mane
> Hung fifty silver bells and nine.

And I no longer remember his exact words when he spoke, for I seemed to see the things he described. I saw upon a magnificent stallion, the war steed of a man, one who was neither man nor mortal. She was the Queen of the Otherworld, riding like a bold flower on horseback, her gown of green silk the stem and her wild red hair the blossom, some of it curled in loving tendrils around her blithe face, some of it flying like red petals in the wind or red birds flitting amid the branches of the oaks, alighting then swooping on—her luminous hair filled the air. And her steed pranced with the silver bells ringing in his mane, and close behind her trotted a vast gold-decked company with glorious horses and flying mantles and with the uncanny glow of the Elfin folk, what is called their glamour, shining all over each of them, but most of all on the queen. Yet amid all that there was to see, still the very fairest thing was the queen's face, a flower within a flower.

The King of Calidon looked enchanted upon her face.

It was no mere chance that made her visible to the golden-bearded king that day, for she had observed him and desired him. But not so that he could rule her realm. There was not, nor ever had been, nor ever would be, a King of Elfland; she desired King Bardaric only as a willful child desires a toy.

She beckoned, and he rode to her in a trance, her captive. His son, his followers, could neither move nor speak nor even think, for she was Queen Theena, and her spell was strong. She invited the king upon her own horse with her, and without looking back, he put his arms around her and rode away with her into a green mist, for hers was a power greater than any mortal monarch's.

So she took him away to the Otherland of swan-blessed blue waters and mossy banks of ferny green, and there perforce he stayed with her. This was a timeless place of ease and pleasure, sweet music and midnight dancing on the clouds, amid the stars. Every denizen of that place was more beautiful than any other, and as they lived in eternal youth, there was no need for them to have hearts, fall in love, or bear children; they lived with neither regrets nor expectations, for past or future they had none; only sunshine or moonglow, music and delight, revels and ease.

Queen Theena gifted her captive with every charm she had to offer; they went flying together like two birds of paradise, they sailed her bonny boats upon lakes and land and air; my father slumbered with her in beds of rose petals, he supped with her upon ambrosia—but even her power could not make him look upon her with desire, nor could it keep him from yearning for his true love, his wife, my mother, and for—for me.

Me, Aric. But as Albaric strummed the harp and told the tale, I saw myself as my father saw me, as the pride of his loins, his crown prince and the heir of his kingdom, a modest, clear-eyed, strong and comely youth, gallant and true.

But I had no time to comprehend this, for the tale went on.

Never before had Queen Theena taken such a captive as this mortal king Bardaric, all noble courtesy yet not fully hers to command, confound him; even as his body did whatever she wished, his mind and soul remained his own. He would not forget Calidon; he chafed in captivity, fretted to be free— these sorrows shadowed his eyes. Because he served her with mere obedience, she could not take pleasure in him. Her frustration grew as her power proved insufficient to make him completely hers. But she knew of another power, a secret and ancient thing, a ring locked in a coffer that had once belonged to the puissant Pandora, a treasure of power so great that even greedy Theena hesitated to touch it. The nameless ring had a life of its own, and she could not predict exactly what might happen if she used it.

But desperate in her pride, at last she dared to touch the coffer, turn the key, take up from its velvet bed the ring of power, and bring it forth. She issued to it her command, then deceitfully, as if it were another pretty bauble, a trifle, she placed it on my father's finger. And it gave her what she wanted, although not in the way she expected. Never could she have dreamed of what was to happen to her, utterly changing her endless life.

In order to fulfill her desire that King Bardaric might feel something for her, the ring caused *her*, Queen Theena of Elfland, to fall madly in love with him.

CHAPTER THE FIFTH

"QUEEN EVALIN," Albaric bespoke my mother, "I beg you to forgive me if this distresses you."

"It dizzies me. I can hardly take it in." But she smiled and lifted her chin. "There is nothing to forgive, Albaric. I reason things out and judge no ill of my husband." She reached toward him.

Father grasped her hand as if he were drowning and she would save him. He looked dazed. "I remember nothing of any of this," he murmured. "It would be hard to believe a word if it were not for the ring."

"Yes. The ring."

"But in every tale of sorcery I have ever heard, a magical ring empowers the person who wears it."

"Mortal stories of mortal magic. Little does anyone, mortal or otherwise, know of the ways of this ring. It is like. . . ." Aric hesitated, as if he meant to say something more. But then he plucked the harp and resumed his tale.

Like the folk of Othergates, Elfland, call it what you will, the ring was neither good nor evil but whimsical and fey. The denizens of the fair, timeless place enjoyed one another's company, singing, combing each other's hair, and decking themselves and their horses with flowers; they played with one another as if playing with toys or pets, they tumbled together like puppies, they danced in air or floated amid water lilies, but they did not fall in love.

So when they saw on the face of Queen Theena the passion they had never seen before, and tenderness, and yearning, they did not know what to do or think. And when they heard her asking where was King Bardaric (for love had compelled her to let him roam Elfland free; she could no longer confine him to stay by her side) and when they saw her riding her vehement stallion—it is said that the horses of Elfland are made of wind and fire—riding alone, or flying alone like a red bird amid the glory of her own hair, they felt much perturbed. And whenever they witnessed the moment she found the mortal king, her love, when they saw the timid fervor in her eyes as she approached him to offer golden trinkets, cups of nectar, and herself, they were disturbed. They whispered among themselves, attempting without success to understand what was happening to her. They had never seen the like. They were scandalized.

The only one who understood, and felt compassion, was King Bardaric.

Always before, when perforce he lay with her by power of her command, he had done what she had bid. But now, when he lay with her, although still by power of her command, he saw that she strove with all her wiles to give him pleasure, she lavished upon him all her love, hoping he would love her in return; she became almost ensouled in her adoration; she nearly could have melted into him.

He could not love her, but he pitied her, and he held her as he would have held a crying child, comforting her, trying to ease her pain.

As his heart responded to her need, her body responded to him in a way unforeseen.

And despite her sure knowledge that King Bardaric still loved Queen Evalin and only Queen Evalin, nevertheless, Queen Theena of Elfland began to feel a happiness, a ripening, a fulfillment such as she had never imagined. She accepted this new joy as an Elf accepts any pleasure, without question, without understanding—at first. Only when she began to feel the butterfly stirrings of life within her belly did she surmise, with greatest wonder, what might have chanced.

The Queen of Elfland was with child.

Never in forever had this happened in that world. Where there is no growing old and no death, the idea of birth—it was beyond comprehension. Scandal turned to shock, then to awe, as the queen enlarged in girth like a ripening pomegranate, as her glamour increased in warmth and loveliness, as her belly swelled like blown glass, like a bubble, until she grew so translucent that when she unmantled herself, one could see the baby within, a perfect folded flower of—of uncanny life. Elf melded with mortal! The denizens of timelessness could not bear the sight; terrified, they fled from the presence of their queen. She began to fear, for no one stood by her, and when her time came, what did she know of giving birth? She or any of the others? There would be pain and danger, both unthinkable to her. Would another great change come upon her? Would she—could she die?

Trying to comfort her fears, King Bardaric remained with her constantly. He, and only he, stood by her when she gave birth, although he knew little more of it than she did, having always been chased away by midwives—but he had heard the screaming, screaming from Evalin, his beloved wife, who never otherwise cried out in pain, and although he concealed his dread of childbirth from Queen Theena, it perhaps exceeded hers.

But to the relief of both, it was not such an ordeal. Instead of hard labor, there was a simple sort of opening like that of a flower blooming, and the infant came forth, not amid blood but amid a stream of white light, and the newborn child's nakedness needed no bathing but glowed with white glamour; he was the most beautiful of all possible babes. His father held him for long moments before handing him to his mother, whose breasts ached to suckle him. For she lay swollen now with milk—milk! Like a mortal—and the king looked on in wonder as the baby boy, his son, nursed at the breast of the Queen of Elfland.

Then he thought of his true love, Queen Evalin, and of how many times she had lain in a blood-soaked bed nearly dead after childbirth, and how it had broken her heart each time another child had struggled for life only to fall victim to some sickness, until at last one had lived: his son, Aric, for whom he ached every day and whom he might never see again. He felt how unfair it was and how wondrous that the Elf Queen's birthing had been so supernaturally bloodless and white.

He reached out to his new son, and the baby's hand met his, and the boy's strange blue-gray eyes looked straight into his eyes, and this time it was the king who fell in love.

"I know what I would like to name the child," he said softly. "There is an old word, 'alba.' It means 'white.'"

"You wish to name him Alba?"

Thinking of his other son, whose name the Elf Queen did not know, the king replied, "I wish to name him Albaric."

I am not stupid, although I sometimes choose to appear so. My heart had started pounding when Albaric spoke of Queen Theena's being with child, then racing when the babe turned out to be—yes!—a boy, and when he said the name—

"Albaric!" Taking him into my arms, harp and all, I hugged him and felt him trembling. "My *brother*?" I whispered, even in my joy not yet able to comprehend—all my life alone, but now I had a brother? The most magical of brothers? No wonder that I felt I would do anything for him, that I had felt thus from the first night I met him.

"Aric." Father's voice, displeased.

I would have disobeyed the tacit command, but Albaric pulled away from me, still trembling but trying hard to keep his head up and his face steady, the way he had done when he had asked my father—*our* father—"Sire, do you not know me?"

Father sat motionless with Mother clutching his hand, nearly as pale as he; above his golden beard, his skin had gone the color of chalk. In a low voice he warned me, "Be not so hasty. We do not know whether he is telling the truth."

Astonished, I forgot respect, lifting my head to cry at him, "How can you say that? He saved your life!"

"Yes. And I have not yet thanked him." The king rose to stand, a great golden man. "Albaric," he spoke straight to the—visitant, the marvel, my brother—"fair youth, I owe you greatest gratitude for my life. Yet it is a life dedicated to protecting the throne of Calidon. If you claim to be my son, it could be for the sake of taking the throne."

Albaric stiffened as if he had been hit, but he faced Father levelly. "Sire," he told the king, his voice soft and straight, "you fear treachery, as any king must. But I promise you, there are no schemes in me. From this moment, I renounce any claim upon your throne or kinship. Prince Aric, Queen Evalin, you are my witnesses."

I dared not speak, for never had I felt so angry with my father.

The king settled back into his seat next to my mother. "Only tell me this: if not for gain, then for what reason did you come here?"

Lackwit! I barely controlled my face and kept silence, aghast at my father's question, for how could he not know Albaric had come only to save him?

But Albaric—my brother!—merely took up the harp again, playing and singing softly for a few minutes:

> Up the hilly northern lights
> Down midnight's milky glen
> Fares the bonny starry road
> I shall not ride again.

Although it was hard to tell in a place with no birthdays, he had grown much like any mortal child, because his father, the captive mortal king, was the only one who cared for him. The others had no use for him, a half-human oddling, and aside from giving the breast, Queen Theena scarcely knew what to do with him, never having been a mother or known one. But the king held the baby to hush his crying, rocked him to sleep, cared for him as he grew, watched over him, spoke with him in the language of mortals, taught him the handling of lance and sword—skills unknown to Elfinkind—and took him hawking and fishing and shared with him whatever wisdom he could.

They were nearly always together. As the boy grew in understanding, the king told him their own mutual story, so that Albaric should comprehend why he was shunned by those around him—although truth to tell, he was not very different than the others in appearance, only in manner. He possessed to the fullest an Elf's carefree, feckless, thoughtless beauty, yet he possessed also a heart; he knew affection and loneliness and longing. Worse, within his brilliant eyes could be seen a keen mind and perhaps even a soul. He was an embarrassment to the immortals, much as the behavior of their queen was a scandal and an embarrassment, the more so because King Bardaric's true love of his own mortal Queen Evalin endured.

The king told his Elf-son of his cherished wife, and of Dun Caltor his home, and of harsh, lovely Calidon his kingdom, and of Prince Aric, his son and heir. And as Albaric grew, as he became no longer a boy but the most comely of youths, a great sadness seized King Bardaric, for Albaric reminded him so strongly of Aric he could think of nothing but the family he had left behind. How he missed them, and how he had missed their lives! Were they old now, Queen Evalin silver-haired or perhaps even dead? Was Aric a goodly man with a wife and children of his own, or had life been unkind to him? Did Dun Caltor still stand, or had it fallen to the ever-threatening tribes from the Craglands? Thinking these things, the king brooded, and ceased to eat, and he—he wept. For the first time, Queen Theena saw him weep.

And so it came to pass that she showed the extent of her love for him, how she had come to cherish him so truly that she wanted only his happiness, no longer her own.

She set him free.

She let him go back home.

Because time runs differently—indeed, not at all—in Elfland, she was able to send him back to the same place, the oak forest atop the hill, and to the same time, the exact same moment. All was just the same, the hawks, the blue sky and singing wind, his son Aric on horseback at his side—only this time King Bardaric did not see the Queen of Elfland a-riding with her fair and eerie retinue.

Such was her love and her unwonted mercy that she spared him all memory of her. He did not even know he had ever been gone from his own world.

Nor for several moments thereafter did he notice the shimmering, eerie ring that had somehow appeared on the finger nearest his heart.

CHAPTER THE SIXTH

"SHE TRIED AND TRIED AGAIN to remove it before she returned you to your mortal world, Sire," Albaric explained, "but it would not let go its hold of you. It is a contrary thing, and by then its power far exceeded hers. I stood by and watched her struggle and secretly hoped you might stay with me after all—but she sent you away ring and all, hoping that in the mortal world it would become only a mortal trifle, a bauble you could take off and throw aside as a matter of no moment. So in the end she said the spell, and you disappeared as if you had never been.

"And I. . . ." Albaric faltered to a halt. His head hung.

"How could you come here and take off the ring," Father demanded, "if Queen Theena could not?" And little as I liked it, I followed his reasoning. Could the ring have been put on him to sicken him, then Albaric sent after to make him well and be a hero?

Albaric flung up his head, not in defiance but in a wild sort of whimsy. "Why, Sire, shortly after sending you away, my mother became a stranger to me, changing back into what she had been before she knew you, the puissant immortal ruler who cared not a whit for anything, least of all her child. All of Elfland rejoiced to have its queen back. But great was her vexation that she had lost the ring, when with her returning powers she realized how she could have kept it."

"So you came to get it back for her?"

I could not bear more misunderstanding. "My father," I burst out, "when he set foot on the ground, his horse turned to air. When he took the ring off you, his fire went out. His light is gone. He cannot return whence he came. He has thrown in his lot with mortals now, and he will someday die, and he has made this sacrifice to save you."

The king looked at me sharply. "Aric, how do you know whether this is true?"

"He knows, Sire," Albaric answered for me, "just as I knew you had need of me. From the moment I set foot in Dun Caltor, Aric has shared a sympathy with me such as. . . ." He hesitated but said it. "Such as I once shared with you. Even from Othergates, I knew that the ring had turned against you, I knew you lay ailing, and I—I was frightened of what might befall me in this world, knowing I could not return to my own—but in the end I came to you."

"Frightened," Father said.

"Yes. I am frightened still."

"It takes courage to admit of fear. I commend you, Albaric, but still my own fears bid me beware, for I know not what is true."

For the first time, my mother spoke. "Dearest, this much at least is true, that Albaric came here to save you, for he brought with him the device he needed remove the ring."

"Device?"

She went on to explain to him how Albaric had forced the ring to move by winding a filament behind it. "It seemed as fine as floss yet stronger than any human hand, with no end to its length. Although I could not see it in the night, I judge that it was no ordinary thread."

"Wise Queen, you judge rightly." Reaching into his tunic, Albaric brought forth a sizeable coil of some filament that seemed to glow with an inner life, like fire, like gold flowing red from the furnace. Albaric held it with ease in his hands, but had he asked me to touch it, I think I would not have dared. That uncanny glow—it was glamour. This thread came from no mortal hand or land.

"What is that?" Father asked hoarsely, and I saw that he and Mother had drawn back.

"It is a strand of my mother's hair."

I know my eyes widened, and I think I gasped, glimpsing within my mind the immense grandeur of the Elf Queen.

"It is fey," Queen Evalin said in low tones of judgment. "It belongs with the ring."

"Please, no." Albaric shook his head as he tucked the fiery filament back into his tunic. "It is all I have left." Although wistful, nothing in his tone asked for pity; he spoke merest fact.

"The ring," I blurted, startled by a twinge of alarm. "Where is it?"

My father knew not. Even a king will forget, I suppose, what he does not wish to believe. Nor did anyone else remember more than I did, that he had laid it aside in his bedchamber.

In a manner that, I am sure, caused comment throughout the castle—it is uncommonly lacking in dignity for royalty to scuttle hither and yon—but trusting no servant to run the errand for us, we all hurried to the King's Tower and up the stairs, into the chamber lit by its window of glass from which sometimes one could see the dragon-prowed longboats of the Norsemen sailing by.

In the king's chamber, plain to see in the daylight, an old woman scattered fresh rushes—every bedchamber floor is strewn with rushes for the sweet smell, for softness underfoot, and for the discomfiture of fleas. Frightened by the sight of Albaric when we stampeded in like so many royal cattle, she gasped, dropped her basket, and fled. But as she scuttled past me, something caught—not my eye so much as my breath. It was a sense of the ring's presence, or at least a sense of the presence of something not from my own world. I hastened after her and overtook her on the stairs, placing a hand on her arm to stop her, touching her gently—but I could feel her quaking, and she looked up at me with her toothless mouth agape, incapable of speaking.

"The ring," I said to her in a whisper, not wanting my father to hear, for the servant's sake.

Her wet old eyes calmed, and she was able to speak. "'Twould fall from me apron," she said, "so I put it on me fist." She raised her hands, and my heart stopped to see the ring of power gleaming darkly on one of her fingers. Dreadfully I feared she would die—but in the same moment, quite simply and easily, she took it off and handed it to me, then curtsied and hurried on her way.

I stood there, stupefied, with the ring, the color of mud, lying in the palm of my hand.

"It is sulking because you captured it," said a voice like moonlight; Albaric stood by my side.

I turned to him, demanding, "You saw? Why did it spare the old woman?"

"Why not? No voice of command bade it do otherwise."

I ogled like a dolt. By good luck my parents could not see me; I heard them moving furniture in the bedchamber at the top of the spiral stairs.

Albaric explained, "It possessed our—your father by the force of Queen Theena's most puissant command."

"She wished him *dead*?"

"No! No, she loved him. What happened—afterwards—I do not understand."

"Aric?" cried my mother from the bedchamber.

With a sense that I must protect the old woman, Albaric, myself, everyone, I stooped to place the ring on the floor at my feet. "Here!" I called back. "I've found it on the stairs. Bring candles."

Mother and Father came back, each with a candlestick, and we stood looking down upon the ring that lay glowering on the stone step. Darkly it smoldered as if with green lightning, then turned to lustering the dull red of dried blood.

"How came it here?" Father sounded shaken.

I said nothing. Albaric said, "Unless restrained, it will act of its own will, Sire—"

"Do not call me Sire!"

We stood stunned to silence by his vehemence.

His glare raked us all. "And tell no one anything of—of this fairy tale, of adventures in Elfland, of a supposed son or a supposed brother, none of it! Aric, Evalin, and—and you, Albaric—I command it."

Albaric bowed his head, I dare say I flushed with anger it would have been most unwise to express, and the ring blazed a merry scarlet.

"Now look how the pesky thing rejoices," said my mother in the tone of one dealing with troublesome children. "What are we to do with it?"

"I relinquish charge of it," said the king, "for already I have been neglectful."

"I do not want it," said Albaric, "for you trust me not." Yet his tone was level and without rancor.

"I will take it and—" I was going to say lock it in a box for safekeeping.

But Father commanded, "No, Aric, I forbid you! We know not what it will do to you."

"Oh, fishheads," said my mother, as was her wont when vexed, and she crouched on the steps with her girdle-dirk in her hand. Picking up the ring upon its tip, rather as if removing a toad from the kitchen, she stood and strung through it the end of a chain of gold she wore around her waist. Then taking the chain, she transferred it to her neck, clipped its ends, and tucked the dangling portion beneath the outer tabard of her gown so that the ring hung hidden in her clothing, unseen.

"Men," she grumbled, "fuss over the simplest things. What is Albaric to call you if not Sire?"

She and Father stood staring at each other. Standing a step above him on the stairway, she fronted him eye to eye, hers chilly gray, his blazing blue.

"Surely you will kindly excuse us, your Royal Highnesses," I said as formally and woodenly as a servant, with an exaggerated bow. Before either of them could react, I fled, with Albaric at my side, and once downstairs and safely in the great hall, I could not help laughing.

Albaric stood watching me with a quizzical smile. Wondering whether he had ever laughed, I tried to sober.

But he understood better than I knew. "Father always said you were wont to tweak his beard. You are brave, my brother."

My throat tightened when he called me brother, and I could not speak.

"You are the only one here who is brave enough." Lifting his head, Albaric regarded me steadily. "Small wonder if my— if the king wants no part of me, but what if you had thought me a rival? There is mercy in this mortal world, Aric, and it has given me you."

Much moved, I reached out, and we gripped hands like warriors going into battle. From that moment, I knew that my quest in life must be to find him peace.

CHAPTER THE SEVENTH

E WERE BOTH ABASHED, I think. We walked outdoors in silence, and by happenstance we passed through the walled garden. Seeing the harp still lying on a bench, I picked it up, because, even though the sun shone, at any moment clouds might blow in from the sea and it might be soaked in rain, so changeable was our weather in this far northern kingdom called Calidon. It was not uncommon here to host sun, thunder, rainbow, sleet, and windstorm all in one day. Such as the day Father and I had last gone riding.

I blurted to Albaric—my brother!—"Would you like to see the horses?"

He nodded, smiling, so harp in hand, I led him toward the stables. The grooms stiffened to ashen silence as we walked in, but the horses thrust their heads eagerly over the half-doors of their stalls to welcome the newcomer. And my favorite, my shining red-gold Valor, whinnied in greeting to me.

"Beautiful," Albaric murmured.

"You think so? Not one of them can compare to the steed

you rode hither." A thought struck me. "Do you miss him?" I would have missed Valor.

"A steed of white wind? Nay, it was a thing of no significance, no heart."

He stood by as I stroked Valor's tawny face. Then I led him down the aisle, showing him Father's war horse, Invincible; Mother's gentle palfrey, Marzipan; and Trueheart, Daisy, Black Diamond, many others.

"You like them all," Albaric remarked, rubbing the forelock of an old skewbald cart-horse, "whether cob or pony or charger."

"True. Am I boring you?"

"Boring?" He did not understand the word or, I suppose, the concept, being unaccustomed to time or pastimes.

I was spared trying to explain, for men shouted from the training yard outside, and we heard a scream all the more frightening for not being human. A horse's cry of fury or despair, it struck me like a lance, sending me dashing to see what was the matter, with Albaric at my side.

The horse trainer had already found safety atop the tall, stout fence, but the massive blue stallion still reared and struck with his deadly forehooves, outraged. A rope lay in the dirt. The blue steed bore not a stitch of harness.

Blue?

Blue roan, really, its mane and tail black, but on its body the dark hairs blended with white so that in certain lights it looked blue—so I told myself. But never had I seen a horse so blue as the one inside the fence.

Nor had I ever seen this horse before. "Whence came *that*?" I exclaimed.

At first no one answered, for those standing nearby edged

away from Albaric and me or found sudden reason to return to tasks inside the stable. But the horse trainer, Todd, dropped from atop the fence and limped over to speak with me. It came to me that he must be getting old, for I had known him all my life. He had taught me to ride. I knew his temper to be patient and his skill to be great. "Are you all right?" I asked, for he moved as if in pain.

"'Tis but a blow and a bruise, my lord Prince."

"Where did he hit you? Are you sure there's nothing broken?"

"On the shoulder. Nothing that hasn't been broken before," Todd said with a wry look that gave me to understand I should stop fussing. Todd greeted Albaric with a bowed head but no show of fear; indeed, he looked him over, taking his measure, as if he were a colt. Then turning back to me, he said, "As to whence came the wild beastie yonder, Prince Aric, the week before last a peddler of horses stopped by. I thought it best not to trouble you about him."

"You thought rightly," I assured him, for at that time my father had lain abed and seemingly dying. "What sort of peddler, to sell steeds like this?"

"An ordinary swindler, my Prince, with ordinary nags, except for this one, hobbled all four feet in chains. Given up by a grand lord of the southlands, the fellow said, as impossible to train." Todd smiled ruefully. "I rose to the bait like a fish to a cricket. And now I could have lost my life for the sake of my daring, trying to put a rope on him."

We looked at the blue stallion pawing the earth, all shining with sweat like—

"That *is* sweat, is it not?" I murmured.

Albaric said quietly, "I think yon windflower-blue stallion

and I might understand each other. May I borrow the harp, Aric?"

I passed him the instrument, and cradling it, he walked to the gate, raised the latch, and slipped into the training pen while we stood watching him as if in a trance. At the last moment, Todd cried out and would have prevented him, but I held up my hand.

"Strange chance brought us here with a harp," I told him. "Watch."

Facing the frothing, snorting stallion across a few scant rods of earth, Albaric fingered the harp strings, and notes flew up sweet and swift as honeybees amid larkspur and hollyhocks.

From everywhere in the castle yard, folk hurried out to see whence came the wondrous music. And the blue steed halted his raging to stand as still as a statue, head high and ears pricked forward, listening, his white-rimmed stare fixed on Albaric.

Steadily answering the stallion with his own eyes, as if mindful only of the blue steed, Albaric began to sing, and wine of Elfland could have been no finer than his voice:

> Son of the wind, son of the thunder
> Fleet are your legs, son of the lightning
> Son of sky raining, shod with silver
> Son of the dayspring, shod with gold.

I sensed that he was creating the song as he sang and would have liked to pay better attention to rhyme, but there was no time.

> Your mother the rainbow, your neck arched bold
> Beloved by the rainbow, beloved by the lightning
> Both shine in your eyes, sheen your shoulders
> Cerulean blue, steed of the high sky

Gasps and murmurs sounded from the crowd that had gathered, for the renegade stallion, ears at a wary angle, began slowly to walk toward Albaric, who stood where he was and sang on, gazing into the great eyes of the steed—uncanny eyes, I saw with scarcely any surprise amidst so much strangeness. No longer ringed with frightened white, the horse's eyes shone the color of blue violets after rain.

> Lapis your hue, and you were born
> With a jewel on your forehead, finest sapphire
> A jewel like a star between your wide eyes

Indeed, I saw, this was no hammer-headed Roman-nosed war horse. The blue horse's head, handsome, straight-lined, and small, could fittingly bear a jewel or a star.

> And on your fetlocks the wings of Otherwhere,
> Of rare blue eagles, of—

The giant steed approached within two paces of Albaric, within one pace, then stopped.

Everything stopped. Albaric stopped singing, stopped strumming the harp, and I feared for him, although the sympathy that connected us told me he was unafraid, and I could see ease, comfort, in every line of his slim body as he stood looking up at the horse and waiting—but even though he feared not, I scarcely breathed. I think no one did. All sound stopped; I heard not even the chirp of an errant sparrow.

The stallion's nostrils quivered, flared, and I could hear them fluttering as it lowered its head to sniff at Albaric's flaxen hair.

Cries broke out; the spell was broken, and the stallion retreated with a snort.

Albaric turned to me, and through the boards of the fence, he handed me the harp. I glimpsed his glowing face, sensed his hope.

"He should come out now," Todd blurted. "Prince Aric, please make him come out."

"It is not my place to tell him what to do, Todd."

My old riding master gave me a startled glance, then turned to study Albaric again, whispering, "What is he?"

I gave no answer, only watched Albaric watching the horse—no, talking to the horse with his eyes, strange youth and stranger steed conversing without words. At the same time, each took a step toward the other, close enough to touch. But Albaric did not reach out, although he badly wanted to; I knew this, felt it in him as I had felt it myself the many times I had wanted to lay a hand on his shoulder but refrained for the sake of his princehood. Similarly, he refrained for the sake of the great stallion's pride. He waited, and the steed took the leadership, extending its lapis head, nostrils flared, to explore his face, his ears, his neck, arms, and hands.

Then and only then, Albaric raised one arm, one hand, to smooth the black mane wildly strewn upon the stallion's curved neck. He stroked the steed's massive blue shoulder, and I saw how the sheen of the horse now glimmered on Albaric's hand. I heard Todd beside me swearing steadily and very softly in sheer wonder. I heard the whispering, nearly silent awe all around me in the many watchers. And I felt no fear anymore, only joy for Albaric's sake, as he stood beside the tall steed, touched its withers, and waited for permission.

The blue stallion bowed to one knee in assent. Folk gasped at the beauty, the grace of the odd-hued steed as, gripping a fistful of black mane, Albaric vaulted onto the charger's back. The horse straightened, snorted, pranced in place, lifted its head, and bugled a neigh of victory.

"He wants to run," Albaric called to me and Todd. "He has been tied, chained, hobbled, and haltered for so long that he's half crazed. Is there a place—"

"The tourney fields!" I pointed to the stone archway that led thither. "Todd, open the gate."

"My Prince Aric!" he cried, aghast.

"Do it." And as my command drove him to obey, I shouted to the multitude, "All stand aside!"

Only just in time. The stallion charged out of the gate and swept past like blue fire, Albaric on its shining back as if he were a part of the horse, at one with it, only his hands gripping its mane to guide it.

CHAPTER THE EIGHTH

"WHAT IS THE MATTER WITH ME?" Albaric clutched my shoulder as we made our way out of the stable. "I can barely stand up or walk, my legs hurt so."

"Sore muscles are the price a mortal pays for galloping a blue stallion bareback for an hour or two."

"An hour, or two? What is the difference? And must the stallion be blue?"

I could only shake my head and smile as I helped him toward the wooden tub outside the kitchen door, scullery girls filling it with kettles of boiling water as I had ordered. I put my hand in, cautious lest I be burned, but a few buckets of cold water from the well had cooled it enough. "In you go, clothes and all," I told Albaric, only snatching the boots off his feet lest he ruin the leather.

"Ai!" he cried more in surprise than pain, for it was the first time he had felt hot water on a body made of flesh. "Bloody blue blazes!"

He sounded just like my father. Our father. I could not help but laugh at him. "Sit down! You will soon feel better."

As his sore muscles soaked in the hot water, he sighed in relief, leaned back against the side of the wooden tub, and grinned at me. "It was worth these, what you call them, sore muscles," he said. "Never in my world was there ever such a horse."

"Or in this world either. He is yours."

"Mine? Is that not for our—is that not for the king to say?"

I felt his pang of longing for the father he could not claim.

"It is merest sense. You are the only one who can handle him. What will you name him?"

He shook his head.

"You don't want him?"

"Of course I want him! But he will not be truly mine until I ask the king."

"I—"

He heard me before I spoke. "No, you will not do it for me, Aric. I must be the one to ask him."

After he had soaked in the hot water for a while, he was able to walk into the keep, up the stairs to my chamber, and put on dry clothing. And he was able, a few minutes later, to approach Father without hobbling.

In his crowded court of law, Father sat on his second-best throne—its arms and back draped with the rare skins of white hart and golden bear—wearing his second-best raiment, across his broad chest his heavy silk baldric of the Calidon colors, slate and crimson, and around his neck the ancient golden torc of the White King. Mighty to look upon even while seated, he loomed on the platform that elevated his throne above the table where scribes recorded his judgments. Every weekday afternoon he sat thus, hearing the problems and grievances of his people. While he had been sick, I had done it in his stead, but it had made no difference that I wore the baldric and the torc; I was an untried youth, and looked like one. I think many folk had held off, hoping the king would get better, and since he was well, there was a great press of people in the court of law today.

I stood at the back of the room unnoticed—no wonder, for all eyes were on Albaric as he awaited his turn. Folk edged away from him, and many were the murmurs of wonder at his beauty and fear of his strangeness.

In due time, Father's castle steward beckoned Albaric forward, and then many were those who gasped aloud, for Albaric neither bowed nor dropped to his knees before the king but stood like the prince he was.

"My Liege," he addressed Father, "concerning a certain stallion—"

Father interrupted, although patiently. "Do not call me Liege. You are not my sworn vassal."

I had known from the start that there would be more than the matter of a certain horse to be settled. That Albaric approached King Bardaric in public court showed his mettle. He could have spoken to the king in privileged privacy but chose not to do so.

He answered, "I would willingly swear you fealty. No vassal could offer greater loyalty, my King." Another gasp, for it should have been "Highness" or "Majesty."

But father let it go, gazing quizzically into the eerie gray eyes that met his so levelly. "I would as soon have the birds of the air swear me fealty, Albaric, as you. Is it the blue roan stallion of which you spoke?"

"Yes. You heard?"

"And saw, issuing forth to watch you riding him like an eagle riding the wind, for folk could speak of nothing else." Father's smile twitched his beard; beneath that concealment, it could have been either admiring or rueful. "You wish me to give you the horse?"

"Queen Evalin offered a boon, my—my King."

Father waved the words away. "This boon is mine. I give the blue roan stallion to Albaric. So let it be written." A command to a scribe, who dipped his quill and began the document. "Doubtless Prince Aric will wish to ride out with you tomorrow."

I stiffened, bitten by the bitterness in those words.

Albaric protested, "My beloved King—"

But he had gone too far. Father leaned forward in this throne, and his tone darkened. "Beware, Albaric. I know you only as an unaccountable being come to trouble me."

"I beg you, blame not my—blame not your son in my stead. It is for pity of me that Prince Aric cleaves to me, my—King Bardaric, it is because I have no place. His heart is great, and cherishes you, and I have not stolen it from you, Sire." The forbidden word slipped out. Albaric's face flamed. "I beg your royal pardon." He bowed his head and dropped to one knee.

For a long moment, Father studied him. "So," he said quietly, "you *will* bow if you displease me."

Albaric raised startled eyes. "Of course! I wish only. . . ." I knew what he was going to say and felt his struggle as he thought better of it.

"You wish only for what, Albaric?"

"I wish only to please you, King Bardaric."

No lie, but not the entire truth. That for which Albaric wished, for which he yearned on bended knee, was the love of his father.

Our father.

Who dismissed him with a flick of a hand.

That evening, Albaric went early to bed, aching and exhausted by his wild ride on the blue steed and perhaps also by his audience with our father. He affirmed that the king had given him the horse, saying, "I shall call him Bluefire."

"A fine name. Simple and sooth. Did you tell Father?"

"No." And he said nothing more of his audience with the king. I am sure he did not know I had seen and heard all.

After Albaric was asleep, I sought out Father and found him in the barracks, quaffing ale with the castle steward and the Captain of Guards and Todd and a few others. They welcomed me, gave me a mug of ale, laughed when I got foam on my face, and said it was a white beard, for I had been wise beyond my years (so they told my father), taking charge and rendering fair judgments while he lay ailing.

"Well," Father grumbled, "it's all playtime for him now that I am back. When did you last ply your sword, Aric, or study your Tacitus?"

Hardly a fair response, but I smothered the heat in my heart, for if he made a quarrel between us, I wanted to mend it. "I'll spar with you tomorrow, Father, if you like."

"High time you got back into practice, for the Domberks buzz like a hive of wasps, so I hear."

Lord Brock Domberk was a vassal of my father's, but an uncommonly troublesome one, scheming always to take the throne of Calidon for himself. "Truly?" I quipped. "More so than usual?"

"Certainly. The crops are in the ground; warrior hands do not care to go idle until harvest, and they have heard that I am sick and weak. Did you not think of that?"

It was unlike him to berate me in front of others. But again I attempted a quiet answer. "I could think of little other than you."

"And now you think of me little, but much of another."

The listeners laughed half-heartedly. In their unease, I saw a reflection of my own. Trying, I am sure, to turn the talk, Todd spoke of Father's charger, Invincible, how he was growing lax in his training, how he needed his master's weight on his back and his master's hands on the reins again.

"Ay, well, then, he's not the only one."

A jab at me again. Enough. Finishing my ale, I rose to take my leave. "I will see you tomorrow in the training yard, Father?"

"So long as you leave that pet goblin of yours behind."

I turned to ice. I am sure my face went frost white. Honorably, I could make no defiant reply before the others, and the silence lay like snow upon us, for they also were struck dumb in shame and fear. Shame for their liege lord's spleen. Fear of his temper.

I made ice move, walk toward the door. As I spoke to Father over my shoulder, my voice was smooth. "Until tomorrow, then."

But what to do on the morrow, I had no idea.

"Pet goblin?" Albaric was my brother! Albaric had saved our ungrateful father's life!

Once well away from the king, I raged through the castle, striding hard, striking the stone walls with my fists. I had thought I was rampaging at random, but somehow I found myself approaching my mother's chamber, and there she stood in her doorway awaiting me.

I melted like a spent candle, hugging her, taking comfort in her embrace. Neither of us spoke a word until I stood back and asked very softly, "Mother, does Father seem oddly changed to you also?"

"Yes," she said, simply, somberly, but she lifted her chin in defiance of the change. "Perhaps this unaccountable ring"— she gestured toward its hiding place beneath her plaid woolen kirtle—"has harmed him. Or perhaps his life has changed so greatly . . . but I do not blame Albaric. And whatever bedevils your father, Aric, I mean to deal with it."

CHAPTER THE NINTH

WE SPOKE AT LENGTH of Father and Albaric. The queen reminded me that believing in Otherwhere and fey things was not in the nature of a king; indeed, a king differed from lesser men by his lack of fear of ghosts and spirits and midnight shadows. A king dealt in lands held, conflicts won or lost, measures of barley, sides of beef. A king's power depended perhaps more on strength of mind than on the sword, and if any king said he had encountered Elfin kind—one could scarcely imagine the scandal.

"Mother says it is easier for her to welcome you than it is for Father," I told Albaric later that night, for my clumsiness awoke him as I reentered my chamber. "She says a woman learns all her life to accept changes."

"Such as her husband's by-blows," he muttered.

"Mother does not think of you that way, Albaric. You're no mortal brat but a savior from Othergates, and she embraces you as I do."

"Queen Evalin believes me, then?"

"Of course." Mother's was a mind that saw clearly, and pondered well, and judged truly.

"You asked her?"

"Yes. She knows you speak truth, and if she had her way, you would dine on the dais with us."

"But the king—one cannot blame—him—"

"Your father. Our father. Go ahead and say it."

Albaric shook his head. "Not until he permits it. Perhaps not ever again."

A brave truth I could not deny.

"He was not unkind in granting me Bluefire today," Albaric added.

"Yes? Good." Let him think so if he liked; he did not need to know I had heard and seen. Nor did he know that the "not unkind" king had called him my "pet goblin." Nor would I tell him. Not ever.

I lay silent on my side of the great canopy bed, and Albaric slept, but I slept little. My heart hurt. While Father had lain dying, I had desperately wanted him to live. I had not been able to imagine going on without my father who loved me, my father noble and kind. But now, even though he lived, I felt bereft of him.

Morning dawned as cold and windy and gray as the day before had been sunny and warm. Very early, so as to outwit Father, I dressed for the training yard, inviting Albaric to spar with me; he accepted happily even as he inquired, "More sore muscles?"

"Ay, but your arms and shoulders this time." I must be

careful, go gently with him, I thought. "Breakfast first, but eat lightly."

We passed through the kitchen to filch some bread and cheese. Although the servants avoided us, no one screamed or ran away any longer, I was pleased to note. Perhaps in time they would become accustomed to Albaric.

We ate as we walked to the barracks, where each of us chose a leather helmet, a leather shield, and a wooden sword. Albaric hefted several swords before settling on a lightweight one such as striplings use. "There's no use pretending I'm warrior-thewed as you are, Aric," he remarked as we entered the yard.

"Many are the folk who believe strong muscle means weak mind."

"If they think that of you, then they are badly mistaken."

We squared off, and as I raised shield and sword, reminding myself not to knock him about, he sent his weapon darting like a bird through my defenses and gave me a light poke in the belly. First touch for him.

"Wake up," he said with a smile.

"How did you do that?" I exclaimed.

"Quickly." As he came at me again.

I just barely fended him off. Never had I faced so swift a sword. He sparred with the cunning of a serpent and the speed of a viper's strike. By the fifth bout, I was sweating, panting, and had managed to touch him only once. But I began laughing so hard at myself that he cried, "Hold!" We ceased combat, and as I leaned on my heavy wooden weapon, gasping for breath amidst laughter, he said soberly, "'Tis not honorable to cross swords with an opponent who has lost his wits. Are you weak-minded after all? What's addled you?"

"Lightning smite me, you are the best swordsman I have ever—"

Then I became aware of a tall figure standing nearby as if he had been watching for a while. Silenced, I turned to the king. But Father spoke first to my brother, and only a little gruffly.

"Aric speaks truth, Albaric. You are a superlative swordsman."

Albaric bowed his head courteously at the compliment but then raised his eyes to gaze straight at Father as he said, "Small wonder, my King, for you taught me."

The words struck like a sword, staggering the king. "What?" he roared.

But Albaric replied in the same quiet tone, "You are the one who taught me my swordsmanship, all the while I was growing up, my—" I knew he struggled to keep the word "father" unspoken upon his lips.

I think Father knew it too. "Silence," he ordered, then turned to me. "Aric, come with me. I would speak with you."

Leaving my gear with my brother, I obeyed. Father led the way almost to the middle of the tourney field, to an isolation where no one could hear us.

When he stopped, I expected to withstand his long stare before he loosed his royal wrath. But he surprised me. He said at once, quietly, "My mind is reeling. I see his heart in his eyes, yet I remember him not, and the more I admit there is truth in him, the less I feel for him except to shudder at his freakishness." But his tone changed. "Aric, could you not spare me his presence for a few hours? I told you not to bring him."

Lightly I retorted, "You told me not to bring a pet goblin, my Sire. But I have none."

"You knew what I meant."

I took a deep breath. "Father," I said, "Albaric told me that you said I was ever wont to tweak your beard."

"He *said* that?"

"Yes. And I think never has it needed tweaking more than now."

"To the contrary. I know not what to think, and you jest? Never have I had less stomach for your impudence."

"Then I am sorry." I had wanted to teach him not to call my brother, his son, by hateful names, but now I felt at fault. "Come, Father, have a few bouts with me," I coaxed. "Whack me upon the head, and you will feel better."

He shook his head, averting his eyes. "I'm likely to 'whack' too hard. Some other day," he muttered, and he strode away.

The day proceeded, like many a Calidon day, from wind to rain to rainbow and sunshine. Under that painted sky, we rode forth, Albaric and I, he upon Bluefire and I upon Valor. Taking my advice, Albaric persuaded Bluefire to accept the lightest of saddles, so that he might brace his feet in stirrups and spare his sore legs. But not so much as a string restrained the blue stallion's head as we galloped up pastures cropped short by sheep, and onward to the meadowlands wet after their shower, smelling greenly sweet, then to the wooded hills. Wary of the blue steed, Valor made no attempt to press ahead of him, nor do I think he could have. When I felt Valor tiring, I called to Albaric, and we slowed to a walk—although truth to tell, Bluefire pranced more than walked.

"Is this country very strange to you?" I asked my brother. "Very ugly compared to whence you came?"

"Ugly, no. Odd, yes. The piles of stone—"

"Cairns. Burial mounds."

"And the great rocks set on end?"

"Ancient peoples put them that way."

"Ancient?" He did not understand the word.

"Long ago." I struggled to explain. "Dead and gone so far in the past that we know nothing of them."

"Long—is large time."

"Yes."

"I am unaccustomed to a land with time and life and death in it. These mighty trees, is it the weight of time I feel in them?"

Giant oaks loomed around us now, rainwater gently dripping from their crowns far above, and even Bluefire quieted in their shadows, passing their mossy trunks of great girth. I, too, felt a sense of awe. "Perhaps. They stand like the rocks, yet they live, they grow, they have been here longer than any man, and sometimes I have fancied that I could hear them whispering among themselves as they listened to the news of the wind."

"They seem to me beautiful and wise," Albaric said. "I feel at home in this place. Is this where—where my mother came a-riding?"

I blinked, wondering at myself, for I had thought only to gallop the blue stallion uphill to sap his wild energy, yet I had led us straight to the wood where Father and I had gone hawking that day—little more than a month ago, yet I felt as if a lifetime had passed.

"Yes, this is the place," I answered as our horses paused to drink at the spring, and then as if the wisdom of the giant trees could help us, I blurted, "My brother, what are we to do about this disgruntled father of ours?"

"I wish I knew." Albaric stroked the blue roan's neck, and for once the steed stood still, so that we could face each other. "When I came here, I quested only to save his life," Albaric admitted. "I never gave a thought to the way it is with mortals, that there would be the next day and the next."

"Afterwards."

"Yes."

"But you hoped he would still be a father to you."

"Yes, like a fool. How should he remember? Yet here I am."

"Knowing what you do now, would you have accepted the quest just the same?"

"Of course! I could not let him die."

"But now *you* will die."

"Right now?"

"No." I most certainly hoped not.

"Then what matter?" He shrugged, yet gave me a piercing stare. "Aric, if you pity me, stop it, for there is no need. Even if I could return, which I cannot, there is nothing in Elfland for me. My mother would rather I were never born, and the others shun me; I am an oddling there just as I am here. To all except you."

I murmured, "Perhaps not."

"What? You're not saying—"

I felt his keen alarm. "No, no, I will never forsake you, my brother! What I mean is, perhaps you are not an oddling to all people. Perhaps we should go somewhere else. To a place where no one saw you ride through a barred gate, where no one saw your white horse return to the air, where no one has heard of a fey ring. To a place where perhaps no one will see you as anyone or anything except—you."

When I saw hope dawning in his eyes, however faint the glimmer, the dayspring, then I knew we had to do it.

CHAPTER THE TENTH

I BADLY WANTED to speak with my father alone, heart to heart, and not hide like a child behind my mother's skirts, but for Albaric's sake, I put aside my pride. I hardly knew Father anymore; I needed Mother for the sake of her good sense, and moreover she had as much right to hear what I proposed as Father did. So, as I wished them to understand it was a serious matter, I petitioned both King and Queen of Calidon, in writing, for an audience.

"Do you know how to read and write?" I asked Albaric as I penned this missive in the privacy of my chamber.

"Yes."

"They have books in Elfland, then?"

"No. Fa— I mean, King Bardaric taught me. He would write on sand with a stick and I would read. In Erse," Albaric added.

I paused, my quill dripping upon the blotter, to gawk at him.

He smiled, amused. "There is no writing in Elvish."

"But. . . ." I struggled for understanding of what it might have been like for him, growing up. "But your mother spoke Erse?"

"When she was in love with the King of Calidon, yes. But the moment he was gone, she forgot it."

I shook my head and returned my attention to my writing. But once my missive was completed, blotted, folded, sealed with wax, and delivered, I sought out the castle scribes, who unlocked for me the chest where the books were kept, for they were few and precious. Untold years had gone by since the Romans had left behind what little learning they had brought here, and throughout the Craglands and the southern lands near the wall—Hadrian's wall—all had returned to ignorance and greed. There, barbaric tribes painted themselves and hacked at one another with huge swords so heavy it took two hands to wield them. Wild, fierce peoples, they fought against anyone they pleased, including the Norsemen with dragon-headed longboats who raided the shores.

Here to the far north, in rugged Calidon, we lived as if in a different land, a mortal Othergates; here was mostly peace, aside from occasional defiance from the Domberks. But they were a petty enemy, while the fearsome Norse seafarers with horned helmets passed us by, for their runes, which we could not decipher, had at some time been chiseled into our sea cliffs, and there were legends of the founding of Calidon by a flaxen-haired White King who had come from the sea and would come again to welcome back a time of peace and plenty. The legends claimed that this was why the Norsemen let us alone: because we were the descendants of one of their ancestors, if not one of their gods.

This much was true, that we of Calidon, like the Vikings, were tall and fair, while the people of the Craglands and the other southerners were short and dark.

Nor did raiders from the Craglands often venture this far

north. No one greatly desired our chill, stony kingdom where arable land was sparse and the growing season short. We possessed little for anyone to covet; we fished the sea, hunted, herded sheep, and while we kept ourselves reasonably equipped for war, we tried to preserve peace and civilization of a sort.

Civilization. Books.

The ones in Latin and Greek I left with the scribes, but I took an odd old volume bound in piebald-spotted leather with the fur yet on, and this I offered to Albaric.

He did not at first understand what it was. When I opened it and showed him the leaves of parchment and the words inked thereon, he gasped, turned to the beginning and began at once, albeit with difficulty, to read.

Thus he spent the two days before my audience was granted. He could hardly raise his eyes for the wonder of the words. "These are songs!"

"Ancient ones. They may once have been chanted around the holy bonfires on the quarter-days when the year turned."

"Year? Turned?"

"A year is like a wheel, a great turning circle of time. Winter, spring, summer, autumn, and then another year, winter and so on all over again."

"This has been going on for a large—um, long—time?"

"Since time began."

"Time *began*? What came before?"

Perhaps my mind was a wheel; it seemed to spin, or wobble. "I do not know."

"I do not know some of these ancient words either. What is 'troth'?"

I sighed with relief; this was easier. "Troth, like both," I corrected his pronunciation.

"Troth, like both of us?" A sober joke that was perhaps no joke at all, and he said the word correctly.

"I think so, yes."

"Is it the same as truth?"

"In a way, yes, but more. Troth is. . . ." I searched my mind. "It is honor and valor and—and uncommon loyalty. Utmost faithfulness."

"A great weight of meaning for one small word."

"Yes. Where did you find it?"

He sought a page and read aloud, haltingly,

What is a friend?
Troth without end
A light in the eyes,
A touch of the hand—
I would follow you
Even to Death's dark strand.

The catch in his voice, I realized, was partly from emotion. I touched his hand.

"I mean that," I said, but then I had to turn away and leave the room, for I had taken myself by surprise, and I felt embarrassed to face him.

Often, those days, I tried to see my father alone, no avail. I think he avoided me.

So as the appointed time for my audience approached, I took great pains to dress as if I had not a care in my heart. I wore youthful clothing—fur leggings, a jerkin instead of a tunic, and over the jerkin a gaily checked short cape, and over that a woolen neck kerchief of a different plaid—here in Calidon we did not weave only plaids of exact design, as the Craglands folk did their clan tartans, but we enjoyed any bright-colored work of the loom. I put aside my sword belt, and in what I hoped was winsome regalia, I went to meet my father and my mother in the council chamber.

To Father's credit, when he saw me, he took off his torc and baldric, and he and Mother descended from their thrones. More humbly seated, they waited for me, standing before them, to tell them what I wanted so very formally. What permission, what favor, what boon.

I had determined that this should not be the sort of audience they expected.

I had seen to it that nearby, on a sideboard, stood a sconce of many candles, unlit. I lifted this, took out one of the candles, and lighted it at the hearth fire. When it burned strongly, I carried it toward my father and dropped to one knee before him.

"Sire," I said to him, "see this flame, how it shines? It is my fealty for you."

He raised his brows. "Why should it be necessary for you to bespeak your loyalty?"

By way of answer, I arose to set the sconce back where I had found it, for I needed the use of both hands to loosen another candle from the sconce and light it from the first. When it burned strongly, I handed it to the queen. "Mother, here is the flame of my love for you."

She smiled.

"Has the one flame taken away from the other? Has my love for you taken away from my love for my father?" I held up the first candle. "Sire, does this flame burn any less brightly than it did before?"

"Bah! Of course not! Aric, why such talk?"

"Because it is needful." I took another candle from the sconce, lit it from mine and handed it to him. "That is yours, Sire, for all the warmth in your heart. Do we now have less light?"

"Son, you weary me, speaking in riddles."

"Why is it, Father, that I have felt so little of your warmth of late, when my own has not changed?"

In a low voice, he said, "I feel a change."

"But you can see—" I lifted my small beacon. "There is no lessening of my love. I swear it, Father. I could light candles for my bookmasters and weaponmasters and for Todd and his grooms and my horse and my hawk—"

"Pray do not so!" And praise be, he laughed.

"Only one more, then." I chose a fourth candle and lit it. "This is for Albaric."

Father's laughter stopped like a stone, dropped. "Place it far from me."

I put it back into the sconce, and my own alongside it.

"No," Father said.

"Yes, if I am worthy to be called your son," I said quietly, turning to face him.

"Bah!"

My mother then astonished me. Without fuss, as if she performed the most ordinary of daily tasks, she rose from her chair, her wide-sleeved silk gown rustling like wind in oak leaves as she walked to place her candle in the sconce beside mine. And as she returned to her seat, she took the one out of my father's hand. "I think I must safeguard this for you," she remarked. "You were just about to blow it out, were you not? In anger? When I smile on Albaric, are you angry at me too?"

"I do not pass judgment on anyone!" The words sounded like a plea, and I could not at first understand the look on my father's face, for I had never seen it before. "But a king must think like a king. An oddling comes and claims to be my son. What can I think but that he schemes to take the throne?"

Mother drew from beneath her gown the golden chain on which hung something that looked like a black ember glowing red. The ring! Like a coal of fire pendant upon its own prison, it danced. "See how the mischievous thing rejoices in your suspicion," Mother chided. "I can almost hear it chuckling."

"Put that monstrosity away from me!" said Father in a voice as harsh as a rasp. Yet his face reddened, and now I recognized what I saw there: shame, with which he struggled clumsily, unaccustomed to guilt, to error. Never in my memory had such self-doubt afflicted him before.

I felt for him, terribly. "Father, let me see whether I can help." Like a child, I sat on the floor at his feet. "Please hear me, my Sire. Do you remember how, as you lay dying, you rallied for a moment to say good-bye to Mother and me?"

"I have told you, I remember naught—"

Mother did an odd thing. Onto his still-burning candle, she slipped the ring, which settled upon the taper like a belt around the waist of a tunic. As if something had bespoken him, Father turned to gaze into the candle's flame.

"Yes," he whispered, his face harrowed by memory. "Yes, terrible, my self watery weak, my body the merest fragile shell. Aric, I wanted to tell you—" He hesitated, remembering some deathbed message, some words from the heart he no longer wished to speak. "I wanted to tell you something, but you ran out of the room."

"I needed to tend to uproar in the courtyard," I said. "Darkness hung overhead that night, Father, the spirits were singing around the tower, and then one rode in on a fey white steed." He had heard the story, of course, but now he was listening, and perhaps seeing, as never before. So I told him all, from the moment I first bespoke Albaric until the moment Albaric cozened the eerie ring off his finger. "And then you opened your eyes and said, 'What in bloody blazes is going on?'"

I imitated his voice. He laughed as if he felt the joy of that moment, and as he turned to me, Mother snuffed the candle with her fingers, slipped the ring off, and laid it in her lap.

"Father," I asked, "do you remember the first moment you saw Albaric?"

"Yes. The comeliest youth ever to walk the earth. And he still is," Father added in wonder. "Why, now, do I no longer regard him so?"

"Never mind that. He asked you, 'Sire, do you not know me?'"

"Yes, and the pain in his eyes—it should have broken my heart! Yet I could give him no fair answer."

In a sense he had returned to me again, as if from death. I dared to take his war-hardened hand between my own. "Do not blame yourself. You were newborn to life, heedless as an infant. Father," I added, "look at the ring."

The unaccountable thing lay on Mother's sky-blue skirt, innocent and crystalline, as clear as tears.

After a moment, Father breathed out. "Well," he said in a dry whisper, "that is a bit better."

"Sire, I must tell you the rest now, while you are fit to hear." I spoke with difficulty, hating to distress him anew. "The servants brought a surfeit of food, do you remember?" Gazing down on me, he nodded. "In the confusion, Albaric slipped out, and when I noticed he was gone, I went looking for him. At first I feared he had left Dun Caltor, but then a sudden sureness led me up the tower to the very top. I had no torch and I could see nothing in the dark, for Death still hovered there, blocking the stars. Yet I walked straight to him and touched his shoulder. Standing at the edge, he asked me whether a fall to the rocks below would put an end to him."

Both Mother and Father gasped, and in the throes of reaction, Father's hand clenched so hard I had to let it go.

"And I answered him," I went on, "that indeed it would, and it would put an end to me also, for his heart was mine and would take me with him. Father, you did not recognize him, but I did, instantly, soul to soul. Please, Sire, can you understand?"

Silence. Father sat with his head bowed, perhaps thinking of what I had said. I hoped so, although his shoulders jutted hard and still as stone.

"Albaric would have leapt to his death but for you?" Mother asked me softly.

"Yes, Mother. And still he is in dire straits, stranded in this world."

Father spoke at last, hoarsely, "Wonders and marvels unnerve me." He cleared his throat to say more strongly, "Aric, I understand a little, for a moment, tonight, but in the morning, I may be testier than ever."

"That is why I petition you tonight concerning Albaric. He

has one hope: that if he travels someplace where no one knows of wonders and marvels, perhaps he will find peace."

Father gave me a piercing stare. "And you will go with him?"

"Of course I will go with him." I rose to my feet. "I am all he has."

"Folk will think you are a pair of molly boys," Father muttered.

"Bard!" Mother sounded more amused than shocked.

I myself smiled. "No, they will not. Albaric will be a harper. I will be the Prince of Calidon on cavalcade from vassal to vassal in search of a wife. Who knows?" I added as an afterthought. "I might even find one."

"That would be nice," said Mother pensively.

"I wish I could say I will miss you," Father muttered, and although his words smote me to the heart, they did not offend. He attested but the simple truth: lately, my presence caused him nothing but misery.

Such was the manner in which he gave assent to my quest.

CHAPTER THE
ELEVENTH

SOMEHOW EVERYTHING WAS MADE READY in less than a
week. Mother found suitable clothing—plain but not
poor—for the harper, Albaric, in the myriad chests
of which she was mistress. Also she passed along some regal
things for me, tunics and tabards in the Calidon colors that
had been Father's "when he was younger and a bit slimmer."
Albaric and I battled cobwebs searching dusty turrets until we
found for him a fitting harp, rosewood inlaid with gold, its
tone sweetened by age. Father selected four of the strongest,
steadiest, most mature, and humorless of his guardsmen to
accompany us and provided them with the sturdiest horses in
the stable.

There was a bit of a rigmarole regarding horses. Albaric
insisted that I should ride Bluefire. "A harper on so fine a
steed?" he argued. "'Twould defeat the purpose."

The covert purpose, he meant, which was to gift him with
being seen as just another mortal.

I retorted, "Yet the harper will not hear of leaving the steed
behind, here at Dun Caltor?"

"Aric, he cannot be parted from me now!"

True, for the blue horse was likely to break down his stall, or break his own legs trying to do so, or trample anyone from a groom to the king if he became wild to follow Albaric. Still, I teased, "Don't you have that backwards? Isn't it *you* who cannot be parted from *him*?"

"I beg you, Aric, stop tweaking my beard, especially as I do not even have one."

"But how am I to ride that thundering blue gale of a storm?"

"On his back."

"Albaric—"

"My brother, as you trust me, you can trust him. I promise."

And so it proved. What sort of soundless communication took place between Albaric and his steed, I cannot say, but when the time came, I mounted the saddle, took up the reins, and felt the horse's assent beneath me. The bridle was made of the finest and softest of leather, with some jingling metal studs and rings at the sides, but anyone who looked closely would have seen that they attached to nothing. No one who knew Bluefire was fool enough to try to put a bit in the stallion's mouth; the headgear was all for show. Bluefire did what I wanted because he chose to.

All of Dun Caltor turned out to see us off, a small but colorful cavalcade: I in a crested helmet and crimson plaid mantle upon the blue steed, Albaric fair and bareheaded in a belted green tunic on a bony gray cob he had chosen for its winsome ugliness, and four mounted men-at-arms wearing metal-studded leather tunics with Roman skirts, on their pike heads pennons of the Calidon colors, crimson and slate. Piebald packhorses carried our supplies, plus Albaric's harp protected within a waxed leathern sack.

Atop the stone steps of the keep, the king and the queen bade us to fare safely and return soon, Mother in her ermine cloak despite the warmth of the sunny day in late June, Father resplendent in golden torc and golden crown and bold crimson cape lined with slate-colored silk. Our private words of farewell had been spoken earlier; this was a formal appearance, meaning nothing except that their finery plus mine made Albaric in his unadorned green look less awesome in the eyes of the castle folk. Or so Father hoped.

Once we were out of the gate, I grinned at my brother. "Would you like to borrow my hat?"

He eyed the metal monstrosity askance. "Not for all the strawberries ripening on yonder hillside."

"My Prince, you're likely to need the helmet before day's done," said a deep and dour voice from behind me—Garth, leader of my little troop of guards. "You too, harper." He spoke the word "harper" with a certain emphasis as if to say that he knew better. "I've packed you a leathern one. And where's your sword?"

"With my harp." Albaric spoke courteously. "I'll strap it on when you give the word, Captain. But a sword is of small use against the arrows of robbers."

"True. What would you have us do about them?"

"Doubtless the same as you would. When we reach the forest, speak not, but pay heed."

"Pay closest heed," Garth agreed in a growl, and for a goodly while he held forth, to his men as well as to Albaric and me, on the significance of bird cries or silences; the shying of horses, which can mean everything or nothing; the proper way to approach a fallen tree, which might conceal an ambush; and so on.

"We could have gone by sea," I remarked at one point, soberly tweaking Garth's beard, for to landsmen the sea was more fearsome than the hounds of hell yelling a death chase in the sky. "There are no trees at sea."

"No, only sickness and gales, whirlpools, waterspouts, pirates, whales, and death by drowning! Mock me not, my puckish Prince, but listen to me."

I listened meekly, for I sensed that Albaric was listening not at all but riding alongside me as happy as I had ever known him to be, happy with the sun on his shoulders and swaying to the cadence of a horse's gait and counted as one in the company of others.

First we left behind the castle village, then the farmed furrows boxed within hawthorn hedges or stone fences against errant swine, then the pastureland cropped short by sheep, then the higher unfenced meadows where the grass grew tall amid wild blossoms, where barefoot children watched over milk cows, geese, and goats. Then we followed narrow tracks through patches of forest where hogs rooted amid the hazels and rowans and the oak trees. But we did not reach true forest that day, only long shadows and a shambling inn called the Rooster's Tail. We all ate well enough, but we chose to "roost" like the horses in the cowshed, on straw, because the bedding of the inn heaved with lice.

"Worse than fleas," I explained to Albaric.

"How is that possible?" He had not yet learned to accept the inevitability of fleas in mortal life.

"Fleas one can see and kill. Lice, not so."

"They are *invisible?*"

"Not the way you mean."

"Harper, go to sleep," grumbled Garth from the straw of the next stall, "or go lie under the horses' feet, where there will be worse than fleas or lice either."

"Truly? What might that be?"

"Bah! Be silent and let us rest."

We did so.

The next day, the track we followed entered the primeval forest of outlaw legend, wilderness untamed by pig herders or peasants seeking wood; only deer could find ways through the dense thickets beneath the towering trees—they, and the wild men who lived there, who would wish to rob of us of whatever our pack ponies carried, and of our horses, and if necessary, of our lives.

The track was just wide enough for us to ride two abreast, and the great trees arched across it entirely.

"I like not this tunnel," Garth said even before we had left the sunlight behind. "Enemies drop like catamounts from above. Prince Aric, here your guards should ride before you."

Call it foolish pride, but I could not allow that. "Would my Father hide behind guards? Hardly, and neither will I."

"But His Majesty bade me—"

"Silence, Garth." Although I did not speak harshly, my words bore the force of royal command, partly because of what I sensed in Albaric: more than mere calm, it was utter confidence. He knew something I did not. Yet.

"Onward," I ordered, "at the walk, and be quiet."

Perhaps an hour passed, slowly. The farther into that wilderness we fared, the darker seemed the shadows of the trees and the narrower seemed the track, twisting around hills and down deep valleys. It was difficult to keep a brave heart, for we were too richly arrayed not to be waylaid; attack menaced as we rounded every bend.

All this time, Bluefire had carried me steadily without a sign of fear, but suddenly he halted, ears forward, with a snort.

"Scofflaws in the trees ahead!" shouted Albaric gaily, and then I understood: he had known all along that Bluefire would give ample warning.

At once I snatched a fist-sized stone from a sack hanging on my saddle and hurled it at a likely clump of leaves. A yelp sounded even as I threw another stone. Not the most princely weapon, perhaps, but effective, for with a howl a rough-looking churl fell down on his rump in the middle of the track, his bow and arrow pointing skyward. At once the others, eight or nine of them, dropped, landing on their feet, to defend him.

They bent their bows and let fly their arrows at us. But we gave them no time to shoot a second volley. Even before I could think what to do, Bluefire charged, and as I smote enemies with my sword, my steed reared, striking with the deadly points of his forehooves! Nor did the horse and I fight alone, for dimly I grew aware of Albaric and the others beside me doing battle. It was all over in a few minutes. The ruffians fled into the forest, dragging their wounded with them. Bluefire stood again on four feet. We travelers took breath and looked at one another.

"I was unaware, my Prince," said Garth soberly, "that you threw stones with such force and skill." Confound the sour old pickle, commenting on my less-than-royal choice of weapons—yet it gladdened me to see him almost smiling.

"Nor was I aware," he added, "that you or any warrior could fight from a horse on its hind legs."

"A simple matter of flour paste on the saddle," I told him, mock serious.

"Aric," asked Albaric, truly serious, "is it customary to wear an arrow the way you are doing?"

"What?" I had not even noticed I was wounded, but there was an arrow indeed, through my upper left arm.

"No, Prince Aric, don't touch it. You will only make it worse," Garth warned as I reached to pull it out. "Wait. I will tend to it." He dismounted and beckoned for me to do so also. "Where's the bandaging?"

Another guardsman was already bringing a bundle of linen strips from one of the pack ponies.

"Is no one else in need of that?" I asked, looking around, but all my men appeared undamaged.

"Yon yeomen suffered naught, thanks to your remarkable horse and your even more remarkable missiles, my Prince."

"And my remarkable harper."

Garth looked at me strangely but said nothing except, "Stand still, Prince Aric," as he drew his dirk. It speaks for my trust in him that I did indeed stand still. But he did not cut me, only the arrow. Severing its shaft, he let the feathered end fall and drew the arrow out of my arm by its head. At once, blood flowed down my tunic sleeve, but rather than trying to staunch it, he watched.

"Good," he said.

"Good? How?"

"The blood does not spurt or flood. Yet it washes the wound so that one can trust it will not fester. All should be well."

I hoped so. Men had been known to die from the slightest

wounds, ludicrous hurts such as a blister on the heel, if the injury festered, swelling and reddening, filling with foul-smelling poison, killing with fever.

Garth wrapped the wound tightly, had me flex my fingers and my arm, then nodded. "Now you're a blooded warrior, my Prince."

"You'll not hear me bragging of a skirmish with robbers," I said. "Let us ride on."

As we mounted, Garth asked, "My Prince, what ever made you think to carry a bag of stones?"

Of course he did not know that all my boyhood, I had played at hurling stones. "They reach farther than a sword, do they not?" I retorted. "Praise be, my throwing arm is not wounded." A jest—I should have said "sword arm." "Silence, now," I added as we left the scene of the outlaw attack behind.

Nightfall found us still in the wilderness, which was vast. Near a goodly stream, other travelers over countless years had made a clearing by chopping trees for firewood and for safety. We stopped there, bathed in the water of the stream, made a blazing fire, ate dried smoked haddock and oat cakes, but there was little talk and no merriment; we all hearkened to the sounds of the forest. We stood guard two at a time by turns—I for one had no trouble staying awake, for my hurt arm ached like a sore tooth—but night passed with no more than the usual dew and drizzle, and morning dawned peacefully, if a bit wet. Garth changed the blood-stiffened wrapping on my wound, nodding at it in a satisfied manner, and after we had breakfasted on the remnants of the previous night's meal, I assembled the company.

"We may reach our first destination today," I told the guardsmen. "If so, or whenever you find yourselves in the company of strangers, these are my orders: tell no one, by word or glance, anything peculiar of our harper." Albaric stood nearby; I put my arm around his shoulders. I seldom touched him thus, for the sake of his pride, but I wanted the men to hearken to my heart as well as my words. "Say nothing of a white horse vanishing in the night, or of a dying king miraculously recovered, or of a wild stallion tamed, or of any tales or freakish imaginings that might be flying around Dun Caltor. Heed my command: say of our companion only that he plays superlatively upon the harp."

"And that he plies superlatively the sword?" asked Garth. "May we say that also?"

"Indeed." He had noticed? This pleased me, but it should not have surprised me. "You understand me? Good. Let us ride on. Cautiously." For we were not out of danger of outlaws yet.

But late that afternoon, we at last reached the thinning outskirts of the wilderness, and by putting our horses to the canter, by nightfall we entered the palisade wall surrounding the hill fortress called Dun Narven.

CHAPTER THE TWELFTH

THIS WAS A TIMBER STRONGHOLD belonging to one of my father's more humble vassals, Lord Kiffin. Because Father, days earlier, had sent a messenger, a warm welcome awaited us. Lord Kiffin did not appear, as was courteous, for he knew I would be weary and sweaty and grimed with three days' journey. But his steward and servants provided a late dinner and hot baths for all, most welcome, before they showed us to bed.

We had but one room in the officers' quarters over the barracks, one bed none too sumptuous, and some straw ticks on the floor. I shared the bed (and its resident fleas) with Albaric and Garth, wondering why we had not been better lodged in the main fortress.

All too soon the next day, I discovered the reason: to my discomfiture, seemingly every marriageable aristocratic maiden in the kingdom had journeyed to Dun Narven to meet me.

"The ladies, as is the privilege of ladies, took over the bed-chambers," explained Lord Kiffin, a florid, jovial man whose excess flesh attested to the good kitchen he kept. Sweet buns and baked eel pie for breakfast, forsooth! Along with us ate his two sons of about my age.

"You throw stones with great skill, I have heard," said one with condescension, as if he were the prince and I the minor noble.

I said nothing and barely wondered how he had heard. Where there are servants, there are few secrets.

"And I have heard, Prince Aric, that you took an arrow wound to the arm without even noticing it," added the other hastily and humbly. Whether attempting to shield his brother or appease me, he seemed good of heart. The other, I sensed, would grow to be a bitter and envious enemy even to his own kin. How odd, that brothers could be so opposite and opposed, so unfeeling of their good fortune in each other.

"I have arranged for music tonight after dinner," continued Lord Kiffin in high spirits. "There are eleven ladies and you three handsome youths. You like not to dance?" He chuckled at our rueful faces. "But I trust each of you can manage?"

"Perhaps Prince Aric could bring stones to reduce the numbers," quipped the bitter-hearted brother.

I took no offense and made no reply. I had long known that there was something about me less than princely, some boyishness that let servants smile on me even as they obeyed me, that let common folk easily approach me and speak with me, that would make it difficult for me to be feared or revered as a king. I knew this quality in myself, and at times I had rued it, but now I rejoiced in it, as it had let Albaric into my heart. What I saw in my father and even sometimes in my mother, armor of spirit tempered by sad memories and distrust—that could wait.

After breakfast, the young lordships found business

elsewhere as Lord Kiffin showed me around his fortress, jesting about the rigors of courtship—as well he might, for at every turning we "happened" to meet a maiden (chaperoned, of course), blushing and curtseying and chiming, "Good morning, Lord Kiffin! And surely this must be his most Royal Highness Prince Aric?"

Their fawning embarrassed me, and then introductions had to be made, pleasantries exchanged, and I needs must withstand the most overwrought adulation while finding a way to compliment the maiden, be she bony, freckled, stout, buxom, chinless, long-nosed, foul of breath, or a dried-out spinster nearing the age of thirty. How I envied Albaric, my servant the harper, free to chat with the cooks in the kitchen, watch the soldiers at drill or the smiths at work, wander to the stable and commune with Bluefire. Even from afar, I could sense that my brother felt exuberantly content. What matter if folk saw his beauty and thought he might be a mollycoddle? At least they assumed him to be human. It was as we had hoped; folk here accepted him.

Then, during the midday meal, he played his harp for Lord Kiffin, and from all who heard, whispers of admiration arose and rippled outward to the others. Wisely, Albaric did not yet sing, only plied the harp strings softly and gaily, butterfly notes darting one moment, drifting the next.

During the afternoon, Lord Kiffin needs must show me every inch of his estate, prattling of cabbages and turnips and such. The summer promised poorly, he said. Many lambs had been stillborn, the cows were giving much less milk than usual, half the onions had rotted in the ground, and the carrots flourished not. I paid no heed, for I was a young fool uninterested in carrots; I did not understand the significance of what he was saying. I admit I thought the day to be among the most tedious I had ever passed until, as we rode out to view the pasturelands, Lord Kiffin looked over at Bluefire and said, "That is no ordinary horse."

I readily agreed.

"A magnificent steed, and blue, yet. It reminds me of a tale my grandfather used to tell of—oh, blast it, I'm sure to get it wrong, for he told it like poetry and I speak the way I look, as plain as a peat bog." It was an apt comparison, and indeed I could not imagine a note of poetry to ring anywhere in Lord Kiffin, who was frowning with effort to remember the story. "It was something about the White King and how he and his blue horse came to Calidon out of the sea."

"The White King?" I knew him only by the name of the torc my father sometimes wore.

"I think that was what Grandfather said, but what he meant by it, I have no idea. All I remember is that the fellow, the king, you know, came sailing in a blue longboat in the midst of a gale, the stormwind tearing at the great square white sail, and the prow of the ship was carved like a horse's head. And it ran right up onto the black shingle of the beach, but as it touched land, it turned to a great blue horse upon which the king rode, and the white sail became his vast white cloak. And he wore a crown of white—white something-or-other. So they called him the White King."

"Where did he come from? And why?"

"That's the rub and gall of it, my Prince, I don't recall! All I remember is how the blue horse came out of the sea."

"Oh, well." I reached forward to stroke Bluefire's black mane. "Perhaps this one is a descendent of his," I said lightly, although my thoughts hung heavy with wonder.

With far less than his usual bluster, Lord Kiffin said, "I could well believe it."

But once we finished speaking of Bluefire, it became a long day—the peas were not sprouting well, either, I seem to recall—and at the end of it, I had no chance to tell the strange tale of the White King to Albaric.

In the evening, for the dinner music and the dance, Lord Kiffin had provided three ancient men, one with a viol, one with bagpipes, and one with a wooden flute. To me, their combined scraping and puffing sounded like a corn mill at work, and as for the ladies fair, I would rather have faced outlaws again. Those maidens who favored tradition came all draped in plaids, their hair in two long braids clasped in gold, while those who liked the modern ways wore their hair in curled tresses over dresses fitted to their upper bodies then flaring into skirts with elaborate borders repeated on long, hanging sleeves. But whether sewn into their dresses or modestly draped, all seemed to vie for the most ornate jewelry, the brightest colors, and my attention.

It was a mercy when the dancing began, for then I could deal with them singly, if at all. There being but four noblemen, including Lord Kiffin, we could dance only in circles or squares of four couples, stepping as lively as we could while the surplus ladies chattered together along the walls, pretending not to watch or mind. The arrow wound in my arm gave me some pain, and the evening became a garish blur to me. Despite gowns of peacock hues, brooches bigger than goose eggs, and hair decked with ribbons of gold, I cannot clearly remember any dance partner except one who demanded of me, "Are you really the Prince of Calidon?"

Startled, I met the gaze of earnestly shining brown eyes in a thin face that narrowed to a tiny chin. Why, despite the elaborate pile of brown hair on top of her head, my partner was hardly more than a child. Her green frock swept the floor, and I would have wagered that beneath its concealment she wore built-up shoes to make her look inches taller.

"Yes, I am the Prince of Calidon, for my mother tells me so," I answered the girl gravely. "Why do you ask?"

"Because you don't look like a Prince."

"How not?" Secretly, I agreed with her on this galling point sore to the touch, but her honesty amused me more than it pained me.

"Why, because your eyes scorn nothing, and sometimes you even smile," she declared all in a rush.

"Great prickly cockleburs, we can't have that. Am I smiling now?"

"Indeed you are. Quite a bit."

"What if I were to frown? Would I look like a prince then?"

She answered doubtfully, "Perhaps a little more so, but your face is too candid and kind."

Candid? If she saw me as honest to the point of being a simpleton, she had hit upon another secret sore. The dance had us circling like combatants as I challenged my slender young partner, "Why, then, what *does* a prince look like?"

"Like that." She aimed her small, pointed chin toward someone, I could not tell whom, as we continued to move about the floor.

"Like what?"

"The harper."

"Ah!" She saw truly! My interest in her increased. "Tell me, what is your name?"

"Marissa of Domberk."

Now this was worth noting. The Domberks constantly raided to steal Caltor cattle, yet they had sent a young maiden—*very* young indeed, and quite artless—to become acquainted with me?

"At your service," she added as an afterthought.

"Really? Would you marry me?" I teased.

"I am too young to marry! I'm here because Mama wanted to come."

"How old are you? Ten?"

"Thirteen! Almost fourteen! But why would I want to marry you? I told you, it is the harper who should be prince."

I smiled toward Albaric perched on the corner of the trestle table, watching everything with catlike interest, his long legs dangling and his harp by his side. "I quite agree with you. He is handsome almost beyond words, is he not?"

"Yes. But that is not it; you are handsome, too. He seems a prince because—because there is something melancholy and distant about him. Some mystery. I could never, ever speak with him the way I am talking with you."

I laughed aloud in delight, and so that she would not take my laughter amiss, I squeezed her hand and kissed her cheek. "Would you like to hear the harper sing?"

"Yes! Very much!"

"Then you shall have your wish, my lady fair." I left the dance, taking her with me by the hand, and like a table with only three legs instead of four, the dance collapsed without us. In mild confusion, the couples halted where they were, the bagpipe and viol and flute ceased playing, and the guests ranged along the wall turned to stare at me.

Meanwhile, my eyes met Albaric's, and a wordless understanding passed between us that all was well with both of us.

"Albaric," I addressed him, "this is Lady Marissa of Domberk."

As she was the noble and he supposedly but a servant, I should have done it the other way around, introducing him to her. Yet without hesitation, she curtsied to him.

I went on, "Lady Marissa would very much like to hear you sing."

"Of course, Milady," he addressed her gravely. "What sort of song do you desire?"

"What do you call a song that tells a story?"

"A ballad."

"Yes. One of those, please. . . ." But speaking to him, suddenly she resembled a hollyhock flower bending in the wind, a thin stalk with a pink, pink face. "Thank you, Prince Aric," she said faintly as she turned and ran across the hall, most likely back to her mother.

As he turned to get his harp, Albaric told me softly, "Your arm is bleeding, my Prince."

I glanced down. "Blast. I should have worn a red tunic, so it wouldn't show."

"Won't you have someone tend to it?"

"In a little while." Turning to the gathering, I announced in my most princely voice, "Ladies and lords, a ballad in honor of Lady Marissa of Domberk."

But really Albaric's song was for me. I knew it from the first touch of his fingers upon the harp strings, the first words of his voice soaring on golden wings.

He stood, facing them all, and this was the story borne by his song:

> Let me tell you a merry-go-sorry,
> Let me tell you a bittersweet tale
> Of a royal youth and his loyal companion
> Who pledged to him his service and hand.
> "My Liege," he said, "you are made of legend.
> I will follow you to the ends of the land."
>
> "I have a quest to the Mountains of Doom,"
> Said the prince, "that lie beyond the dark tide.
> Will you follow me there?" The other smiled.
> "You doubt it, Liege? How can that be?"
> "The way is long and the crossing strange."
> "I will follow you if you walk into that sea."
>
> *What is a friend?*
> *Troth without end.*
> *A light in the eyes,*
> *A touch of the hand—*
> *I would follow you even*
> *to death's cold strand.*

There were no seas or seaside strands in Elfland, I sensed from Albaric's mind. He had looked upon the cold northern sea that washed Dun Caltor, and he had seen how small looked the coracles of the fisher folk who braved the fickle waves, but mostly he understood what he was singing only with his heart. The words came from the peculiar old book

I had given to him, but the melody was his own, and so uncannily beautiful that it laid hold upon me as no song had ever done before. Judging by their breathless silence, it had a similar effect on the others.

> So they rode afar to the kingdom's sea-reaches
> And came in the end to the sundering strait
> And by that dim shore swam a ghost-gray ship
> Low in the water but nothing within
> Except shivering scent of fear insubstantial
> And mournful voices of folk unseen.
>
> "That is our vessel." But the comrade blanched,
> His breath came tight, his knees gave beneath him,
> He could not go on. "Liege, help me,"
> He cried from the stones of that far cold strand.
> "I am not of the stuff of legends," said he.
>
> A touch of the hand.
> "I understand."
> For all friends fail
> All loyalties quail
> When they reach the end of the living land.

Yet Albaric, my fair, fey brother, while mindful of death, was a stranger to it. He had never known the death of kin or companion, had never shot a stag or slain a hare, had never even to my knowledge seen a chicken's neck wrung for the cook-pot. Was this song his way of trying to fathom the fate he had chosen for himself, his mortality?

"I will go alone. Now get you up,
Go home, be happy, live long and die merry."
He kissed him, the kiss of forgiveness and love,
Then he boarded the gray ship. The vessel set sail.
His companion stood chill and watched it go.
In his ears rang a single living farewell.

And the gray ship sailed on the cold dark tide,
Heavy and slow on the dim washing water
Then gone like mist—how could that be?
The other stood on the land looking after
Then followed his prince—and walked into that sea.

What is a friend?
Troth without end.
A light in the eyes,
A touch of the hand—
I would follow you even
to Mountains of Doom beyond
Death's—cold—strand.

A silver, shiversome tone had crept into Albaric's golden voice, eerie, like the ringing of bluebells one can sometimes hear when spirits pass in the wind, when someone is about to die. He put down his harp amid silence as deep as a grave.

Then it was as if everyone awoke, everyone babbled at once, applauding. Throngs gathered around Albaric, warming him with praise; I could feel it, counterpoint to a shadow the song left in him. But as I stood thinking about my brother, my arm gave me a stab of pain. I made toward Lord Kiffin to ask him if there were a healer in his household.

"Prince Aric!" he exclaimed, staring at the bright red stain on my tunic. "What is that on your sleeve?"

"My heart, I think," I told him.

CHAPTER THE
THIRTEENTH

ONLY A FEW DAYS THEREAFTER, Albaric became more closely acquainted with death.

We had left Dun Narven on a day pleasant enough once we got away from endless thanks and wearisome ceremony. With relief in my chest at least, our little cavalcade passed out through the palisade gate, questing toward the next vassal holding. As before, I rode Bluefire, Albaric rode quite inappropriately beside me on his homely gray cob, and the four men-at-arms followed, tending the packhorses. But we had not gone half a day before we left the hillsides close-cropped by sheep behind us, entering the skirts of the forest. All the world from here to Rome so far as I knew was like Calidon in that respect, all the land a great green ocean of wilderness billowing with trees, its scattered islands the pocks of cleared land men had made, where peasants huddled around an overlord's stronghold.

As the forest thickened, Garth of course recited his litany of warnings, and we would have been foolish not to pay heed. In the open, we had ridden careless and bareheaded to the breeze, but once in wildwood shadow, we put on our helmets and armored tunics—plates of metal held together by leather, with Roman skirts—over which we belted on our swords, and we hung our shields from our saddles, close at hand. We rode on in silence, our horses' hooves clopping softly on dirt deep with leaf loam.

But all went peacefully the first day, of course. Robbers and outlaws are not fools; they know that travelers grow weary of watchfulness, and sleepier after each night that they must stand guard; the farther into the forest, the more likely they are to be taken unawares.

So might we have been taken if it were not for Bluefire.

The forest track meandered around hills and boulders, narrow and dark beneath towering oaks. Every curve of the way had to be approached with caution, for who knew what lay beyond it, just out of sight? But there were so many bends in the path, so many false alarms, and it was so wearisome walking the horses in silence, that by mid-afternoon of the second day, we were thinking—or at least I was thinking—mostly of when we might stop and what we might then eat—

Bluefire halted, quivering all over with fury, not fear. He half-reared as if to charge, yet made no sound. I pulled on his mane to restrain him as we all came to a confused stop, snatching up our shields and swords. Ahead of us, the narrow track took a sharp bend, and beyond the bend most likely the robbers had felled a tree too bushy for the horses to jump, while they waited to drop on us from above when we reached it. But this time, Albaric did not cry, "Scofflaws in the trees!" Instead, he whispered, "Listen."

Indeed we did listen, with all our ears, for we could see nothing. We listened to the wind soughing in the leaves, the heedless hum of insects, the silence where there should have been birdsong, the—faintly, a metallic clanking sound—and was that the creaking of leather?

Robbers do not wear armor or shift in their saddles.

I cupped my hands around my mouth and roared, "Show yourselves, cowards!"

Echoes joined the shadows under the oaks, and along with the echoes, I heard several startled voices, the whicker of a horse, and a clash of metal as swords were drawn. A moment later, half a dozen men-at-arms in metal helmets and tunics of—of chain mail, forsooth!—rode into sight and ranked to confront us, just a little more than a stone's throw away.

"Whom do you call cowards?" bellowed the one at their fore.

"It is hard to tell," I shot back, "as your helms shadow your faces and your shields show no device."

"It is a sad and shameful day," added Garth's strong old voice from behind me, "when mounted warriors lurk in ambush like brigands to rob travelers."

"It's worse than that, Garth," I spoke quietly over my shoulder to him, but the enemy heard.

"Indeed it is," sneered the foremost foe. "Prepare to die, puppy Prince!"

But before the words were out of his mouth, Bluefire charged with the speed of a falcon in flight; had I not been holding his mane, he might have left me behind. It was the sneering man who needed to prepare to die. Bluefire leapt and struck him like a lance, unseating him to trample and crush him. As for me, even though I had gathered that these were no random raiders, it took a moment for my wits to catch up with those of my horse, and Bluefire had already struck to kill as I raised my sword, fending off an attacker's strong blow by instinct. After that, it was nothing but clash of metal upon metal, strike and parry. There was no time to think. I felt more than saw Albaric fighting close by my side, his sword a falcon of death, darting and swift. I became aware that my men-at-arms had made use of their pikes, charging and unseating three more of the enemy—but then another six warriors armored in chain mail appeared! Cowards indeed, they had been waiting, concealed behind the trees, and how many more might there be?

Now it was often two swords of theirs to every one of ours. No chivalry. And no room to maneuver in that strait passageway between thick walls of forest. The pressure of two attackers unseated me; with a cry, I fell. Instantly, Albaric leapt to join me on the ground, taking a sword slash while defending me as I got to my feet, then setting his back to mine so that no one could take either of us from behind. Mounted foes charged us—but while Albaric's cob bolted, as any normal and sensible horse would do, Bluefire reared and attacked the attackers! No one on horseback reached us, but Albaric and I fended off swordsman after swordsman, I felt my helmet dented by more than one blow, and I saw the blood spurt as I nearly beheaded an enemy, I smelled it, felt its hot splash, and hardened myself as it sickened me. I fought on against a red blur of flashing swords and took care not to think either of living or of dying.

But suddenly I was hacking at air. Not yet daring to lower my sword, I blinked, clearing blood or sweat or hell knows what from my eyes, looking about me.

Bodies, some of them groaning, crowded the narrow byway beneath forest shadows. Some of them strangers, some not.

"Albaric!" I cried.

"Right here."

We turned to look at each other. He had taken a gash from cheekbone to chin.

"Your *face*," I choked.

"It's nothing. Are you hurt?"

"No more than you. Bluefire saved us." Now the horse stood browsing at the low boughs as if nothing had happened.

"That blue stallion and you two," said a hoarse and panting voice, "fought off more of them than I could count."

I turned, crying, "Garth!" He crouched with both of his arms wrapped around his stomach. I ran to him, eased him to the ground, and yanked off my armor and my tunic to wrap the latter around a wound I could scarcely bear to look at.

"You and your friend made a two-headed monster," Garth managed to say. "My Prince, I am sorry I ever doubted him."

"Hush. Save your strength." I looked around wildly for help. Albaric, I saw, stood with his sword dangling from his hand, staring down into the blank-eyed bloody dead face of one of our guardsmen, and I sensed that he needed me even more than I needed him. He was watching the gray ship sail; he was walking into the sundering sea. He who had been born not from a mortal woman's pain but amid milky white without a cry, he now stood awash in red, stricken that he yet lived. I felt all of this in him yet could not go to comfort him; there was no time.

At least I did not need to call upon him. Other figures stirred, shadowy, beneath the trees: outlaws, alerted by the clamor of battle, coming to loot the bodies. "You!" I commanded with a shout. "Come here!" Most of them ran away, but two came into the open and walked hesitantly toward me. Not all outlaws are evil; many are innocent victims of a lord's spleen. I looked into the eyes of each man and saw fear there, but no ill will.

I lowered my voice. "Water," I demanded of one who had a flask. He gave it to me; I held up Garth's head and tipped it to his lips. After he drank a few swallows, I told the man, "Stay with him, help him; I will reward you." To the other, I said, "Come with me." We began to make the rounds of the dead and wounded. Those close to death, we left to die. But we found one big fellow lying face to the ground, crying in a droning way, like a weary child. At my direction, we rolled him over to see what ailed him. He made no move to assail us or prevent us as we stripped the chain mail off him. But we saw no wound beneath it, and no blood. Instead, we saw a tabard of black and copper green.

I knew whose were those colors.

"Domberk," I breathed, and the image of artless little Marissa swirled wildly in my mind.

I looked down on the Domberk man-at-arms, his face red and contorted. I looked him in the eye. "Why?" I demanded.

He covered his face with his hands. I yanked them away.

"Do you wish to live?" I suppose it sounded like a threat, but truly it was more that I cried for understanding.

"I will die no matter what you do to me," he said, his voice hoarse. "I am broken. Within."

I nodded, believing him; many a strong man had been known to die after battle without a visible wound. Thinking how dry his throat was—for mine, too, felt parched from the panting of combat—I took the flask still in my hand and tilted it to his mouth, giving him water.

His eyes widened, and he gazed at me.

I waited until he was finished drinking. Then, "Warrior, if you wish to die with honor," I addressed him quietly, "tell me truth. You men of Domberk awaited us in ambush here?"

This time, he did not try to hide his face. "Yes."

"Why?"

"Because we were so ordered by our lord."

"Again, why?"

"To kill you, Prince Aric."

I felt a great chill, as if gripped by a hand of ice; I managed not to shiver, but I could not speak. I only stared at the man.

"Lord Brock wanted you out of the way," the fellow rasped, hoarse again.

I gave him more water. "Why?"

"Because," the man spoke on slowly, "having heard that King Bardaric seemed less than strong after his illness, and that you had gone traveling, the lord seized the opportunity."

I gasped. "Domberk did what?"

"Marched upon Dun Caltor."

CHAPTER THE FOURTEENTH

M Y MIND FROZE in the grip of those words, but my body kept moving. I stood, not knowing where I was going, and walked to a still figure with a dripping sword.

"Albaric."

He looked dazedly at me. I poured water down the wound upon his face, then gently, with my hand, I tried to clean the blood away.

He blinked, then sheathed his dark-stained sword. From a far fearsome place, he came back to me, saw me, and somehow knew at once how badly I needed him. "Aric! What has happened?"

"Domberk." I led Albaric toward Garth so that I could tell them both, wasting fewer words. "This ambush came from Domberk. Lord Brock is marching on Dun Caltor. I must ride there at once."

"And I," Albaric said.

"With me then, on Bluefire," I said, "for no other horse can keep pace with him."

"My Prince," Garth protested, "what will you do at Dun Caltor?"

"I will know when I get there." I pulled two golden coins from the pouch hanging at my belt and gave one to each of the two silent outlaws who looked on. "I wish you to take good care of him." Meaning Garth, who, I feared, might not live, but I would not leave him to die alone.

The men nodded.

"Speak. Promise."

"We promise. We'll carry 'im t'our hut," said one with a countryman's thick burring speech.

"Aye," said the other. "But what. . . ." He gestured with his head toward those who lay wounded.

My other guardsmen were dead. But some of Domberk's henchmen still lay moaning. "I haven't the heart to give them the death blow, as I ought," I admitted. "If any will live, let them live. The horses, the supplies, take what you wish. If brigands will loot, let them loot. Only care well for Garth." I bent over the faithful guardsman and kissed his forehead, much as the royal youth must have kissed the friend left behind in the song called "Troth." Then I stood to shout, "Bluefire!"

Rare is the horse that comes when called, but this stallion displayed a fey loyalty to Albaric and me. When he trotted to me, I stripped the nonsensical bridle off his head and threw it to the ground, then the saddle; the less weight Bluefire bore, the better. Albaric vaulted onto the steed's bare back and gave me a hand to mount behind him.

"Farewell, my Prince," said Garth faintly.

"Prince!" blurted one of the outlaws in gruff surprise as Albaric and I galloped away.

———————

The Domberk dastards had indeed felled a bushy tree across the trail; no ordinary horse could have passed it, but Bluefire soared over without an instant's pause, galloping on. No ordinary horse can travel ceaselessly at a gallop, either; walk and trot are the way to cover long leagues of open country. More than ever, I felt eerily sure that this steed was not entirely of this world.

Albaric lifted Bluefire's mane, combing it with his fingers and holding it in his hands to coax him to slow to a canter, more for our sake than his; weary from battle, it was all we could do to ride the gentler gait.

"Where did Bluefire come from, Albaric?" I blurted. "Do you know?"

He nodded, but did not speak for a moment, only became deeply still. I could feel his inner focus turn to something other than himself or me, and by that, and Bluefire's fox-pricked ears, I knew that he and the horse were having one of their silent conversations. I felt sure that he was asking the horse's permission to tell me. Then, relaxing and drawing breath, he spoke, his voice soft and windy in my ears from the speed of our passing. "Bluefire is a horse of sky, from the vast herds that gallop atop the clouds, accompanying the winged golden horses of the sun. Sometimes, if you watch the shifting sky with patient eyes, you can glimpse them. I had been lucky to do so a few times, so I guessed. . . . Do you remember how I sang to him when we first met?"

"Yes. The crest of his neck, friend of the rainbow."

"Something like that. But I did not then understand that

sky is like sea, an Otherwhere rife with strife and mishaps. Lightning was not his friend. An errant bolt struck him to the ground when he was only a colt and had not yet earned his wings."

"So, like you, he cannot go back to his home?"

"Say rather, my brother, that his home, like mine, is with you."

Much moved, I laid my head for a moment against Albaric's neck, and my hand on Bluefire's flank.

After I lifted my head, I kept silence and tried to pay attention. We sped along the wilderness track for what was left of that day, and a few times Bluefire snorted and plunged into his headlong gallop again as I glimpsed arrows whizzing behind us. Heedless of the outlaws, we forged on until at last, as the sun sank low in the sky, we reached the fringes of the forest and I saw a hut, perhaps that of a charcoal-burner or a woodcutter.

"Let us stop there a few minutes, Albaric." I pointed.

As we rode up, a peasant woman came to the doorway and stood trembling, her hands wrapped in her apron, her children clinging to her skirts.

"Water, my good woman, please," I coaxed her as Albaric and I dismounted stiffly from Bluefire. "We mean you no harm."

But she seemed frozen in place, wordless. "Never mind. There's the well, brother," Albaric told me, taking me by my bare arm—having given my tunic to Garth, I rode naked to my waist and chilled, barely noticing, for memories of bloody combat chilled me also, and fear of what lay ahead at Dun Caltor.

Albaric cranked the windlass and drew up a bucket of

water. After we drank, splashed some upon our wounds, and washed off our bloody swords, we gave the rest to Bluefire, who had been vehemently grazing. No one with any sense would give water to a horse after a long hot gallop; 'twould cause colic. But Bluefire was no ordinary horse. Scarcely sweating, he dipped his muzzle into the bucket as delicately as if he were a lady sipping mead.

"Your face, Albaric," I murmured, still wincing at the sight of the gash, dreading lest it fester to kill him.

"Hush. You need to eat." He reached into the pouch hanging at his belt, then placed money in my hand. "You're not such a fright as I am. Give the poor woman a coin and ask whether she has any food to spare."

The setting sun dappled the sky with shining clouds and made everything seem golden, including, I suppose, me. As I offered the coin and made the request, the shaking peasant seemed scarcely able to comprehend. Making no move to grasp at the money that would make her rich, only flinching as she looked up at me, she whispered, "Are ye mortals?"

I laughed, mocking not her but myself and company. "More or less. Please, my good woman." I pressed the gold piece into her hand, knowing she would be able to buy a year's worth of provisions with it. "Some apples, or bread?"

"There be oat bread," piped up one of the children suddenly. "And berries." The mother stood aside and let the little ones, who had somehow lost all fear, take care of us.

So we rode on at a walk, munching oat scones and juicy brambleberries. Mortal comfort, as Albaric would say.

The sun set, and at the same time, a full moon rose. Only when the moon is full do moon and sun face each other across the world that way, one lifting his rays like reaching arms as he sinks, the other arising to gaze from too far away, like lovers parted, doomed never to embrace.

"Better?" Albaric asked as we finished eating.

"Yes. You?" Already before I asked, I knew the answer.

"Not—not so much," he admitted. "Something sickens me."

"Blood, perhaps, and death?"

"Yes. Swordplay in earnest is no play, my brother."

"You saved my life."

"You save mine every day. But this—men fighting, killing—this ugliness—why? I do not understand."

"A nobleman must seek glory in war and win followers to fight for him."

"But *why?*"

I struggled to answer, realizing I did not understand, either; I only accepted what I had been taught from birth. My father—our father—had been the youngest of four brothers: Ardath, Lehinch, Escobar, Bardaric. Yet he, the last in line, had won the throne. Glory? Or bloodshed? "Each one wants what the other one has," I said at last.

"Glory is another word for greed, then?"

"It would seem so." A new thought, and not a comfortable one.

If Domberk took Dun Caltor, Albaric and I would have a father no more.

"We had better ride through the night," I said.

"You hope to reach Dun Caltor ahead of Domberk? Warn the king?"

"On this marvel of a horse, yes, it is just possible." We had been gone seven days, but our course had circled around Dun Caltor; we were not too far away. "If Bluefire can see in the dark," I added in woeful jest, for—wending through woodlands and cantering across moors in the night—if the horse stumbled into a pit and lamed himself or broke a leg, we were lost.

"I will ask him," Albaric responded, and he sat once more motionless and focused. Bluefire tossed his head and snorted.

Albaric relaxed. "Our Bluefire sees his way by night as readily as he does by day," he reported, matter-of-fact.

Weary beyond marveling, I simply resumed my figuring. "So," I said slowly, "to march upon Dun Caltor from Domberk would take Lord Brock—seven days? Eight? We do not know for sure when he set forth, but if he was at all delayed—as is commonplace during a march—perhaps we might get there in time to sound the alarm."

"Perhaps." Albaric sounded as colorless as the moonlight. "But if we are too late?"

"Then at the very worst, I expect to find Domberk's army laying siege to Dun Caltor." I knew the castle to be almost impregnable. "Our father is the most fearsome of warrior kings. And I will think of something—some way. . . ."

Feeling a chill, I let talk go. Bluefire lifted into a canter, speeding us through darkness.

CHAPTER THE
FIFTEENTH

T HINKING HAD GOT ME NOWHERE by the time the sky put on dawn's blushing glamour, but in the slowly growing light, I could see that Bluefire had brought us to the outer woodlands around Dun Caltor, the oak and hazel groves where lads herded the pigs. "We are almost there. Walk," I whispered to Albaric, and Bluefire slowed, setting his hooves down quietly in the forest loam.

Then as we came to the edge of a meadow, we could see the towers of Dun Caltor rising in the distance.

And at the sight, my heart seemed to stop for a moment, and I tried to say it, "Stop," but I had no breath and could not get the word out of my mouth. Albaric knew anyway, or Bluefire, for at the edge of the trees, hidden in their shadows, the horse halted.

Albaric whispered, "What is it, Aric? You've turned to stone."

Still I could not speak, staring at Dun Caltor, for atop its stone towers waved flags, and even at the distance, I could see that they were not as they should have been.

Not bold banners of slate blue-gray and crimson.

These were narrow flame-shaped flags snaking in the wind, and against the sky they looked black, but I daresay there was poison green in them also.

Finally, hoarsely, I managed the words. "Domberk has taken Dun Caltor."

For one who knew almost nothing of the ways of war, Albaric reacted swiftly and with wisdom. Turning Bluefire, he retreated into the woods.

Stupidly, I protested, "But this cannot be! Domberk could not have defeated Caltor so easily; it is impossible." Unthinkable. Unnatural . . . and into my head spun crazed echoes of Lord Kiffin's plaint: stillborn lambs, carrots, peas. . . .

"What has happened to Father?" I begged.

Perhaps Albaric knew as well as I did that they had probably already killed him. I could not yet envision my father, the king, slaughtered, his head on a pike. I could not yet think anything clearly. But Albaric said, "You are in great danger. We must hide you."

Turning from stone to water, I steadied my head against the back of his and hung on to him for strength.

Thinking aloud, he murmured, "Which also means hiding a rather large windflower-blue stallion."

"Pig-herder's hut," I whispered.

"Verily? Where?"

It was not far, just a crude shelter with three log walls and a canvas roof thatched with straw, a refuge from rain and a place to warm oneself by a fire. Not large enough for stabling, but large enough to block the sight of a horse browsing behind it. I stumbled down off Bluefire by myself, but then I stood unable to move from the spot, scarcely seeing anything around me. Fearsome images had taken over my mind. It was Albaric who stood forehead to forehead with Bluefire, giving the steed silent instructions, then caressed his crest and let him go. Likewise, it was Albaric who piled dry leaves into the shelter, cleared away twigs, and told me, "My brother, lie down before you fall down."

Shaking my head, nevertheless I sat on the ground.

So he sat down facing me and said, "Tell me."

With an effort, I focused on him. "Tell you what?"

"Domberk has taken Dun Caltor. Tell me all that it means."

Facing him, I no longer winced at the sight of the sword cut on his face. It spoke to my wounds within. "So long as it heals clean, 'twill leave quite a dashing scar," I remarked. "No one will think you less than man any longer. Maidens will swoon over you."

"Tell me," he repeated just as gently as the first time.

So I told him. "Our father is dead."

"Are you sure?"

"Almost certainly he has been slain, and his head paraded like a prize."

I sensed that Albaric did not understand how vile this was, that he knew nothing of the respectful care of bodies after death, and how should he? Where he came from, there was no death. Yesterday in the wilderness, we had left our dead guardsmen lying on the ground. He thought about our father for a while, then asked, "What else?"

"My mother is likely taken prisoner. Perhaps dishonored."

"Dishonored?"

"Perhaps Brock of Domberk has—forced her."

Again, while the sun rose above the horizon and coaxed birdsong from the trees all around us, he thought about this.

"He has taken her, you mean," he asked, "somewhat as my mother took your father?"

"Yes, but by force of hand, not—" Suddenly I loathed the thought of Elfland's glamour, beauty even in evil, but I did not speak of that. Instead, I went on. "Other women within the castle have perhaps been taken. Other men have died."

"The villagers?"

"Terrified, likely, but not killed. Peasants are needed to till and harvest, care for cows and sheep and fowl and swine."

"And horses? Do you think Todd is alive?"

"Perhaps. One can hope so." Albeit painful, my brother's bleak questions had done me good, as I think was his intention. They had given me back to myself.

Albaric studied me. "What will you do?"

"I must save Mother."

"How?"

"I do not yet know. Tonight, when darkness comes, we will try to find out."

He nodded. "Until then, rest." He betook himself into the shade of the shelter and lay down. "Bluefire will warn us if anyone comes near."

Lying on the bed of leaves beside him, I said, "Now we are both homeless, my brother." I had felt it in him often, the rue of having no place, and now I felt it in myself as well, what it was to be an outcast. More: a fugitive. They would want to kill me.

Albaric had no harp anymore, but he opened his mouth and his singing rose to the sky as if on softly feathered golden wings:

What is a friend?
Troth without end.
A light in the eyes,
A touch of the hand—
I will follow you unto
The ends of the land.

I was glad he had changed the words. I wished to live.

Such was the strength, the comfort of his presence that I felt able to sleep. Drowsily, not for the first time, I marveled that I, the most ordinary of mortals, could sense his thoughts, when he was the magical one, power in his eyes, his touch, his voice. . . . The echo of his song in my mind turned to a dream. I slept.

He slept beside me, I think, until past midday, when Bluefire's soft nose upon our faces awoke both of us.

Alert at once, neither of us moved except to turn our eyes, then our heads, to where the horse stared. From the meadow beyond the fringe of the forest came muffled earthy snorting snuffling sounds.

Pigs.

Contented pigs rooting, up to their eyes in dirt.

And with the pigs, to keep them out of trouble and herd them home again at nightfall, would be—someone. A boy, most likely.

If he wandered into the forest, he might stumble upon us and make an outcry. I would not let that happen. First, I needed to find out who he was.

"Wait here," I whispered to Albaric, feeling for my favorite weapon—a stone—as I eased up from the ground and crept as softly as I could to where I could see—yes, there was the lad, looking up at the sky, hoping to spy a hawk or an eagle, perhaps—or maybe even cerulean winged horses.

I breathed out, for he was a happy sight to me.

I hurled a stone, but not to strike him, only to bounce in the grass at his feet, alerting him. Another made him look my way. Holding my forefinger to my lips—shhhh!—I let him see me. He almost cried out anyway but managed to be silent except for sobbing as he ran to me and flung himself upon me. Never had I experienced such a greeting, and it touched my heart, especially coming from a shy peasant boy. I lifted him off his feet as he hugged me, carrying him back to Albaric. He was Todd's grandson, Toddy.

"Prince Aric, oh my Prince," he gasped, weeping, "they all say you are dead!"

"They do, do they?" I murmured, ruffling his hair, patting his back. "Keep your voice down or they might come and kill me yet."

"Prince Aric, they—Domberk—came and—"

"Yes, I saw the flags." Easing myself out of his embrace, I set him down and myself sat beside him. "Hush, Toddy, now be calm, my good lad, for there is much I need to know."

"Toddy?" Albaric asked me, seating himself on the leafy forest floor a little farther away. "Todd's son?"

"Grandson."

"He—Grandpa—he died in the fighting." Staunch and true, like Todd, the boy had got control of himself. "Out with the horses, he was the first to see them coming at dawn, cowardly sneaks, and he raised the alarm, and he and the

115

grooms died to the last man, fending them off while the soldiers assembled. But it was all confusion, and they—the enemies—got ladders up before the guards could properly man the walls. . . ."

"They took you by surprise and overran you." I summed it up for Toddy, for his small face had gone very pale beneath his freckles. I could imagine; it had been just another dawn to a sleepyheaded boy, then suddenly screams, swords clashing, bloodshed, his grandfather dead. "Did Father—did King Bardaric die in battle?" I assumed so. I knew my father would fight to the death before surrendering Dun Caltor.

"No, Prince Aric, he is yet alive!"

CHAPTER THE SIXTEENTH

IMPOSSIBLE!
   Unless—
   The thought hurt me like burning iron. Feeling it bleed the color from my face, I forced out a single word. "Torture?"

"No, my Prince! He is not being harmed." Toddy's wide eyes could not have been more earnest. "All the castle marvels. He is in the dungeon, alive and well with not a mark on him, for the scullery boys see him when they take food to him."

"Bread and water?"

"No, good food! The best the kitchen can offer!"

"And my mother?" I asked, dubious and dazed, for so far the narrative made no sense.

"Locked in the king's room, my Prince, and we know this because the kitchen folk take food to her there also."

"You mean the room at the top of the tallest tower."

"Yes."

The room in which my father had lain dying when Albaric

117

came. The room with nothing but stone wall and stony cliffs and cold sea below.

As it was the king's room, likely Brock Domberk had taken it for himself. What he might have in mind for Mother. . . . But I held my voice carefully in check. "Lord Brock? Does he enter that room?"

"He rages outside the door, Prince Aric, but only to go away again because the queen will not have him. Indeed, he rages everywhere, at everyone. He is a pig, that one."

"An insult to honest swine. You should know better."

Listening, Albaric smiled, but I don't think Toddy understood my joke. Vehemently he repeated, "Lord Brock is a stinking pig. Always shouting. Yet. . . ." His young voice faltered, puzzled. "Yet he punishes no one."

"And he does not force himself upon the queen."

Toddy looked blank, as if he did not entirely understand the question, but answered, "The queen says he may not come into her chamber, so he stays outside and swears."

"For a stinking pig, that's very odd."

I talked with the boy awhile longer, learned that his father had wounds but would live, obtained his most solemn promise that he would tell no one, not even his family, that he had seen me, and all the while Albaric sat by, silent, forming a plan. I could feel it in him and wondered greatly what it might be, for how could we two hope to rescue Father from the dungeon or Mother from the tower?

"The hogs have scattered everywhere by now. I must find them," said Toddy regretfully, getting up to leave.

"And what will you tell your mother, Toddy, when she sees your shining face?" I still worried that he might betray me without meaning to.

"Why, she shan't see me for a few days, nor will anyone else, for I sleep in the meadow with the swine. But my Prince, will I see you again?"

"It is most fervidly to be hoped."

"Let us go," said Albaric as soon as the boy was out of sight.

"Go where? Albaric, what are you scheming?"

"I'll show you in a few minutes. First, we need Bluefire."

We walked toward where we had last seen the horse, not daring to call him aloud, yet in a moment he trotted up to us.

"Good. You first, my brother." As always, the words "my brother" warmed my heart.

"We need to go quietly through the woods down to the sea," Albaric said when he was seated behind me on Bluefire, and it did not surprise me that the horse at once started forward, walking in the correct direction. Albaric spoke on. "No one from the castle will observe us if we approach Queen Evalin's tower that way, after dark and hidden by the cliffs."

True enough. "And then?"

"And then we can take a coracle and make our way to the base of the tower where the queen is kept."

True, again, yet insane. "Albaric," I inquired dryly, "can you fly?"

"Not in this body."

"Then how are we to scale the tower?"

"I will show you," said Albaric simply, but then added with a sudden change of tone, "if it works in this world. Cockleburs, I am a dolt, I hadn't thought it might act differently here. Halt Bluefire a moment."

Even before I pulled on his mane, the horse stopped, and my oddling brother leapt down, drawing from under his tunic a relic, a vestige of his Elfin past, that I had almost forgotten: a red-gold coil of Queen Theena of Elfland's hair, still with all the glamour on it that was ever there, so bright in the late-day light that I blinked, looking upon it.

Albaric took a deep breath. His eyes closed for a moment, then opened, intent. With the coil of Theena's hair cupped in both hands he caressed it, whispering to it. Then he took a loop and tossed it skyward as lightly as a child tossing a pebble into the air. He laid the rest on a patch of moss, patted it, then started to climb.

"Praise be," he breathed, "it works."

"What!" I exclaimed, for I had not known the strand of hair awaited him in the air, so fine it was all but invisible, and attached to nothing. Yet hand over hand, he climbed it without apparent effort, surging well above me within a moment. My head tilted backward to its utmost, I called, "Albaric, stop!"

Holding on by one hand, he did so, looking down to ask, "Why?"

Seemingly unsupported there between earth and sky, his flaxen hair floating, against all sense, so as to halo his head—I had almost forgotten how fey he was, but surely I remembered now. "You terrify me!"

"Fear not." Lightly he slipped down again to stand on the ground, smiling. "Try it, and you will find it is not hard."

"As soon as I am done shaking." The strong reminder of his otherness had set me trembling.

His smile faded. "Brother, do you love me—or not?"

It was not a dare, but a plea, and of course, there could

be but one answer. Swinging my leg over Bluefire's neck, I jumped down, walking on unsteady legs to stand beside Albaric. I took hold of what looked like a spider-web filament glinting in the air and tugged it lightly, just to see whether it would give way—then found myself a foot off the ground! Hastily, I grabbed with the other hand and bobbed even higher. Somehow, the strand of Elfin hair made me weigh no more than a feather, so that I could climb more easily than I walked.

"It would not be strong enough to hold you otherwise, you see," said Albaric as if explaining something very simple.

As preparation for the night ahead, I kept climbing, feeling dizzy not with height but with the strangeness of being Aric. Aric the butterfly, whimsical spirit, warrior on the wind. . . . Something of Elfin insouciance seemed to enter me from the shimmering fiber I climbed. "How high does it go?" I called to Albaric.

"As high as it must. I aimed only for the treetops. You'd better come down."

I did so, feeling far better than when I had gone up. "How did you know?

"Oh, I used to play in Mother's hair when I was little. . . ." With an odd look he turned away.

"Is that a mortal pang I see?" I gibed gently. "Meseems I am growing more like you, and you more like me."

"Hush, you scamp. We must ride."

This time he sat in front. I made sure of it, knowing Bluefire would comfort him. Keeping to the groves and woodlots,

silent, we rode at a walk towards the sea, and at last, far out
in the country, with no one to see us and nothing in sight but
moors where a few sheep fed, we reached it. At the edge of
the sea, we turned and cantered along the gravel shore toward
Dun Caltor.

Albaric broke silence. "So this, this narrow passage between
the sea and the true land, this is the strand?"

"Yes." On one side of us, the moors rose gradually into
cliffs, and on the other side washed the glinting gray-green
endless water, its chill waves lunging as if to grasp but then
falling back, frothing and falling back, foaming and falling
back.

"And the sea, it frightens you."

My pride stung, I did not answer directly. Instead, I asked,
"Why are there no seas in Elfland?"

"How do you know that?" He was all innocent surprise,
and I regretted my challenge.

"I know because I know you."

"Well, it is true. There are none. Yet—yet this is beautiful."

Sinking as if to swim in that western sea, the sun glossed
it—and the towers of Dun Caltor, now visible in the distance—
with glamour worthy of an Elfin cavalcade.

"It is beautiful whether in sunlight or moonlight, and I fear
it," I admitted, "although I have a few times ventured onto it
with the fishing boats and have suffered no harm except salt
spray and slippery odors. I think you have no sea in Elfland
because no death is there."

A hushed moment passed. Then very softly he sang:

> By that dim shore swam a ghost-gray ship
> Low in the water but nothing within

Except shivering scent of fear insubstantial
And mournful voices of folk unseen.

"Hush," I said. "Please."

He hushed only his singing. "Is this where the dead go, then?"

"To far western isles, folk say."

"So death is beautiful, like the sea?"

"Perhaps someday death may seem beautiful to me. Not yet."

As the sun sank lower, the cliffs rose higher, at first to shield us from the view of anyone, especially the invaders from Domberk, but then to threaten us, for the strand grew ever narrower.

"Where are the coracles?" I blurted, for we had reached the place where a steep path—long ago carved into the rock—made its winding way down the cliff from the village. I saw ropes for tying, and posts. This was where there should have been boats drawn up upon the shore—yet there was not one to be seen.

Albaric drew Bluefire to a halt, and I dare say that, although I could not see his face, he stared as blankly as I.

"We are a pair of lackwits," I said finally. "Of course the fisherfolk saved their wives and children from the invasion. It was dawn. They were still ashore, or not far from it. Likely they've fled wherever they could."

We sat a bit longer in silence. Then Albaric asked, "My brother, can you swim at all?"

"Nary a bit. Can you?"

"Only to paddle in pretty Elfin pools. I look on this smother and fear it as you do. But all horses swim. Bluefire fears it not."

"You asked him?"

"Yes. He is willing to dare it. What say you, Aric?"

Just ahead, the wild waves slammed into the cliffs, and there was no gravel strand anymore, no footing; perforce we must take to the sea. I could think of no other way to reach Mother, nor did I think long. This was no time for thinking, only for action.

He turned to look at me, questioning. I reached out, and with a silent grip of our hands, we agreed; we would risk the venture.

"Troth for both," I remarked as I loosened my belt, passed it through Albaric's and fastened it again, binding us together. "Would that there were a way to bind both of us to the horse."

But there was none.

"Bluefire," Albaric addressed him whimsically, "can you not turn into a blue coracle with a prow carved in the shape of a stallion's head?"

"You're daft," I told him. Both of us laid our hands on the horse's shining slate-blue flanks for a moment in a kind of blessing or an appeal. Then Albaric said, "Hold on tight, my brother."

"You also."

We both hung on—Albaric to Bluefire's mane, I to Albaric—and like a three-headed beast, we leapt over the breakers into the sea.

CHAPTER THE SEVENTEENTH

GIVE ME ANY FATE, any I say, but death by drowning. Such a betrayal, that nose and throat will perforce accept the fluid that does not belong there, liquid that burns, sets lungs on fire for air, only to breathe nightmare instead. . . . *He followed his Prince—and walked into that sea?* I could never do it. Were I not bound tight to Albaric, I think I would have deserted him when, no matter how I tried to cling to him with my arms and Bluefire with my legs, the first sideward slam of brute water knocked me over. Alas, Bluefire had *not* turned into a boat, and seawater made the horse as slippery as an eel. And the strength of seawater is like that of a halfwit giant. It pushed me down and pulled me up again and battered me about, filling my ears with the ringing of harebells, blinding my eyes, threatening to suck me under the horse's churning, cutting hooves—for Bluefire swam so savagely, he was nearly as dangerous to me as the sea. Somehow, Albaric stayed with him, while I hung like a dead weight from my brother's belt. I must have caught a breath of air from time to time, or I would not have survived, but I do not remember. I recall only banging my head against rock, and being dragged over gravel, and the salt water stinging in wounds I didn't even know I had as I wobbled up to my hands and knees, as I retched and coughed and gasped and heaved, ribs aching.

"Here, Aric. Here, my brother." Albaric laid me face down in something dry and rough, and I felt him rubbing my ribs hard with the same stuff until I stopped vomiting and enough water had run out of me. Then I rolled over, he dropped beside me, and we both lay gasping for breath in a patch of coarse seaside grass. Along with a mouthful of gravel, I managed to spit out words. "Bloody hell!"

"Quite."

"Bluefire?"

"Left us here, went back. . . . You had the worst of it, Aric. I clung to Bluefire's neck with arms and legs, and even so I barely—Aric, I could not help you."

All friends fail. "Whoever—made that song—"

"Knew what he was talking about. Yes."

We lay side by side, panting, a while longer, until our breathing calmed, until my eyes had cleared and my sight at last returned. Night had fallen, or nearly so. I gazed up at a tall, tall moonlit tower against a deep indigo sky curdled with stars.

The King's Tower. Behind the window at the very top, we might find my mother alive, whole, and—dare I think it—somehow able to help us free Father?

It would have been good to lie in the dry grass much longer. But I lurched to my feet.

"There is no fear anyone will see us," I answered Albaric's question before he spoke it. "The walls of Dun Caltor rise sheer above this cliff, without battlements, crenellation, or guard posts, for the builders gave no thought to fighting the sea."

"Which, I have come to agree with you, Aric, is quite fearsome enough to serve as fortification upon its own." Albaric rose to stand beside me. "More fearsome, to my mind, than yon tall tower. Shall we?"

"We must."

"Then here." Pulling the coil of his mother's hair from its sanctuary by his heart—in the night, it glimmered the color of hot embers—Albaric told me, "Find a good rock for throwing, my brother."

"I?"

"Yours is the arm most devoted to flinging them."

Already bending and feeling along the cliff-shingle at my feet, I had found a sea-washed stone of an inviting shape and heft. I held it out toward Albaric, and he wound the uncanny filament tightly around it several times, then knotted it.

"Now, Prince of Caltor," he instructed softly, "take careful aim, and throw the stone directly at the queen's window.

"Albaric, I cannot possibly throw so high!"

"Tonight you can. Remember, it is my mother's hair you fling. It will soar as high as it must. Only be sure of your aim."

I needed to stand a few minutes, inhaling the night, making myself stop exclaiming within my mind, stop thinking of anything except the strength and direction of the sea breeze and how it might affect the stone's flight. Then, coiling, I hurled the stone and its light burden as high and true as I could.

Somewhere far above, I heard it strike. But what if it had merely bounced off the side of the tower and hurtled into the sea?

"Can you tell where that went?" I whispered.

"Beautiful," Albaric breathed.

"What?"

"A spire glimmering as dim as rushlight, one thread for you and one for me."

"I can't see them."

"Here." He took my hand and guided it to something that felt no thicker than spider web. "Climb; I'll be right beside you."

Pushing away thoughts to the contrary, I obeyed, climbing quickly, guided by touch, allowing my sore and weary body, now weightless, to lie spread out upon the air, resting—although I took care neither to look down nor to contemplate what I was about, floating upward by means of a filament and my fingertips. Should I lose my hold on Queen Theena's hair, my mortal weight would return, and I would plummet to the seaside rocks and my death.

Another dire thought struck me. I blurted, "What if the thread has only caught on some projection in the tower's stone, a beam, a coign—

"Hush. You are on your way directly to your mother's window," answered Albaric, his face turning to me, a pale oval in the night.

"But what if I missed—"

He shook his head at me. "You believe in Elfland, so why can't you believe in yourself, Prince Aric? Your stone flew true. Were it not for the shutters, you would have shattered the precious glass. You will see."

And within a few moments, I did see. Unmistakably above my head, I could make out a rectangular shape illuminated from within by the dim golden flutter of candleglow.

Within a few moments, I reached the window, its aperture the thickness of the castle wall, making a ledge three feet deep. There on the ledge lay my stone. And it would appear that the sound of its impact had aroused my mother, for there she stood with shutters and windows flung wide open, standing straight and pale as a statue. In a moment, I realized what great courage she displayed.

"Spirit of my son Aric," she addressed me in a low, controlled voice, "why come you here?"

Startled at first, then I understood how I must look seemingly floating on air in the darkness outside her high window. Doubtless Lord Domberk had taken pleasure in telling her his henchmen had ambushed me to kill me. And if I were dead, she had every right to be terrified of me, because only those who have died unjust and evil deaths return to haunt, and their spirits are vengeful. Even though I had been her loving son in life, she could no longer trust me.

"No, Mother, no, I'm not a haunt," I told her with my heart in my voice. "I am alive! I am flesh and blood. I used an Elfin device to get up here, that is all." Reaching the window ledge, I crouched there, offering her my hand.

Her mouth opened like an oval, and after a slight hesitation, she took my hand, and when she felt my warm and solid fingers close around hers, she gasped, gripped me by both arms as if I were a toddler, and hauled me inside, tears running down her face. I hugged her—not as tall as I had thought, she stood with her head tucked beneath my chin. Stroking her hair, which was plaited for slumber, I noticed serpentines of silver woven into the braids. When had her hair started to gray?

"No handwomen?" I sensed we were alone in the shadowy

room—except that Albaric now crouched on the window ledge, gathering his most precious remembrance of his mother into a coil.

She shook her head—a movement against my collarbone. "They took them away."

"To leave you alone with fear." My feelings for her squeezed my chest and choked my voice.

"With despair. Oh my son, I never expected to see you again alive." She clung to me.

Kissing her, then holding her by the shoulders, I studied her, trying to assess how much harm she had suffered, but in the wavering candlelight, I could tell little.

"I am as strong as a sword now that you are back," she told me, guessing my concern, "and you, Albaric," she added, turning to the window. Then she gasped. "Oh, Albaric, they scarred your face!"

He gave her a smiling glance. "It was hard battle."

I said, "But they were not expecting so swift a sword, or so fierce a horse."

With her head high, gazing at both of us, somehow she managed to look every inch a queen even though she stood barefoot, clad only in her shift. It was her strength that gave me strength to question her. Taking her hand, I led her to her broidery-chair, seated her there, gave her a blanket off the bed and knelt to gather it around her feet, then forced myself to ask, "Mother—what has that pig named Brock done to you?"

"Nothing!" She straightened her spine, defiant. "He has not laid a hand on me. He can take away my clothing and my baldric and my dirk, he can lock me in this room, but he cannot set a foot inside it. Nor have I let him harm so much as a hair on your father's head, Aric, for all that he's shut him in the dungeon."

"*Let* him?"

"I should not boast, lest I be bested." Her voice lowered, sobered. "I know not what may happen next. We are prisoners, and the ring is a tricksome thing."

CHAPTER THE EIGHTEENTH

THE RING!

The wayward ring of Elfin power. No longer, I realized, did Mother wear it on a long golden chain around her neck.

Albaric came in the window, another sort of Elfin ring—the glimmering red-gold coil of his mother's hair—in his hands. He tucked it back into his tunic and sat on the floor beside me, his silence asking many questions.

As did mine. But before I could settle on one, Mother said simply, "It was like this," and she told her tale.

Clash of metal on metal, sword upon sword. Screams of men in rage or mortally wounded. Those were the sounds that had awoken her and her handwomen from sleep two mornings ago. At first, Queen Evalin had remained calm, albeit dressing quickly, for it was not the first time Dun Caltor had been assailed—but this time was different. Frightened servants ran in to tell her that the wall was overrun, King Bardaric unhorsed and unhelmed, his warriors leaderless and in disorder, the keep itself under attack.

"I could scarcely believe it," she said, her face bleak as bone with words unsaid.

Nor could I say the words. I could barely bring myself to think them: Father, hauled down from Invincible and captured without a wound? *Without a wound?* This was not the Sire I knew.

"Yet, even when the mind is stunned, one must prepare for the worst."

Mother had taken the Elfin ring of power off its gold chain and carried it concealed in the palm of her hand.

The ring. I should have known.

"The quirky thing was very pink," she recalled, "and merry. During the past month or so, I've become well acquainted with that ring," she confided to Albaric and me, "and begun to feel a certain understanding with it, and I resolved that if I had a chance to make use of it, I would do so."

The chance came all too soon. Hearing sounds of battle near at hand, Queen Evalin issued forth from her chamber to meet whatever fate awaited her. "I would not have them take me in my hidey-hole like a mouse." Soon enough, it was all over; Domberk's men seized her by the arms and hurried her to the great hall, where Brock of Domberk slouched on the tall throne carved of Calidon stone. Stripped to his smallclothes, Bardaric knelt before him. Rough hands forced Queen Evalin to kneel by her husband's side.

"What has happened to you?" she whispered.

"Courage, my Queen," was her husband's reply. "They say Aric will not return."

"Silence!" roared Brock of Domberk, glorying in victory. "Do you swear fealty to me, Bardaric, as my vassal?"

"Never shall Caldor bow to Domberk."

"But you *do* bow!" Gloating glee oozed from the conquering lord like slime. "Why not face defeat, swear to obey me, and spare your life?"

"Never."

"You would rather die and leave your widow at my mercy?"

"Lord of Domberk," Mother cried out as if in great agony of emotion, "I beg you, spare my husband's life!" She bowed her head and raised her hands as if begging for pity.

"Evalin, where is your pride?" protested my father.

But she ignored him. "I cry upon your sovereign grace for our lives, conqueror!" she appealed to Lord Brock, inching closer to him on her knees until she clutched at his robe.

Domberk, quite enjoying this, told Father, "Behold, your once-so-haughty wife knows the next king when she sees him. Bow your head, Caldor!"

"Never!

"Bow, or you die!"

"Never."

"Oh, mercy, please, great my victorious majesty, spare him!" Almost in Brock's lap by this time, Mother heightened her frenzy, grasped his left hand, and drew it toward her as if to smother it with kisses. Much flattered, he allowed this—but as her head bowed over his hand, she rammed the ring of Elfin power onto the finger closest to his heart.

"You shall kill no one!" she shouted as she sprang to her feet. "You shall harm no one in my household!"

At the same time, but with far less dignity, Lord Brock sprang up also, jumping and jigging as if wasps were stinging him, flailing his left hand and clawing at it with the other. Bellowing curses, he managed to snatch the ring off his hand, but he could not keep hold of it; it flared scorching orange, and as if it were a fiery ember, he flung it away.

Then greatly Mother feared that her ploy had failed. "What have you done?" Domberk roared. "What have you done to me? Witch!" he cried, striking at her with his fist. Leaping to his feet, my father lunged to stop him—too late—but it mattered not: Domberk struck only air. As if a wall of invisible stone stood between the angry lord and Queen Evalin, he could not touch her. The power of the ring protected her.

"But where is it now?" I exclaimed.

"I do not know." In the dim candlelight, I imagined more than saw Mother's rueful smile. "It flew off into the shadows of the great hall, no one knows where. My victory was partial and short. Lord Brock cannot harm any of us here at Dun Caltor or order us harmed—it enrages him constantly that he cannot ravish or torture or slay us, enrages him all the more because he cannot comprehend what prevents him, and while his rage seemed amusing at first, I like it less and less with each passing hour. How long will he imprison us thus? What is to become of us? What if they turn the power of the ring against us?"

"First," said Albaric softly, "they would have to find it."

"Surely, if Brock is no fool, they have already done so."

My brother smiled up at her and shook his head. "The ring is particular about the company it keeps. You are greatly honored, Queen Evalin, that it has befriended you. I think it will not allow Lord Brock to lay hands upon it if he is as porcine as I understand him to be."

"But you could find it," I said to Albaric, for I knew him.

"Yes, and I should do so."

"How?" Mother asked.

"Just go padding about. I will feel it."

"But my dear, we are locked in this chamber."

She called him "my dear" as if he were a beloved child. Getting up, I had to smile. Shuffling in the darkness, I made my way toward the chamber door.

Mother asked, "Aric, what are you doing?"

"Didn't someone lock me in my chamber as a punishment on occasion when I was a child?" I teased. "And didn't I generally get out?" With the tip of my dirk, I probed the keyhole of the clumsy old lock, and sure enough, they'd left the key in it on the outside; I felt it give way and heard it clang on the floor. Then I took my sword and slipped it under the door. I tried to sweep the key inside the chamber with it, but the sword grated against the stone, sticking. I muttered something that made Mother tsk her tongue at me.

"Try my sword," Albaric offered.

More slender, it did nicely, coaxing the key under the door until I could seize it. Standing, I warned, "Shush, everyone," and waited until Mother had blown out the candle before I turned the key in the lock and eased the door open.

For several minutes, I stood listening with weapon at the ready, in case some Domberk guard had been alerted by the scrape of the sword or the clack of the lock. But no sounds of alarm disturbed the silence. Finally, I stepped forward.

Albaric whispered, "First we must find the ring."

"I must go to Bard!" Throwing a dark shawl over her linen chemise, Mother pattered forward, on her bare feet as noiseless as a spirit.

Standing with my arms spread across the doorway, I blocked them both. "How will you see where you are going? And first, before anything, we must capture Brock Domberk.

Once we have him, we can do what we like. Mother, do you know where he sleeps?"

There was a moment's silence as they accepted my leadership.

Then Mother said, "I *think* behind the throne." She meant in a small chamber where kings slept during travails when they might be needed at a moment's notice—although I had forgotten there was a bed behind the throne; in my lifetime, that chamber had been used only as a repository for royal paraphernalia.

Mother added, "And I *know* you both had better take off your boots if we are to go skulking about."

We did so, and after that, we three moved almost wordlessly as one. We gathered a supply of rushes from the floor, then felt our way out the door and down the stairs, single file, one hand to the wall. When, at the landing, we found a torch flickering in its bracket on the wall, we reached up to light the rushes, which burn not with a flame but with a slow smoldering glow, a whisper of light.

By rushlight, then, we ghosted on bare feet down the tower stairs and along the passageways of the keep, hastening past torches and pausing in shadows, until we reached the great hall and neared the room where Mother thought our enemy slumbered.

She was right, I could see that at once, for guards flanked the door, one standing on each side. From a shadowy corner, we studied them. Both had disobediently laid aside their helmets for comfort. Both stood leaning against the wall, dozing if not actually asleep on their feet. Albaric and I had our swords; we could easily have whacked the heads off the pair of them before they so much as squeaked.

But I felt in myself, as much as in him, a shudder at the thought of more bloodshed.

As I hesitated, Mother whispered, "Let me deal with them." Motioning us to stay where we were, she herself padded forward. As if stealing toward the dungeon to see her husband, she slipped nearly past the two guards before she "happened" to brush against them with her shawl.

That feathery touch startled them as if they had been awakened by a spook. One straightened with a hoarse grunt; the other nearly fell over. Mother gave a ladylike little cry and ran.

"What—who—" croaked a guard.

"The queen!" snapped the other one, and both of them ran after her. I felt Albaric's fear for her.

"She is enjoying herself," I whispered to him. "She knows every secret turning and hiding place; she will make fools of them. Come."

Albaric and I darted to the door the guards had deserted. On the inside, I knew, it was barred; no mere key could give entry here. I jammed my sword through the crack, thought of my father in the dungeon below, and heaved the blade upward with all my might redoubled by the force of my rage. The wooden bar lifted and clattered to the floor. As Albaric stood by my side, the door swung open.

Instantly, a hooded shadow, a man in dark clothing, I knew not who, shot out with such force that his shoulders knocked me and Albaric sideward in opposite directions. Before we could think or blink, he was running like a deer across the great hall, gone.

And forgotten, by me at least, for within the room stood Lord Brock of Domberk.

Apparently he had lit a candle from the embers of the hearth fire, set it on the mantelpiece, and there he stood in his nightgown, reaching for his sword. Such was his astonishment upon seeing my face that he nearly dropped it, scabbard and all.

The usurping, would-be-murdering pig, I felt no compunction lest I spill *his* blood. "He's mine," I told Albaric as I lunged into the traitor's room. It was an even match; like Domberk, I had a sword but no shield, no helm, no armor; indeed, I remained naked from the waist up, like a wild man. Certainly, at the sight of him, I felt like one. "Defend yourself, villain!" I barked, and as soon as he had drawn his blade, I attacked him with far more vehemence than sense. He was clever; he wounded my shield arm, which I had not so much as wrapped with a cloth, and he dodged behind furniture and snatched up a dirk in his other hand; now he had two blades to my one. Albaric had taken the candle to safeguard it, or without light I might have been lost. But in the end, Domberk could not best me; my sheer fury overpowered him so that I struck the weapons from his hands and drove him to his knees, the point of my sword at his throat.

"Yield!"

"I yield." He said the words with distaste but no hesitation. He was no warrior, Domberk, just a greedy vassal eager to seize an opportunity.

"Hands behind your back. Albaric, can you find something to bind him?"

The rope tassels from the bed canopy served nicely. Knotting them, Albaric said without looking at me, "Aric, you're bleeding."

Barely feeling the wounds, I grabbed up some sort of

garment, Lord Brock's smallclothes perhaps, and wrapped it around my left arm for Albaric's sake. "To the dungeon with this one!"

One on each side of Brock Domberk, with swords drawn, we marched him down the stairs, and the guards he had posted shrank away without needing to be warned; I think my face spoke for me: if anyone interfered with us, Domberk would die.

Rounding the corner to the dungeon, though, I nearly smiled, for there stood Mother kissing Father through the prison bars. Guards surrounded her as if to seize her but hesitant to touch.

They jumped back as I entered with my captive. I put my sword to Lord Brock's throat. "On your knees to the King and Queen of Calidon, every one of you!" I ordered.

As they complied, "Aric!" Father cried with more heart than I had ever heard in his voice.

"I *told* you," Mother chided him happily, "but you would not believe until you saw." She looked around her at the kneeling soldiers. "Who has the keys?"

The captain did. No keys make such a harsh clangor as dungeon keys, but their sound was sweet to my ears as my father stepped out of the cell, and Albaric and I shoved Domberk in to take his place. Father embraced me. "They told me you were dead!"

"Albaric saved my life."

"Then I am grateful to him." Nearby, Albaric had taken away the weapons of the kneeling men and stood with his sword drawn, on guard, silent. And although his face remained hard, in his silence, I began to feel something like soft-footed shadows, gray cats of despair, creeping into his spirit. No wonder, for despite what Father had said, he gave Albaric not even a glance. Instead, he asked me, "What of Garth?"

I pulled away from my father's embrace. "He may indeed be dead." I faced him, the king, without ceremony. "Too many have died. No more. I have a plan."

CHAPTER THE NINETEENTH

"AND IT IS THIS." I turned to address the glowering vassal in the dungeon. "Lord Brock, order your men to march home to Domberk immediately." The light of dawn showed through the bars of the dungeon window high above his head; his army could get an early start. "You shall remain where you are. A small force, no more than six, of your people shall return here, bringing with them your daughter Marissa as a hostage for your release. If she is willing, and if you will swear to keep the peace thereafter, I shall marry her. Her son, your grandson, will grow to rule Calidon, as has been your ambition."

My mother gasped. My father stiffened. Of all concerned, only Lord Brock Domberk seemed not to be shocked. He stood stroking his beard, as if he had a choice in the matter.

Father growled at him, "I would rather kill you like the treacherous dog you are."

Domberk's eyes smoldered, but he spoke to his captain. "Carry out Prince Aric's orders. Go."

Silently, the defeated soldiers rose and filed out, with Albaric at their heels—dangerous for him, one on guard over many. I sprang to go with him.

"Aric," Mother cried after me, "you're wounded!"

"Later," I called back.

But not too much later. Within moments, as my fury abated, my strength finally gave out. Father had gone to release and rally the forces of Caltor, and I dimly remember being back in the throne room, by daylight now, overseeing the transfer of Lord Domberk's clothing down to his new and less pleasant quarters. Albaric was saying, "I wonder who it was that so desperately ran away when we stormed the door. For an instant as he came out, I thought it was King Bardaric. There was some resemblance."

"Bah. Probably just a manservant saving his own skin," I tried to say, but the words slid together, the world began spinning, and as I clung to Albaric's shoulder, everything went black.

I awoke in my own bed, my own room, to candlelight, a confused mind, a parched throat, and an empty belly. "What, it's night already?" I said—to no one, as it turned out. Sitting up to open the bed canopy, I found I was alone in the chamber. My wounds had been bandaged, and someone had put on me a knee-length tunic, soft and comfortable from long wear and many washings. But I could not stay in bed, could not go back to sleep, because I felt famished. When had I last eaten? Had it been the oat bread and berries from the frightened peasant woman? Getting to my feet, I felt lightheaded and, thinking only that I must eat, I made toward the kitchen, carrying the candle to light my way.

As I trod the stone passageways, no one seemed to be about, giving me an eerie feeling of not quite knowing what was real, and I began to think that I had been killed and was a ghost, because clash of swords and blood of combat, evidenced by the bandages on my arm and the bruises on my body, seemed dim as a dream, a memory from another life—but as a ghost, I felt lonely, incomplete. How could I be a spirit when I knew not how to sing? I was a person of earth and daylight things, sun on my shoulders and a comrade's whack on my back—without Albaric, I felt incomplete. He was my spirit, my soul, my song, my brother; how could I be parted from him, even in death? Did the dead hunger as I hungered, weakness making me hold on to the walls as I walked? Wobbling without that support, I started to cross the great hall—

A voice cried from the shadows, "Aric!"

Before I could even think, "It is Albaric," my heart swelled almost beyond bearing. As he ran to me, I pitched toward him and hugged him with all the small strength I had left, laying my head on his shoulder as if I were a child, tears in my eyes from sheer love of him.

"Aric, you oaf, get off!" he said, resisting the clumsiness of my embrace, "What are you *doing*? It's not yet dawn."

"Looking for something to eat." Which, I realized, meant I was far from being a ghost yet. I tried to let go of Albaric but had to hold on to him or fall down. "What are *you* doing?"

"Looking for. . . ." His eyes widened, gazing over my shoulder and upward. "Confound the fickle thing, there it is," he breathed.

Considerably muddled, I turned to see what he was staring at. Amid the carving of the vaulted ceiling, I seemed to glimpse something glimmering, but with my eyes blurred by weakness, I could not make it out.

"For some reason, it wants *you*, my brother. It would not show itself before you came in. Here. Sit on the floor." He helped me do so. "Stay where you are. I will bring you food."

Taking the candle, he hastened toward the kitchen. Left in darkness, I eyed the small presence overhead, recognizing its glow as Elfin glamour. There was only one thing for which Albaric could have been searching in the night. The ring, apparently, had been hiding on a coign of the wooden vaults since Lord Brock had flung it off his hand.

After what seemed a long time, Albaric came hurrying back, arms loaded, carrying with evident difficulty the candle in one hand and a bowl in the other. "Take the soup, Aric, please, before I spill it on you."

Shaking from hunger, I reached up for the bowl and, without waiting for a spoon, drank from it. The liquid within was hot, for the stock-pot simmered night and day; I burned my lips and tongue but gulped the mutton broth anyway for the sake of its warm strength flowing into me.

Setting down the candle and other things, Albaric laughed at the mess I was making. Rarely had I heard his laughter, as musical as harp strings. "Aric the barbaric," he teased as he sat cross-legged, facing me, "take a napkin and try to behave." He handed me the square of cloth, a spoon, then a wedge of cheese, some light bread, and a pastry oozing strawberries. "Slow down," he said, watching with amusement as I devoured everything. Not until I had licked the last sticky crumbs of strawberry turnover from my fingers did I speak.

"Is it still the same day?"

"Same day?" Albaric repeated. Even now, time had little meaning for him.

I tried my question another way. "How long have I slept?"

"After your wounds were dressed and bound, you slept through sunset and far into the night."

Yesternight at about this same time, then, he and I, dripping wet and half-drowned, had climbed the tower to Mother's chamber. Instead of giving me satisfaction for the good we had done since, the memory jolted an anxious qualm in me. "Bluefire?" I demanded. "Has anyone seen—"

"Our bonny blue horse is in the stables, terrorizing the grooms just as before. At ease, Prince Aric."

From something in his being with me, beyond his words, I knew he had ridden out to find Bluefire and bring him home. At the same time, I sensed his amusement at me, and his happiness in my company, and also that something had made him unhappy—the same old something. Worse, he was desperately weary. "Albaric," I asked, "have you not slept?"

"I am not so battered as you. Yes, I slept for part of the night, but thoughts of yon contrary thing pestered me." He pointed up at the ring. "I came down here, and in the silence and shadows, I could feel it was yet in this room, which comforted me, for I had feared someone might have made off with it. Yet I could not find it! But now all is well."

"Indeed? How will you get it down from its perch?"

The moment I said this, the ring rolled off the coign of its own accord and fell—no, flew gently down like a firefly, glowing, to land on the stone with a sound like the ringing of a distant bell.

Albaric got up, went over, and brought it back carefully in

the palm of his hand. Together, we studied its disposition. It glowed a mild, limpid gold, as peaceable as sunrise.

"Certainly, it is making a great show of behaving itself," remarked Albaric. "I wonder why."

"So do I. Equally, I wonder why I feel that I must keep it."

"Because it wants you to." Albaric cocked a quizzical eyebrow. "You know, brother, it is an oddling in this world, just as I am. Small wonder it takes refuge in you." Albaric handed me the ring; gathered up crumbs, napkin, spoon, and bowl; returned them to the kitchen; then came back with the candle and helped me to my feet. Since eating, I felt both stronger and weaker, able to walk by myself yet uncertain in the area of my belly and feeling also a queasiness of mind. But that was due to the ring. As Albaric walked back to the bedchamber with me, I held the ring beneath closed fingers in the deep hollow of my palm and did not look at it until I laid it on the washstand.

Yes, all right. It was still as golden and serene as dawn.

From the neck of an outgrown jerkin, I pulled a leather lacing, strung the ring onto it, tied it securely, and slipped it over my head onto my neck, hiding the ring under my clothing. "Do not tell anyone, Albaric," I said, "not even Mother, and especially not Father."

He nodded, giving his silent promise without asking why. If he had asked, I could not have answered. I did not know why the ring was now my secret.

CHAPTER THE
TWENTIETH

LBARIC SLEPT THEN. Lumped in the bed like a pair of tired puppies, we both slept until nearly noon the next day.

When we finally got up, a manservant awaited me with word that Father wished to see me as soon as I was ready.

I ordered luncheon brought to the bedchamber, for I required a great deal of washing, even my hair, in addition to many wounds to be redressed, and must needs do all things at once, accompanied by much pain and stiffness and grumbling. Albaric helped as I struggled in the hip bath, shaking his head and cleansing my various cuts with greatest care.

"Some of these are deep and raw," he said as he bound them afterward. "Take care of yourself, my brother, or you will be sick."

"Bah. Worrywart." Young, strong, I had never suffered from a festering wound in my life. Now clean and dry, I ate a slice of kidney pie as I searched for clothing. Albaric perched in the window and strummed a harp—somehow, already, he had got himself another harp—remarking, "The king wants his report only from you. I offered yesterday to give him an account. He looked at me as if I were an odd sort of talking monkey and declined."

"Ah."

Yes, it was indeed the same quiet grief, then, that I felt in my brother. He wanted his father. But his father did not want him.

After I had put on good leggings and a better tunic, being careful to cover the thong whereby I carried the ring, Albaric added, "If the king does not want to know what I am thinking, it is just as well. I am worried about Marissa."

That gave me pause, standing there with a neck kerchief in hand. "Worried?"

"Perhaps I do not much understand about this thing called wedlock. But Aric, should there not be some love?"

"Oh. I see." I knotted and draped the length of tartan. "You are wiser than most mortals, my brother. Of course there should be love; you are right. But when one is a prince. . . ." I shrugged, took a deep breath, willing him to understand. "I like her very much, and I can but hope that in time we might come to . . . love." I tossed on a silk-lined short cape of white fur. "And as a lord's daughter—she has no choice, but I hope—I believe she does not dislike me, at least. She is just a girl, not nearly a woman yet, so it will not truly be a wedding. She is yet innocent, and I would be ashamed not to let her stay a virgin for as long as she chooses. I will be her friend, and wait, and hope that maybe it will turn out all right in the end." I sighed. "And if not, I will try to do what is best for her."

"But what is best for *you*?"

"No need to worry about me. When I get rambunctious, as Mother would put it, there are wenches in the kitchen only too happy to oblige me."

Albaric missed several notes on his harp. Glancing at him, I saw his shock grow as understanding smote him, as he realized where I might have been any one of several times when perhaps he had noticed my side of the bed empty in the middle of the night.

I spoke gently. "Do not the Elfin folk feel such needs, my brother? Certainly your mother did."

"But she is the *queen*."

"So?"

"So—so I do not know!" He lifted laughing eyes to mine, amused at himself. "Perhaps I am an innocent like Marissa?"

"Too young in this world, you mean?"

"How can I ever become old enough for wisdom when I grew up in a place with no time?"

"Stop. When you talk about time, you give me a headache." With a pair of clean and shining boots on now, all in royal regalia, I went to Albaric and touched his hand. "Please do not worry about Marissa, brother mine. I intend to take the best care of her."

Leaving, striding down the ever-dark stone passageway, I wondered whether Albaric ever worried about himself, or if he realized by now how hopeless. . . . He wanted the love of his father who had raised him. He had my love to the utmost, yet that seemed to make little difference; one's father is, after all, Father, not to be replaced. Returning to Dun Caltor with me, Albaric had come home to the same sad yearning. Nor, I sensed, would that ever change.

I had vowed to right that wrong for him. I had made it my life's most important quest to find him peace.

But how?

Formally enthroned, my parents awaited me in the council chamber, and I strode in feeling rather as if I were to be disciplined, which made no sense. They had been told I was dead, but after all, I lived; my return had liberated them from captivity; I had taken that pig Brock Domberk at the point of the sword: one would think my parents should be pleased with me. I had not yet greeted Father properly—the warmth in my heart kept a smile on my face as I walked up to him, but I studied him. He had dressed almost entirely in black; that was unlike him. His smile tried to answer mine and failed. And as I dropped briefly to one knee, bowing my head, I knew my instinct was right; all was not well.

"Aric, please, be seated." It was my mother who spoke, warmly enough. "We would like to hear of your travels."

I sat on the velvet-cushioned chair a servant had placed behind me, and with all seeming innocence, I asked, "How much has Albaric told you?"

Father's stark face hardened, darkened, although he did not scowl.

"We want to hear it from you," Mother said, still speaking just as pleasantly. "First, that wound up near your shoulder—is it from an arrow?"

So I told them of the outlaws, and how Bluefire and Albaric between them had given us ample warning, and how Garth had said I was a "blooded warrior." But with Garth's name on my tongue, I had to tell what had become of him, and skipped ahead to describe the Domberk ambush. I was telling of being unhorsed two against one when Father finally spoke:

"Cowards!" Leaning toward me, with his eyes smoldering like hot embers, he demanded in wonder, "How is it you are yet alive?"

So I told how Albaric had saved me, putting his back to mine, and how we had fought "like a two-headed monster," while Bluefire had unnerved the foe by attacking on his hind legs like giant warrior and had done so much damage that they fled. I told of the aftermath: three men-at-arms dead, Garth's gruesome wound, and how Albaric and I, hoping to reach Dun Caltor before Domberk did, had left him with who I hoped were trustworthy strangers.

"Tomorrow, we will ride to reclaim him, be he dead or alive," Father spoke in tones of command. "You will come to show me the way."

"Dear," Mother interposed, "he's not yet strong enough."

"Nonsense."

"But my love, you did not see his wounds; *I* did. I bound them up, and I implore you to be reasonable: he needs rest. Surely Albaric could ride with you."

"Bah!"

"Fishheads!" she shot back at him. "What ails you, Bard? There's nothing wrong with Albaric."

"There's everything wrong! We have not yet even begun to speak of what's wrong!"

"Then what might that be?" I asked civilly enough.

Father sputtered. Mother told me, "He hardly knows, dear, that's half the problem. He's been like a bear with burrs ever since you got him out of that dungeon."

Father reared up like a bear indeed. "My son marrying a Domberk?" he roared.

"Ah." I softened my tone. "Father, it's not yet done—"

"It should not have been suggested, not thought of, without consulting me!"

"But Father, surely you will agree the circumstances were extraordinary? In truth, when I spoke to Domberk of marriage, it was not a pledge but a ploy. I hope for a period of peace with him, perhaps even some few years, while his daughter remains at Dun Caltor. But as for Marissa of Domberk, she has already given me reason to think she would not marry me, and I'd never force her or any woman. Although she's not yet woman," I added. "She's barely more than a child. She's a wee, bold slip of a lassie." I smiled, remembering how she had told me I did not look or act like a prince.

"You met her at Narven?" Mother asked. "You like her?"

"Yes, I like her the way I would like a feisty terrier pup. Nothing more."

Mother turned wide, thoughtful eyes to Father. "I wonder why Domberk sent her to Narven."

"To set the trap!"

I said, "Father, I doubt Domberk knew anything about it. His wife—"

Lady Domberk had seized the excuse for an excursion, I was about to say, but Father interrupted by leaping to his feet and roaring in a tone fit to terrify me, "I will thank you to remember who is ruler here!"

"Bard!" Mother squeaked, shocked.

"Father." His bellow did not entirely unman me, not quite, for I thought I understood its cause. Slipping out of my chair, I dropped to one knee but tilted my head up to meet his angry eyes as I addressed him. "Father, you were imprisoned in your own dungeon, the last place a king ought to be, when in I came looking like a bloody barbarian and slinging orders around. I apologize, my Sire. In the necessity of the moment, perhaps I overstepped."

The king glared back at me without speaking.

I tried again. "Father, surely you must know I've no desire for glory, or war, or power, much less your throne. You *must* know that."

In a low and terrible rasping way, he said, "I know nothing of the sort."

"Bard!" Springing to her feet, Mother laid her hand on his arm. "You cannot mean it. Aric has bled for you! Why is your proud head as sore as his wounds?"

He flung away her hand without looking at her, only at me, and his eyes seemed no longer blue; they blazed like black fire. Feeling as cold as if turned to stone, I could not speak, and I could no longer think I was not afraid. "Go," the king commanded, his voice clotted with fury. "Hence, out of my council chamber, both of you. You and your precious Albaric."

There was nothing to be done but leave him alone with his wrath.

CHAPTER THE
TWENTY-FIRST

I COULD NOT SLEEP but walked half the night away, alone, unable to talk, trying to calm myself. I went late to bed, taking care not to awaken Albaric. Sometime before dawn, clouds sailed in from the sea, bearing torrents of rain, to my relief, the next morning. Father could not possibly set out to look for Garth on such a day and therefore would not be obliged to change his mind. Carefully respectful, I reported to him as usual and found him dealing with delegations of his people: fisherfolk frightened by myriad haddock floating dead on the sea and peasants worried about a blight in the barley; it seemed nothing was going right in Calidon. But instead of keeping me beside him to learn or help, Father gave me a curt "Good morning" and sent me away.

The rain made it a singularly useless time for a holiday, even had I not felt all the darkness of my father's shadow. Forlorn, I wandered Dun Caltor looking for Albaric and found him, of course, in the stables.

He was having one of his silent conversations with Bluefire, and not wanting to interrupt, I did not enter the stall. But

Bluefire astonished me, leaving Albaric to stick his head over the railings, nudge me, and snuffle my hair, and lip my ear as if he—

"He likes you, Aric!" Albaric declared with greatest joy. "He has missed you, and he's glad you are alive!"

I hugged the blue stallion around his great muscular neck, for I felt much the same toward him, but then I hid my face in his mane.

"What's wrong, Aric?" Albaric came out to stand beside me.

I muttered, "That's my line of duty."

"What?"

"Asking people what is wrong."

"People? Asking *me*, you mean. What is *wrong*?"

I lifted my head to face him. "I don't know." This was untrue; I remembered well enough the things my father had said. But I felt within me a new sort of turmoil I had not yet faced.

"Shall we find out?" Albaric asked, smiling.

"I suppose we'd better."

"How?"

"The same method I have been using since I could walk."

"Which is?"

"You'll see."

We went to consult my mother.

The queen's loom room, usually well sunlit, was only a little less shadowy than the rest of Dun Caltor on that rainy day. Mother had tied a colorful checked wrap around her shoulders and wore ribbons in her hair, as if she were trying to brighten the gloom. She was well pleased to see us, letting her handwomen put away their spindles and leave the wool to be carded another day, sending them away. I seated her in a chair by the hearth, where there burned a small peat fire to dry the damp; and beneath the shadow of the tall standing loom, Albaric and I settled on the thick catamount-skin rug at her feet.

"Mother," I said in sober jest, "you've known Father a good while longer than I. Could you explain him to Albaric? For I can make no sense of him."

"I!" Albaric protested. "'Twas you with the fish face because he spurned your company today."

Mother turned troubled eyes to me.

"A bear with burrs," I confirmed. "Mother, what is happening to Father? Who or what is he mourning in his black garb? He's not himself."

To my surprise, Mother smiled tenderly upon me. "Aric," she said. "My amazing Aric."

I sat slack-jawed and uncouth, but Albaric said softly, "Hear, hear."

"Your father is made in layers like an onion," Mother told me, "just like every mortal I have ever known—except you, Aric. No matter how I watch for a darker core to appear, the sun continues to shine through you, my son."

"I've no desire to be an onion, but a glass window instead."

"Rare and beautiful."

"A marvel," Albaric said quietly. "I've met no one else like you, Prince Aric."

While I sat, feeling heat ascend my neck and face, Mother went on, "If you had jealousies and grudges and petty ill

feelings like most people, it would be easier for you to understand your father."

"A king is not like most people."

"True. He is not." She drew breath, her gaze looking past
Albaric and me, distant, misted with thought. It was a moment
before she spoke. "A king is a man who wears a crown, but after
a while the crown begins to wear the man. A crown, I think, is
a trickster sort of ring of power that fate places around a man's
head. And Bardaric's crown," she said in a way I'd never heard
her speak before, low and bleak and bitter, "is a burden no
man should have to bear, weighty with the fates of his father
and three brothers, Ardath and Lehinch and Escobar. Like
the ring, it is a trickster, and lately I believe it has made him a
bit mad. He wishes to spare you from bearing it, my son. . . ." She
turned back to me, then grimaced and shook her head. "Bah.
I try to deceive myself for love of him, I am so grateful to have
him back after he nearly died . . . but since then, the sad sooth
of it is that he's no better than any other king."

Stunned and speechless, I sensed more than understood
the meaning of her words.

But Albaric spoke. "Queen Evalin, could you explain,
please? For in my native country, there are no kings. Your
husband was but a captive there, and I his mongrel son."

"How interesting." Mother reverted to her usual thoughtful
tone. "What was he like then, Albaric? When he was no king,
I imagine he was quite wonderful."

"To me, yes. But to my mother—shadowed beneath his
pity for her was great anger. Inwardly, he raged as if in chains."

"And he hated the ring."

"Yes. He hated that thing he could not remove from his
hand."

"Mother," I burst out before I even knew I was going to speak, "why is he turning against me?"

Pain of saying it cut me like a sword to the face; for a moment, I thought I wore my trouble like Albaric's scar. For this was definitely the trouble I had not been able to name.

But she seemed hardly able to answer. She sighed, then spoke more to the sunless room and the shadowy looms all around us than to me. "Aric, you have done such deeds and grown so much that suddenly you are no longer a stripling, his youngster, but you are a man, his equal, a rival, a threat. . . ." Perhaps thinking of what he had done to other such threats in the past, she paled. Her voice quavered and faded.

"No," said Albaric strongly. "Aric, you are his mortal son and heir; he loves you. He may not know it right now, but he loves you deeply, and he will never harm you."

Chilled, I protested, "He has not harmed you either."

Mother spoke once more with words flat and bleak. "I pray he never will. Either of you. But I cannot tell, for I no longer seem to know him, he is so changed. Perhaps the ring hurt him; perhaps . . . I do not understand, but this truth I must face: something has gone wrong with my husband. When he rode forth to fight Domberk, he was not the warrior I know him in troth to be. He should never have been taken alive to be shackled in a dungeon. And he has not been himself since you gave him back to me."

CHAPTER THE
TWENTY-SECOND

O N MY GOOD GOLDEN HORSE, Valor, I bespoke the
king riding across the fields with me on his black
charger, Invincible: "So, Father, what will it take
to convince you that I am but a lamb in wolf's clothing?" I
tapped my much-dented helmet.

As I had hoped he might, Father laughed. He also in his
helm, and I in a brand-new tunic of chain mail, so armored in
case of outlaws, we were riding out to find Garth. Riding side
by side, just the two of us. This was due to my suggestion, and
I hoped the few days together might bring him back to me.

"Wolf's clothing is comfortable compared to a turtle shell,"
Father rejoined, referring to his own Roman-style metal
breastplate but not exactly answering my question, as I noticed
without comment.

"All this armor, you mean? Too true. These gloves have to
go." Slipping them off, I turned in the saddle to stuff them into
a pack. I felt my father watching me with some amusement.
When I faced forward again, he was eyeing the sack of stones
hanging from my saddle by my right knee.

"One can't throw them properly with hands encased in leather," I told him, straight-faced. I had brought the stones mostly to remind him how much of a boy I still was.

"How is it that I had never heard of your skill as a thrower of stones?"

I shrugged, my chain mail jingling. "I made no report, Sire, as stonesmanship is not listed among the noble arts of war."

"Nevertheless, I would like a demonstration. Choose a target."

We were jogging the horses across moorland, a wild heathery place where deer grazed along with the cattle and sheep. "Cow or deer?" I asked innocently.

He rolled his eyes. "Try yon standing stone."

The menhir stood almost too near. I struck it squarely, then another farther away, then a third so distant that one could not hear the stone strike, only see the chips fly. Father gave a low whistle.

"Strong arm," he remarked, then added, "You should be carrying your shield on the other one, to build it up again. The muscles grow weak after they are wounded."

I nodded and obeyed, placing the shield on my left arm. Father was right about the muscles Domberk's sword had cut. By the time we crested the next rise, my arm was aching.

Beyond the moor lay forested hills, which I studied. In the distance, they looked random, like green hogs sleeping, but I thought I saw a familiar contour. "Let us ride a little more toward the north."

"Are you sure?"

"No," I said frankly, "I am sure of nothing. That day is a blur to me." A propitious moment; I told my father, "I've sent Albaric ahead of us to scout." On Bluefire, Albaric could ride in one day what would take us two or three. "He'll set me straight if I lead you astray."

"Ah," Father muttered. "Albaric. Always Albaric."

"He has made a great difference in our lives," I said, trying for Mother's thoughtful tone of voice, "and it's up to us, Father, whether it's for better or worse."

Silence. I disciplined myself to say no more; either Father would respond or he would not. And he was the king.

Some moments after I had given up on him, he growled, "At least he looks less like a mollycoddle with that scar on his face."

I laughed. "Speak sooth, Father; he's the dashing warrior and turns the head of every serving-maid who sees him."

"No more so than you do."

I shrugged. "I wouldn't know. There's no competition between us." I waited awhile, then asked, "Do you still find him so hard to accept, Father?"

"Accept in what way?"

"Just as my comrade. You know he has foresworn his birthright to anything more."

"I do not trust his word," Father said softly, "and I do not like it that he cleaves so closely to you."

Although hard to hear, this was what I had desired, this speaking of truth without the scowling face, the hot blood, the raised voice. Father spoke solemnly, that was all, and I answered him just as calmly.

"But we love each other, Father. Not in any shameful way. We love as brothers."

"I hated my brothers," Father said.

For a moment, my breath stopped. How had I not realized; how had I been so stupid? Of course, it was a thing spoken of seldom, and then in whispers, which as a child I was not supposed to have heard, had not understood, had easily forgotten. And even now that I was nearly a man, I still had that childish way—I saw it in that moment—that innocence causing me to regard my parents, the adults, as ageless and unchanging, without any interesting history before I had come along.

I spoke slowly. "I understand you and your brothers hated one another because you were competing for the throne?"

"I suppose. I do not remember ever thinking well of any of them. Ardath, Lehinch, Escobar, then me; I was the youngest, of no account when Ardath paid brigands to kill Lehinch and Escobar. Lehinch died, but Escobar escaped into the brawling Craglands and has not been heard from since. I hope he is dead, for his is the throne by right, and all my life I have dreaded his return."

"Would you go to war to keep the throne, no matter whose the right?"

"Yes. You know I killed Ardath to take Calidon and your mother."

"But that was a duel. A fair fight." So I had been told, once, years ago, by Todd.

"It might as well have been murder," said Father with that same odd calm. "Ardath was more than half drunk, as always, and he scarcely knew one end of a sword from the other even when he was sober. For him to be king, just because he was the eldest, was absurd. He poisoned our father to take the throne, you know."

No, I didn't know. But I swallowed the information in silence.

Father went on, "Whenever he was in his cups, he bragged

of having slipped arsenic into the ale of our sire. Turnabout is fair play, so I killed Ardath and took his wife, whom I loved."

"Mother."

"Yes."

"And she loved you."

"Yes. Her marriage to Ardath had been arranged against her will, but when she laid eyes on me, and I on her—it was like a fated thing. Still, our love was adultery at first. I have sometimes thought—all of our babies dying—it might be a punishment."

Never before had Father spoken with me thus, revealing his inmost thoughts. It was the rhythm of riding, I think, that brought the secrets out of him. There is something about swaying atop the stride of a strong steed that stops time and soothes one into a kind of trance. Still, I felt all the honor of his trust.

Punishment meant he felt guilt. I did not want that for him. Yet I did not wish to quarrel with him.

"Why did I myself not die, if it was as you say?" I asked at last.

"We do not know. But you can see why—when Domberk boasted that you could not possibly have escaped his ambush . . . it shattered us."

Truly, I had my father again, even more than before.

I managed to say gruffly, "Domberk boasted wrongly, for here I am."

"Yes, thanks to Albaric, and I ought to love him for it, yet I cannot."

"Who is to say what you ought to love and what not? It is a thing that cannot be demanded of anyone, much less the king."

This truth flew out of me, startling, like a grouse bursting from a thicket, shaking me with every beat of its wings.

Then silence, during which I eased my shield back to its fastening on my saddle, for my arm ached almost as badly as my heart: Albaric was never to have what he lived for and longed for, our father's love, and I had just admitted it. Was I giving up my quest?

Finally, my father said, low, "I did not dare to think you could understand."

"I understand only dimly, and partially, and at some times, not at others, alas."

Father laughed, a good laugh with harmony in it. "That is much the way I understand you, my son."

We rode on into the first forest.

That night, as my father snored, wrapped in his blanket on the opposite side of the campfire from me, I lay wakeful and troubled. I could not forsake my fealty to my father. Ever. Fealty to a liege is a loyalty even deeper than love.

It did not appear I could reconcile my father and my brother.

Was I to be forced to choose between my sire and Albaric?

But I could not. That would be like tearing myself in half. I had to bite my lip to silence a moan of misery at the thought, and my distress prompted me to pull a constant companion from under my clothing: the ring.

Like a hollow moon, it glowed white—but no, whiter than the mottled moon. White as swans, white as milk, white as the white Elfin glamour amidst which Albaric had been born or the tiny four-petaled flower called Innocence. Never before had I seen the ring so ardently white. Lying on my side, keeping my body between my slumbering father and the ring's whispering light, I studied it.

Today, I had faced a truth: I could not by any means compel Father to love the person I loved. Which made me question, with a queasy feeling in my chest: perhaps I presumed too much, questing for the happiness of another? Perhaps each mortal's happiness is his own quest and his alone?

Yet:

> *What is a friend?*
> *Troth without end.*
> *A light in the eyes,*
> *A touch of the hand—*
> *I would follow you even*
> *to death's cold strand.*

As I thought, the ring subtly changed, half of its white turning from milk to silver until it flowed around its own circle like two fishes, yet blending with each other, very much at one within the ring.

I watched it, blinking, entranced, and somehow comforted, until my own drowsiness warned me to put it away before I fell asleep. I lay and looked up at the stars, circling always but so slowly one could not discern—yet tonight I seemed to see them like distant white horses on the move in a magical meadow vast and dark.

———————

Riding onward the next day, after the morning dew, tears of the night, had warmed away, and also the morning silence, I asked, "Father, was it very hard being a captive?"

I knew he thought I meant his few days in the dungeon at Domberk's hands, but I was thinking of the timeless time when he was the captive of Theena, Queen of Elfland.

He answered promptly, "Insupportable. I nearly chewed off my own beard in pure chagrin."

How infinitely worse that other, timeless, Othergates time must have been. How could he not remember it at all? But this fugitive thought fled when Father spoke on.

"If it were not for your mother's quick wit with the ring," he added, "Domberk could have done far worse."

"I have often thought that Mother would make a good king were she a man."

I heard no mockery in Father's laughter. "You are quite right!"

"Sire, was your sire a good king?"

He turned to me, his face hard, his laughter lost. "Why do you ask?"

"Because I wonder whether you learned it from him."

His heavy eyebrows lifted. "You think me a good king? Despite how I began?"

He had asked, so it was not flattery to answer, "I have always thought you the best of kings, fair in taxation and in the court of law, mindful of the welfare of your people, helping them prosper, protecting them, merciful to the unfortunate. Was your father also merciful?"

"No." He faced straight ahead now, scanning the forest trail, not looking at me. "Your mother taught me the virtue of mercy. Son, you—you honor me. Much I have had to learn on my own, with many mistakes. I have tried to be fair, but I have not often thought of myself as good."

"But you *are* a good king. I can hardly imagine any better. Here you are, King Bardaric of Calidon, yourself riding out to find a hurt yeoman."

He shrugged that off. "Garth deserves no less from me. How much farther?"

"Perhaps half a day."

I would not have known if it were not that Albaric was guiding me, for he had already found the way. When Father and I came to the thinning trees at the edge of the forest, then faced a vast expanse of heather and gorse, we halted to seek a landmark, and I could feel the direction as if I were a compass needle and Albaric were north. But to Father I said only, "We should make toward that tall, dead pine atop which the eagle nests."

"I can barely see it. You yourself must have the eyes of an eagle."

"I'll race you there." A small show of youthful daring.

"And break your horse's leg in a badger's burrow? Have some sense, Aric." A small show of parental authority. Nevertheless, instead of walking on, Father led off at a canter, carefully scanning the ground for the sake of his steed. I cantered a little behind, making no attempt to overtake him, smiling to myself: this was not a race, yet he would win. All was going well. I hoped against common sense that we would find Garth alive—but even if it were not so, even if Garth lay dead, then he had served his king and his prince well in death. He had given us back to each other.

Or so I thought.

Partway across the gorse waste, Father slowed Invincible

to a walk. There was no escaping the sun, which heated that open place like an oven, and sweat ran freely on the horses as well as on us. But as we walked on, we began to see something bright-colored, low to the ground and a little to one side of our landmark. It tweaked our eyes, for we could not tell what it was. Father urged Invincible into a trot, and I, for one, forgot about sun and sweat, trotting beside him, eager to see what that thing might be.

The sun floated nearly overhead before we reached it: a length of yellow plaid tied to a tree limb next to a narrow trail, perhaps made by deer.

"We are to go in here?" Father asked.

"Yes, Sire." Untying Albaric's neck kerchief, I slung it around my own shoulders without comment. Father rode in first, but rather than duck beneath low branches, he drew his sword and whacked them off. I think he rather terrified the two peasants who awaited us.

Surely, Albaric had told them we were coming. In a small sort of glade or clearing they stood as if expecting us, the two good-hearted outlaws I faintly remembered, ducking their heads and tugging at their forelocks. One look at their faces showed that they would be quite incapable of speaking, so Father turned to me. "Aric, is this the place?"

"I think so. Let me see," I answered, dismounting. Among the trees at the edge of the clearing stood a low shelter of logs and pine thatch. I strode over there and peered in at the doorway.

"My King!" a husky voice cried from within.

"Garth?"

"Yes, Majesty!"

Elated that he lived but dismayed by his greeting, I stepped inside quickly, found his cot, and took his hand. "No, Garth, it's only Prince Aric." Another figure appeared in the doorway, a broad-shouldered, proud silhouette one would think no one could mistake. "There's your king."

"Garth," spoke Father's gruff voice, "my heart rejoices to find you alive."

"Your Highness!" As Father also stepped inside the hut. "Majesty, as I live, Prince Aric has grown as tall and almost as mighty of mien as you!"

"Nay, it's only the helm and chain mail that befooled you," I said.

I made way, giving Father my place by the bed while he asked Garth how he had been treated and whether he was well enough to travel. He had taken fever and had managed to live through it but was yet weak. Still, all was far better than we could have hoped, for a bad wound that swells with fever generally kills. The two outlawed peasants must have nursed him excellently well. I went out to bespeak them, thank them and reward them, and make arrangements with them. They had kept, hidden in the woods, two reasonably gentle horses they had caught after the Domberk ambush. With saplings everywhere to choose among, it would be the work of an hour for them to construct a horse-litter for Garth. We agreed that they would do so and come with us to Dun Caltor the next day. Then, if they liked the place, I told them, they could stay as my father's yeomen.

So all was well, excellently well. Yet when my father stepped into the daylight and looked at me, my heart winced, for his eyes might as well have been made of stone.

CHAPTER THE
TWENTY-THIRD

LBARIC RODE INTO THE CLEARING a while later, carrying several burlap sacks in his hands, for Bluefire wore not a strap of harness to which he might have fastened them. Nor did Albaric wear clothing above his waist; the day was hot, swarming with midges, and Father and I had long since laid aside our helms and chain mail. Albaric inclined his head to Father with a shy smile, handed me some sacks with a grin, then lithely slipped down off his tall mount.

"Mortal comfort," he told me.

"Eggs!" I exclaimed, opening one sack after another. Rarely did an outlaw lurking in the woods taste proper eggs from a hen, not some wild bird. "And fresh-baked bread, and— what's in the flasks?"

"Milk, for health. And just in case anyone wanted it, whiskey."

He said this in so droll and sober a way that I laughed, the peasants laughed, even Father laughed. Garth's face appeared at the door of the hut; he stood bent with pain, clinging to the timber.

"Ah," he said, as if the sight of Albaric and Bluefire explained any amount of laughter.

"Garth!" I hurried to him, easing him down to a seat on the dirt with his back against the doorpost. "Eggnog! I could make you eggnog. Would you like some?"

"Sooth, why ruin good whiskey with milk and egg?"

In another sack, the peasants had discovered, with more commotion and laughter, a live hen for our supper. "I thought the meat less likely to spoil if still cackling," Albaric explained in the same straight-faced way.

"You have done very well, Albaric." Father had not smiled on the newcomer, but he tried to be fair, always. I felt his words of praise startle my brother's heart and swell it with hope.

And my own heart shrank, knowing there was no hope.

One of our woodland hosts took the chicken away from the clearing to dispatch it. The other started a campfire by which to cook it. I mixed eggnog for Garth, despite his joking protests, and squatted by him to watch him sip it. Albaric took his neck wrapper back from me and used it to rub Bluefire.

"If there ever was a horse deserving to be groomed with the finest tartan, that would be the one." Father spoke again fairly, and whimsically, but with a dark undertone. That darkness had shadowed him since the moment Garth had called me king, even though I had explained it away.

And just as I thought of it, Garth undid the explanation; indeed, meaning all good and no harm, he was the doom of me. "Prince Aric," he bespoke me as he finished his strengthening drink, "it wonders me yet how, barring the beard, how quickly you've grown to be the spit and image of your royal father."

Everyone heard, confound it, including Father. "Spit?"

Albaric echoed, puzzled. The old country word for "spirit" was "spit," but doubtless Albaric was thinking of spittle.

Father laughed—not a very good laugh in his uncertain mood. "Spitting images spit on the ground. Aric, Albaric," he ordered suddenly, "Come here. Stand beside each other."

We obeyed, facing our sire at a distance of perhaps two paces, while he stood with his fists on his hips, studying us up and down.

Again, I felt hope beating in Albaric's heart, for he knew nothing of the king's chagrin, and he thought Father might at last be seeing us as brothers, almost twins, of the same height, with the same flowing hair—mine golden, his flaxen—and the same straight back and lifted head. The same comely features were ours, except that my brother's were finer, less blunt and common; the same build, except that, again, his was finer, more graceful. The same frank eyes, mine as blue as Father's, Albaric's a bit grayed, as if with distance.

I felt wary. My father's gaze, studiously blank to start with, quickly grew hard to hide fear. He burst out, "By all the gods, Aric, he's like a fetch of you!"

"I am honored," I replied quietly.

"A fetch?" Albaric asked just as quietly, although I could feel the word strike him like a blow. "What is a fetch?"

"A second self." I smiled at him.

"A wraith!" Father burst out. "An unnatural double dogging a living man to—not haunt, exactly, but—"

"To save your life, and mine, and mine, and yours again until I've lost track?" I suggested serenely.

"Bah! No good can come of a wyrd for long." Stormily, Father turned away and strode off into the wilderness.

"Albaric is no wyrd, Father," I called after him.

"A wyrd?" Albaric asked me, troubled.

"Same as a fetch. A weird double."

"But it's—how can he say it's weird?"

Brothers might well look alike, and Father should know it, he meant, and I agreed. But with Garth and two curious peasants watching and listening, I could only shush him with a warning glance.

After Father returned later in the day, we ate well. Conversation was mostly for Garth, telling him all that had happened in Dun Caltor while he was gone. Or it was about Garth, his wounds, how well the two outlaws had nursed him, how lucky he was to have lived through festering and fever, his strength now returning but not yet great. Or it was for the outlaws, who explained that they had been driven to the wilderness by Domberk's demands for taxes and were shyly delighted to learn he was presently lodged in Caltor dungeon. Father spoke readily with Garth, graciously to our woodland hosts, little to Albaric or me. But we refused to sit silent, speaking freely to the others.

At dark, Father ordered that we should take turns standing guard, for so many fine horses might attract unwanted attention. Truth was, with Bluefire about, there was hardly need for human vigilance, but Albaric and I did not say so. We looked at each other and waited. The two outlaws offered to divide the first half of the night between them. Then I volunteered for the next duty, and Albaric the one after, and Father grumbled that he was always stirring before dawn anyhow. So it was settled.

When a hand shook me awake and I got up to stand guard, Albaric ghosted after me within a few minutes, following me quite stealthily and silently to my post. I hugged him, and he laid his fair head for a moment on my shoulder.

"Keep your voice low," I murmured as I released him.

"Nay, you," he whispered. "I've nothing to say. You tell me."

So I did. Leaning against a mighty elm tree, while darkness made shadows of us both and the voices of owls spoke louder than mine, I told him all I had learned on the ride hither: of Father and his feuding family and the bloody way he had acquired his throne. I told him how the confessions had brought us closer to each other until the moment of Garth's mistake. Now I thought my father watched me with jealousy and stony suspicion, regretting having revealed so much. Indeed, I half feared for my own life, having lately learned that my father was a murderer. Although I could not see my brother's face, I could feel his shock.

"This man with his black garb and his dark thoughts is not the father I remember." The words issued from him slowly, softer than moths.

"Yet you have not ceased to love him and yearn to please him."

"Have you?" he retorted.

"A touch," I admitted as if he had tapped me while sparring. "A definite touch. But no matter how cantankerous he acts, he still acknowledges me as his son, whereas you. . . ."

"Whereas I what?"

"My brother, as I love you, I cannot say it. You must bespeak it yourself."

In the silence of the night, I heard sighing wind and a plover's pining cry.

"Whereas," whispered Albaric finally, "he will never so acknowledge me. He refuses to believe. No matter what I do."

For answer, I gave him only the touch of my hand. I could not speak.

"Now he says I am an evil spirit. How does he believe in spirits, yet not in Elfland?"

"Nothing makes sense. I do not know what to think."

"It seems the ring has an opinion," he said wryly. Startled, I looked down to see light issuing from the chest of my tunic. The ring was awake and listening.

"Quite an opinion!" The glimmer of the ring was not usually strong enough to show through fabric, not even at night. I hesitated a moment, fearful of being found out, but the massive elm stood between us and the camp we guarded, so no one there should catch a glimpse of eerie light. Tugging at the thong around my neck, I pulled the ring out so Albaric could see.

"It's pure white," he whispered.

So much so that by its light, I could see Albaric's face hovering in the night like a white butterfly for innocent symmetry, but scarred—how could that be? How could anyone in the world hurt him?

"It's moving," he whispered.

The ring. It had divided itself along the rim, still white but now part soft and part shining, and although I held it motionless between two fingers, it seemed to spin, then swim and swirl, the soft half mixing with the shining half as we watched, rapt, until gradually it glowed once again entirely white.

I put it in the palm of my hand, and it lay there, its white light so gentle now that I concluded it had no more to say.

"When I looked at it yesternight, it was almost the same, like white fishes swimming nose to tail," I told Albaric. "Somehow, it comforts me."

"And me also."

"But I don't know what it means."

I saw his smile as I put the ring away. "As if anyone ever knows what it means? Or what it means to do?"

Darkness now. The ring no longer showed through my clothing.

"But it has settled my heart somehow," Albaric murmured.

"Mine also."

"Go sleep, my brother. I will keep watch." Whimsically, he saluted me. "Sweet dreams."

CHAPTER THE
TWENTY-FOURTH

WHEN THE REST OF US got up in the morning, Albaric was gone.

It took a while to be sure of this, for he could have been on a personal errand in the woods. But when my "Good morning, Father," was met only with a growl and a scowl, I began to worry.

When Garth requested help with his washing and dressing, which were difficult for him to manage alone, I crowded into the hut with him. As I rather expected, he took the opportunity to whisper to me, "Prince Aric, I have no right to ask. . . ."

"Ask what you will."

"Has something gone wrong between you and your—and the king?"

I sighed. "One would think he'd be glad to see me grow in prowess, but no, my helmet's too far from the ground now."

The old captain grimaced. "And I made things worse. I am sorry."

"No need. How could you know?"

"I should have been more careful. Any king can turn into a mettlesome, jealous tyrant."

I sighed. "It would seem that no proud king likes to be rescued by his beardless son."

"No proud man of any rank likes to be rescued by anyone, and that's fact, no matter how truly gratitude may be a virtue."

I thought on this a while, and on other things. "I think he regrets telling me how he won the throne."

"Very likely, for now he cannot help but think you might take it from him in likewise."

"Bah! As if I want his dusty old throne or his heavy crown. But he's full of black bile, so much so that I fear for myself, and even more—have you seen Albaric this morning?"

"No. Nor the blue steed."

Some small time later, over breakfast, Garth bespoke the consternation I dared not voice, for in easy tones he asked King Bardaric, "My Liege, pray tell me, what has become of the lad?"

"What lad?

"Young Albaric."

"The fetch, you mean. When I relieved him at guard, I ordered him to ride ahead on that freakish horse of his, carrying the news to Dun Caltor."

"Aha!" Garth looked far more pleased than I felt. "Will he tell my wife I am alive?"

Father relaxed his grim tone a bit. "He will tell Queen Evalin, *my* wife, and undoubtedly she shall tell yours."

After eating, I went about my business with my jaw locked, saying nothing, thinking much, thoughts I did not like. From now on, I knew with instinctive certainty, Father would seize every chance to separate me from my brother, whom he saw as no son of his, only as an intruder and a rival for my devotion. He would send Albaric into harm's way at every opportunity. He might even scheme to have Albaric killed.

Within the hour, we started back to Dun Caltor, and a wearisome journey it was, all at a walk for Garth's sake. Even at that slow pace, the movement wore him with constant pain; he said nothing, but one could watch the pallor bleach his face and see its lines deepen.

So we were a day longer on the hoof than before, but I could regain nothing of the camaraderie I had enjoyed with my father on the way out, although it was not for want of opportunity. Once we had seen how well the two outlaw peasants took care of Garth and how constantly they kept watch over him, we let them alone and rode several strides ahead of them; we could have talked about anything. But we seldom spoke. Father's attitude made it plain that we were there as a bodyguard against brigands for Garth and his two nurses, nothing more.

Once every hour or so, I ventured a comment. All were answered with silence until, the second day, I hit the right nail on the head.

"The Domberk party should reach Dun Caltor not too long after we do," I remarked.

Father reddened, puffed, then erupted. "Bah! The idea of my son married to a Domberk curdles my liver!"

By now, even such a harsh response was welcome. I replied pleasantly, "But would the idea of five, six, maybe seven years of peace with Domberk cool your liver?"

"*What?*" Scowling, Father darted a puzzled glance at me.

"Marissa is barely more than a girl," I explained, even though I had told him this before; it seemed reasonable to believe that he remembered nothing of it, not in his choler. "I cannot decently propose marriage, only an engagement. And that engagement could go on for several years, and who knows what might happen in that time, or how such a pact might end?"

"Humph." He spoke far more quietly. "You're no fool, and neither is Domberk; he will agree, but do you think the girl's mother will favor this engagement?"

"Perhaps not. Perhaps she wishes her husband to remain in your dungeon."

Father barked out a laugh; I had made him laugh! But then he fell silent again, and I was left with only the memory of the moment. It was the best moment in all that journey.

Except, I suppose, another moment having to do with Garth. Even his weakness, weariness, and pain could not constrain his excitement when he saw the turrets and towers of Dun Caltor in the distance and knew we were nearly home. He tried to sit up in the crude horse-litter in which he rode and might have fallen out had Father not ordered him, "Bloody blue blazes, Garth, lie still!" But the rough words bristled with affection, and beneath Father's beard, his smile was broad and warm. It gladdened my heart to see good King Bardaric again.

Even better, when we reached the village, every peasant had turned out to meet us, cheering without restraint and surging forward to surround our horses. Garth's wife, an ordinary frizzy-haired woman rendered even plainer by weeping, kissed him right there in the street, and great was the approbation of the crowd. We carried him to his cottage, and Father dismounted to oversee—"Gentle! Be gentle, now!"—as a dozen eager yeomen carried him inside. He bespoke Garth's wife, "I shall have the castle kitchen send treats to tempt his appetite."

She curtsied. "Your Majesty, her Majesty the Queen has already done so."

"Then you must send word if you need anything. Anything at all. I command it." Upon the humble woman, he smiled down as warm as the sun.

"Yes, your Highness. Ten thousand thanks, your Highness."

The cheering crowd followed us right to the gates of Dun Caltor, and cheering castle folk awaited us within, and again Father showed how innately he was a kind man, for he turned his attention first to the shy, speechless litter bearers who followed us, thanking them again while ordering the castle steward to welcome them, see to the stabling of their horses, and give them yeomen's clothing, bunks in the barracks, and all the hospitality he had to offer.

Meanwhile Mother, a slim and lovely goddess, with her golden filigree crown holding in place an airy white drapery over her wide-sleeved gown, stood waiting on the steps of the keep, her head high and smiling. And beside her, in regalia befitting her escort, stood Albaric.

As Father was busy, I managed to reach them first, bowing to Mother on bended knee before rising to give her a son's kiss of greeting; as I hugged her, I whispered in her ear, "Bear with burrs."

Turning to Albaric, I felt his contentment, his sense that he had done good service, and I hated to say what I must. But he had to know. "Trouble ahead," I told him by way of greeting, "unless I'm much mistaken."

Then Father strode up the steps to embrace his wife as his people clapped and cheered. Albaric he ignored until we four had turned, entered the keep, and the great doors closed behind us.

Then he turned on him vehemently. "What are you doing in my son's clothes?"

I took my stand beside my brother as Mother said what Albaric dared not. "Dearest, he *is* your son."

"Don't you ever say that again! Ever!" And the look he gave her made her pale. "Foolish woman," he told her, words that must have cut like a dirk, "don't you know a fetch when you see one? Weird, unnatural, evil?" Then he turned on Albaric. "You, take your blasted blue horse and leave here at once. Go."

"Father," I said, "if he goes, I go with him."

I spoke so levelly that for a moment, Father seemed unable to comprehend or react but stood choking on his own black bile, glaring at me. Then his face reddened as he roared, "What! You defy me?"

"No, Sire, I defy you not. You have given me no command. But I say what I must do. If Albaric leaves, then I shall accompany him."

"You—impudent puppy—you say nothing!" My father yanked his sword out of its scabbard, menacing. "I rule here!"

"And I conduct myself with honor, my Sire, as you have taught me." I gazed into his maddened eyes—barely human, his look more like that of a charging bull—I met his glare with mute plea, willing him to see me, recognize me, remember who I was, to come back to being my father. I did not draw my sword, only touched Albaric's arm, signaling him to step back, feeling his reluctance as he did so. But he knew I had the right. This matter was between Father and me.

Father had forgotten about Albaric, all his ire now for me. "You conduct yourself as a traitor! Renegade—ungrateful—viper!" Left-handed, he clouted me on the side of the head. I took the blow silently, barely staggering, standing erect and making no move to counter it.

Father gave a roar without words. His sword swept up. I glimpsed Mother's face, very likely a mirror of my own, white and waiting, knowing this was the only way. I saw the sword slicing down to smite me, and I think I closed my eyes, for after it cut the side of my neck, I only heard it clang to the floor as Father dropped it; I did not see.

I opened my eyes but closed them again, because I could not bear to look upon the scarlet contortion of my father's face, now all horror and dismay.

"What have I done?" he cried. "Have I gone mad? Aric, my son!"

I wanted to look at him and speak to him, but my vision blurred, and something clotted my throat.

Mother stood beside me, examining the cut on my neck. "Not so bad," she murmured. "Albaric, take him and tend to him, would you, please?" Already, she had Father by the arm, leading him away as if he were a distraught child.

As soon as he left, servants crowded in, babbling, exclaiming, the whole keep in an uproar. Some took charge of my father's sword, some cleaned blood off the floor, some had brought bandaging and water for me, and most had come with no excuse but to look.

I found my voice. "Out!" I commanded in a tone not unlike my sire's. "Everybody out!" They scattered like quail.

Albaric took me upstairs, my arm over his shoulder. "My brother," he kept saying in a kind of daze. "My brother." In my chamber, I slumped on the bed as he slipped my blood-spattered tunic off me, lifted a clumsy bandage away from my neck, washed the cut and closed it with gentle fingers, and wrapped it more tightly. It was a wound, I thought, the mate of his, the misplaced twin of the scar on his face.

At the thought—that scar on his perfect face—I bent with pity of the whole world's pain and burst into weeping, trying to hide behind my hands.

"My brother." Kneeling beside me, Albaric enfolded me, and slipping to the floor to lean against him as he leaned against the bed, I wept as I had not wept in years, not since I was a child.

"You know," Albaric said quietly, "it was the weight of the sword only that smote you; he had loosed his grip before it touched you."

I nodded to show that I had heard him, because I could not speak for sobbing.

"Therefore, as he did not lop off your head, I was not after all obliged to become a patricide," Albaric added dryly.

I knew it was no joke; to avenge me, he would have killed Father then and there. His beloved father, for my sake. My brother. . . . With my tears soaking his tunic, I clung to him, crying in his arms, unable to stop until I could cry no more. When I had mostly quieted, he boosted me back onto the bed and knelt to pull the boots off my feet—I protested feebly, but indeed I felt so spent, I might not have been able to do it without his help. "You did it for me once upon a time," he remarked, "and made me rest, and gave me your bearskin for covering." It was too hot for the bearskin, but he helped me slip a nightshirt over my head and made me lie down. Bringing a moist cloth from the washstand, he bathed my face, paying special attention to the bruise on the side of my head. He stroked the damp hair away from my eyes, then sat with me until I slept.

CHAPTER THE
TWENTY-FIFTH

WHEN I AWOKE, my father sat there. A candle burned, and some quality of silence and darkness told me it was very late. By my other side, on the bed, Albaric slept in his clothes. At the bedside sat Father in his nightgown, not at all majestic, with his hair and his beard in a crow's nest.

"I couldn't sleep," he said, his voice very low.

In a whisper, so as not to awaken Albaric, I said, "I'm hungry," for it was so gut-true I could think of nothing else, having missed dinner. I sat up and reached for the candle, already halfway to the kitchen in my mind, before I paused to look at my father's face.

It is hard to describe his expression. Baffled, I suppose, and desperately haunted, yet almost laughing. I asked, "Sire, are you all right?"

"The world could be ending, and you would be hungry, Aric, my son. Why ever should I not be all right?"

I did not venture a response to this. We spoke no more until we reached the kitchen and I had devoured much bread and cheese. Father would have brought me ale, but I drank milk. He himself did not eat, only sat across from me and watched me.

"Would you not like one?" I asked as I finished off a dewberry tart. "They are very good."

He shook his head. "I cannot eat."

I turned on the bench to lean against the table, replete, studying him. Even now, I felt sure, even in pain of spirit, he was too proud to welcome sympathy or advice or declarations of my devotion or even the touch of my hand. "Father," I asked as simply as possible, "how can I help?"

"I scarcely know. It would appear you have already forgiven me?"

"Willingly."

"You are a wonder, my Aric. Yet your goodness makes me feel only more that I am evil. I think crazed thoughts, fly into rages, act like a madman, I do not know myself anymore. I am afraid to wear a sword. I feel unfit to call myself your father, much less King of all Calidon."

"Yet you have been the best of kings."

"So you tell me! So also does your mother!"

"How is Mother?"

"Sleeping, I hope. She says I let go of the sword before it touched you. She said that, even before seeing this, she knew I would not greatly harm you, or she would have interfered."

"I knew the same, standing there."

"Standing up to me. I thought it the worst of insolence. Now I marvel at your courage."

I shook my head. "I wished only for you to see."

"See what?"

I spoke softly. "The troth between us, Father."

After a glimpse of his moistening eyes, I studied my own hands, sparing his pride.

He did not speak. After a long silence, I added, "It is my father I crave, not his throne."

He cleared his throat and said, "Despite my regrettable upbringing, I will try to keep that in mind."

"Please."

"But that is not the only rub. There is this matter of Albaric, on which we disagree."

"Yes. Father, in regard to Albaric, I would ask you to think on this question: why did the ring try to kill you?"

"The ring! I had nearly forgotten that foul thing! What has become of it?"

I pretended not to hear the question, saying earnestly, "What if I were to tell you the ring is not a foul thing, Father, but can be fair? Again, I ask, why did it wish you harm?"

"I dare say I am the foul thing and deserve to die."

"You are all contraries, my Sire. You know that is not so. Please do me this favor, and think. Why was the ring sickening you?"

He sighed, folded his hands, and set himself to the task. His eyes looked for memories. After a while, he said, "I detested that thing, hated it at first sight, especially as I could not remove it from my hand. I wanted to be rid of it."

"You hated it? Why?"

"Because it hated me, uncanny thing! And I did not know where it had come from."

"Father. Could it be perhaps that, while you did not remember, somehow you sensed it had followed you from a place where you had been held captive? A place you therefore hated?"

Like a weary child, he shook his head, uncomprehending. Clearly, he had reached his limits for the time being. I wanted to continue, reasoning with him that Albaric, like the ring, had come from the place he had hated, and for no other reason he hated Albaric—but compassion made me say, "Think no more of anything tonight. Could you sleep now, Father? Or eat?"

"I believe I will sleep. Thank you, my son."

As we made our way back to our bedchambers, he asked, "How badly did I cut your neck? Tell me the truth."

"How can I tell you anything? I cannot see my own neck."

He sighed and rolled his eyes, just as I wished, for I was tweaking his beard. "Bloody blazes, Aric, is it deep? Is it swollen? Does it fester?"

I raised my hand to feel the bandaged wound, with muted surprise finding it very hot, or else my hand was cold. The touch hurt. "It's sore, Father; what can one expect? Will you let it go and *sleep?*"

"Yes, I will sleep. But Aric—tomorrow may be not much easier than today was."

"Perhaps, then, you could remember to drop your sword on the floor directly after you draw it, rather than a moment later?"

He laughed—only a chuckle and a shake of the head, but he did laugh.

Father was right. The next day was bad, although not in the way he had meant. It was perhaps worse, because chills and fever awoke me around dawn. My skin all goose bumps, I sat up to get the bearskin—for at the moment, I felt as if I were freezing—but my head spun so that I almost fell over. I had to clutch the bed with both hands. Blast and confound it all, what was the matter with me? I never got sick.

Therefore, this was a moment's weakness and would pass. Not wanting to awaken anyone, I sat waiting for it to do so—but the next moment, a spasm of dizziness and shaking toppled me back onto the bed, willy-nilly, and my head bumped something.

Someone. Albaric awoke and knew instantly that all was not well, I think, for I heard no drowsiness in his voice. "Aric?"

"Blasted bloody blazing hell." The words might have been strong, but my voice sounded weak.

"Aric!" My brother jumped up, ran to light a candle at the hearth, brought it to my side of the bed, and looked at me. "Aric, what is wrong?"

"I'm sick, confound it."

"The wound! Is it from the wound?" He knelt to look at my neck and reached to undo the dressing, but I stopped him with my hand. "Don't. It hurts," I said, peevish.

"But—but what am I to do? I know nothing of mortal ailments."

"Here." I reached under my nightshirt, pulled off the leather thong holding the ring—it was white, still white—and crammed thong and ring into his hands. "Hide this. Then get Mother."

Running even as he slipped the thong over his own head and hid the ring under his tunic, he darted out of the chamber. Only after the door closed behind him did I think what I had just done by telling him to fetch Queen Evalin, a task that should have fallen to the bleary-eyed manservants who had started sitting up on their pallets. With terror, I knew that I might as well have sent my brother into a dragon's den as to the King's Tower. Father would be sleeping with Mother, most likely, and if Albaric set foot in their bedchamber, I wouldn't have put it beyond the king to take a sword to him then and there.

Breaking into a sweat of terror and fever, I thrashed in the bed, crying out in dismay, and the manservants sprang up and stood over me, gawking as they saw the state I was in, asking each other what they should do. They had not yet settled which one should stay and which one should go for help when the door opened and a tall, robed figure hurried in.

It was Mother. "Albaric!" I cried at her.

"Right here," he said, appearing out of a kind of mist in my eyes, bending over me. With both hands, I clutched at his shoulders.

"Don't leave my side again!" I babbled. "Promise you won't leave me again! Father might kill you!"

Mother said "Aric, hush," and made the admonition sound as tender as a kiss. "There's no harm done. Your father is sound asleep at last." She took my hands in hers, loosened their grip on my brother, and made them lie still, then knelt beside me, bidding one of the servants to hold the candle while she unwrapped my small wound, the insignificant cut Father had given me yesterday. Even before she spoke, I knew from the pain what she would find.

"It's very fiery and swollen." She turned to the other servant. "Go rouse the kitchen. Bring water, and have them send up more, both hot and cold."

"Why not just throw me into a horse trough?" Calmer now, I tried to jest.

"Because you're too big for me to carry, Son." She stroked my hot forehead with a cool hand. "Now I want a promise from you. Do not give way to this contagion. Do not let death take you away from us."

"What? You think I might die from this little thing?"

"It will get worse before it gets better. Promise me all your strength, my Son."

Oddly, I found that I could not speak the promise. Instead, I nodded.

CHAPTER THE
TWENTY-SIXTH

SOMETIME MUCH LATER IN THE DAY, my father's face loomed over me, the skin behind his beard a chalky mask to hide emotion, and my mother's voice was saying, "You slept well, dear? And you ate?"

"Yes, confound it, was that what you wanted? Why did you not tell me about this immediately?"

"Merry-go-sorry," I explained to him earnestly from my pillow, already drunk with fever; I thought I made perfect sense.

"Because you needed rest, Darling," Mother said. "And what good can you do here?"

"The way is long and the crossing strange," I pleaded with him, for I felt Albaric's silent presence somewhere behind me, I saw how Father avoided looking at him, and I felt that I must reconcile them.

"I'm upsetting him," Father admitted, his voice stark and low. "I'll go." He blundered out.

My memories of that time are like shards of a shattered platter in my mind, its pattern all in pieces.

Hot compress on my neck. Draperies soaked in cold water on the rest of me. Mother's hand on my forehead.

Soft harp music that soothed me. Albaric, of course. Yet at the same time, I thought the horses, Bluefire's kin, had come down from the sky. They had wings. Flying, they danced, and dancing, they flew.

Albaric's voice: "Queen Evalin, I beg you, let me sit by him a while. Lie down on the other side of the bed and rest. You shall know at once if anything changes."

Things to drink. Broth. Milk. Wine. My father asking, "Have you tried ale?" I had to be held up to sip at a cup, and I could not swallow anything solid.

The chirurgeon, a bent old man, arriving to lance the wound. Pain, but all the poison did not come out, he said. He placed his leeches, their triangular raspy mouths to my skin and their dark dank eely bodies hanging down, all around the cut on my neck, so that they might suck the swelling away.

Albaric asleep beside me. Perhaps I appeared to sleep, but I languished amid fever dreams. Vividly and vehemently on a blue stallion through my mind rode the White King, his long, thick hair pure white, but his face youthful and surpassing even Albaric's in beauty. His crown, all formed of crystal, shone with white light, and he wore no sword, no armor under his white cloak, for they were not necessary. Just by his being the White King, all was peace, his kingdom a paradise.

But then I heard my father saying bleakly, "He's getting worse. Even I can see the contagion spreading in red streaks up and down his neck."

Promise me all your strength, my Son. I knew that I could not die. Must not die.

Pain. Some sort of ghastly plaster placed on my wounded neck. Then more leeches.

195

Father's voice, grim. "Albaric, I would like some time alone with my wife and my son."

"I swore not to leave his side, my King."

"Aric made him swear," Mother's voice put in gently.

"Why, in all the names of misery?"

"Because he feared you would do away with me, my King."

A silence, and then Father said without ire, "You are as frank as he was. *Is.* Do you really think you will die if you leave this room?"

"No."

"Then will you please do so?"

"No. My King, I once offered to swear fealty to you, but you refused me; do you remember?"

"Yes, I remember."

"You are fair, always. You must recognize that my fealty now is to Aric and the promise I made him, no matter how my heart—"

"Bah. Keep your heart to yourself." The bear with burrs was coming back; I could hear it in his voice.

"My King," Albaric said, "Aric will *not* die. For if he does, I will go with him, and he knows it."

The only answer was the shutting of the door. Father had gone out. Why did he wear black? I was not dead. I had seen black garb on him, although my eyes, like my mind, could see only shattered, jumbled pieces. I closed my eyes, hoping that I could see again the White King.

"Albaric," I whispered.

"Right here." He spoke from directly beside me. Mother must have gone out with Father.

"Albaric," I said again, reaching toward him, and somehow he understood at once what I needed, giving it to me: not the soft touch of a nurse, but a strong clasping of hands into fists, a warrior's grip.

As long as he was there, I could keep fighting.

Finally the fever came down, the wound stopped being swollen or painful, I slept long and peacefully, then opened my eyes to see, clearly now, a smile on my mother's weary face, and I should have felt that I had won.

But I felt no such thing. Now, what I could see most clearly were the wide black wings of death hovering just over the bed canopy.

Father came in. I saw the invisible drawing of swords between him and Albaric; I felt the tension in the close air of the bedchamber. Dark, it was too dark in there because of the shadow of death. Father wore black. He looked at me, his face still a mask, even though he showed his teeth in a smile of sorts. "Well," he said, "I am glad to see those ugly leeches taken away."

Courteously, I agreed. I felt no anger at him or love for him. I felt only hollow, like a seashell washed up on the some far cold strand. After a moment, I closed my eyes.

"Some barley soup, Aric?" my mother coaxed. "Some white wheat bread?"

I shook my head. Servants brought the food anyway, but I could not eat, or would not. What was the use of getting well? Once I regained my strength and got up out of the bed, it would be Father and Albaric again, Albaric and Father, and heartache and constant fear.

I did not want to die, but neither did I want to live. I

hung like a leper in a cage between earth and sky. Albaric played the harp and sang for me to no avail. I do not know how long this went on, for I had lost any sense of time, but it must have been too long, for my father and mother ceased smiling, and without much feeling, I sensed their fear that I might yet be taken from them, even though they, of course, could not see the black wings still waiting.

"Can you see it, Albaric?" I asked when he was alone in the room with me.

"See what?"

"Death overhead."

"The black wings? They have been here the whole time."

"Can Mother see them?"

"I think not. You call them Death. I dare say you are right. Yet why have you not made them fly away?"

I gazed at him, uncomprehending.

"Yours is the choice," he said. "The fever has left you. The wound is calm. Why do you lie shadowed by death?"

"I don't know," I whispered.

Albaric confronted me, his fair, scarred face inches from mine. "Aric, what is wrong with you?"

I shook my head.

"Tell me. What is the matter?"

"I truly don't know," I muttered. Sooth, as my thoughts were far from clear. My heart, usually my best guide, seemed to have left me without so much as a good-bye. I felt like an empty room, a chamber where no air moved.

Albaric put his mouth close to my ear so that no one could possibly hear and told me, "The ring—it fought the fever with you, all golden like a small shining crown, but now it has turned a muddy, bilious yellow."

Not understanding what he was saying, I lay blank and silent.

"The color of cowardice," he told me between his teeth.

Oh. It was a distant concept of no significance. "I don't care."

He pulled back to glare at me. "By my troth, I don't believe you do!"

I looked up at him, mildly interested, for I had not seen him like this before, or never at me. "You are angry, my brother."

"Yes, I am angry, when you are the one who should be!"

"I should be angry?"

"At the one who did this to you. How not?"

How not, indeed? But I had forgiven Father. Now Albaric wanted me to hate him. And Father wanted me to hate Albaric. This was like a black dragon that wanted to nest in my chest, and this could go on forever. This was the reason I lay abed without rising.

"I need some fresh air, Aric." Albaric's low voice carried scorn barely constrained. "As you no longer care, might I be released from my promise? Might I go outside?"

"Of course."

He shut the door behind him softly enough. I did not watch him leave. Already, I had closed my eyes.

"Prince Aric!"

Her brash young voice made me open my eyes wide, just in time for me to see her running, as was her wont, with no ladylike airs or dignity, across the bedchamber to me. Her brown braids loosened from her head and flew. Her great-eyed face bloomed like a flower, a creamy heart-shaped blossom, above her green kirtle. Behind her in the doorway stood my parents, smiling. Father's smile looked real.

"Marissa!" I cried in utmost surprise, for I had forgotten about her, yet knew her at once, to my bones.

"Aric," she scolded, bouncing to a perch on the bed beside me, "I've come all the way from Domberk to see you, and—"

"I thought it was to free your father," I interrupted, teasing.

"Oh. Him." She tossed her head. "He's already gone, without so much as a how-are-you-daughter. I care no more for him than he does for me. But I rode all the long and dusty way here—"

"You rode? No horse-litter?"

"And no sidesaddle either. I rode *astride*. Everyone was scandalized. I brought my own palfrey because I wanted for you and me to go riding together, I on Cherub and you on Bluefire—but you're sick! How dare you?"

She said this without flirtation, but with the honest frustration of an outspoken girl, and beyond her, I saw my father's smile widen. He liked her. That must have been a great surprise to him, to like a Domberk.

"It was not my idea, I assure you."

"Just look at you!"

I quipped, "Do I look like a prince now?"

She all but shouted at me, "You look like something made out of goat's-milk curds and thistledown! You're so thin! What is the matter with you?"

I gazed up at her, speechless with the joy of seeing her.

"Oh, botheration," she complained, and bending over me, with her hands embracing my face, she kissed me full on the lips.

It was not the kiss of a girl.

Nor was it yet the kiss of a woman, but something in between, like nothing I had ever felt before, and it startled my heart so profoundly that I could only gasp and stare.

My heart. It seemed to have returned and taken up residence in my chest where it belonged. Far from feeling hollow and empty, I had barely space to catch my breath.

Marissa turned pink, and no wonder, for I was gawking at her as if I had never seen a girl before. "I must go unpack my things," she said with decision, and away she went in a whirl of brown braids and rumpled green frock.

Mother hurried away with her, to help her with the task, I suppose. Father remained. He still wore black, but my bedchamber seemed brighter than it had been before.

Of course. A shadow was gone. The great black wings overhead had flown away.

Just inside the door, trying to control his countenance, Father said nothing.

I asked him, "Sire, could you send to the kitchen for something good to eat? I'm hungry."

He stared. It seemed to me that he was trying very hard not to say anything he might regret, or to let peculiar emotions show on his face.

Then, turning to stride out of the door, he bellowed at the top of his lungs, as if it were a proclamation, "Prince Aric is hungry!"

The resultant hullabaloo vexed me, because truly I felt famished.

CHAPTER THE
TWENTY-SEVENTH

J UST AS WHEN MY FATHER had recovered from his illness, a plethora of exultant servants invaded my bedchamber, bringing all sorts of fresh-baked bread and pastries; platters of venison, mutton, and codfish; fresh pears; and, of course, ale. And they remained to watch me devour all I could, more exuberant with every avid mouthful. Father sent them away after a while and sat, regarding me peacefully until he was called away on business of court.

A good thing, for he would have expected me to rest, but I had no intention of remaining in bed for one moment longer, hungry now more for life than for food. Wobbling to my feet, amazed at how weak I was, I put on a long tunic so that I need not bother with breeches—in the summertime, most noblemen shed their breeches when they could, while the peasants went about in loincloths—and instead of boots, I wore ghillies, simple footgear of leather laced on. Feeling both better and worse as bread and meat took effect—stronger, but my stomach hurt—I walked out of my chamber and down the stairs, holding on to the wall for balance, careful not to embarrass myself by falling.

Also I was careful to avoid people, for had I been intercepted, I might never have made it to the stable. Bluefire's stall was empty—of course, I thought; Albaric was exercising him after long inactivity. Meanwhile, the stall had been mucked out and piled deep with clean straw. Slipping in, I made myself comfortable to hide and to wait, astonished at how exhausted the short excursion had made me. I actually lay down to rest. Not to sleep, of course. . . .

I was awakened by Bluefire's muzzle on my face, snuffling and nuzzling and licking me from my chin up to my hair. "Ai!" I exclaimed, turning my head, and saw Albaric crouching beside me, joy and laughter in his eyes. As if on its own, my hand stretched out to him, and he gave me once again the grip of a warrior, lifting me so that I sat up as Bluefire slobbered in my ear.

"He's as glad as a puppy to see you at last," said Albaric.

I put my hands atop the horse's muzzle to fend him off. To Albaric, I said, "My brother, I'm sorry I made you angry at me."

"No need to be sorry. Quite evidently that's over."

"My dormouse imitation? Indeed it is over, for the black wings have flown away."

"Praise be." He shuddered. "All mercy be praised that your mother and father are blind to such things."

"So it's over, but you're still annoyed. I can feel it in you."

"Confound it, Aric, I can hide nothing from you." Facing me, he looked rueful, ready to mock himself. "I heard about Lady Marissa," he admitted. "All the castle can speak of nothing else. I am perhaps a bit jealous that a stranger could do for you what I could not."

In no way could I have explained to him what my "dormouse imitation" had been or why he could not possibly have healed it. So I said lightly, "You can't help it that you're not a girl, Albaric."

He rolled his eyes. "Please don't tell me that now you are feeling, ah, rambunctious?"

"She's too young." And, although I did not say so, my feelings for Marissa were no jest. But I smiled and let my brother think what he wanted.

"You mortals," he marveled, all his vexation flown away, "is there only one dependable remedy for you?"

"I won't speak for all mortals." By hanging on to Bluefire's mane, I managed to stand on my feet, but assessing my strength, I said ruefully, "Oh brother, my brother, I think you are going to have to help me walk back inside."

"In a moment." He looked all around, checking for any spying eyes, then swiftly tugged the ring out of his tunic and slipped the thong over my head. "It's been stinging me with impatience to return to you."

The ring glowed a gentle white. "Was it truly yellow before?" I asked.

"Yes." He flushed. "But for me to say what I did—"

"Was quite right," I interrupted him. "Will you hush, now, and get me back to bed before Mother catches me wandering about?"

"And what will she do to you if she does catch you?" he teased.

"Hang me by the thumbs, very likely."

In a changed tone, he said, "Oh my heart, Aric, it's good to have you back," and he hugged me as he had never hugged me before, impulsively, then just as quickly turned away lest I see his face. "If you hang on to my arm, can you manage?"

I could and returned to my room with fair speed, finding

to my astonished relief that no one had missed me except a lazy manservant who had seized the opportunity for a nap on his pallet. Awakening him, I learned that Mother was still busy with Marissa, the two of them rummaging through Mother's hoard of clothing in search of things for Marissa's wardrobe.

I had many reasons to bless the coming of Marissa.

The next morning, after a great deal of eating and even more sleeping, I felt so much better that I sallied forth, barely wobbling, to join my family for breakfast at the table on the dais. Marissa, I was pleased to note, sat with them. No hostage, she; hers was the place of an honored guest.

"Prince Aric!" Marissa saw me first, jumped up, and ran to greet me with a hug around the waist—her head came barely to my shoulder—and, no jest, she nearly knocked me over. Yet, in her linen frock and her willful innocence, she was utterly a lady, a flower, a white rosebud nearly in bloom.

"Aric," Mother exclaimed, "you should be in bed!"

"Sit down," commanded my father at the same time.

I did so, ate oatmeal with milk and raspberries, and teased Marissa. "My lady, if I may ask, how old are you now?"

"Fourteen."

"Then you have had a birthday since we met last."

"I have, yes. Have you?"

The minx, meeting my dart with her own! "I am nearly of age," I said, smiling, "but you're full young to go a-courting. Have you no sisters, that your mother brought you to Dun Narven?"

"I have sisters aplenty, but all younger." She gave a little bounce—evidently any joy of hers required physical expression—and declared, "I am well pleased to be here. Someone else must mind them while I am away."

Mother asked, "Does your mother then stay at her loom all day, Marissa?" Already she was forgetting to title her "Lady."

"No, Mother does what she pleases. When she and Father are not quarreling, she drinks mead with him and Escobar."

Escobar! A shocked silence followed in which the name rang like the scream of a ghost.

It was not a common name.

"Escobar?" I asked Marissa, distracting her while I pretended not to see that Father and Mother sat like two statues of white stone.

Marissa shrugged with elaborate scorn. "A wolfish vagabond, my father's boon companion. He showed up out of nowhere last winter, and Father and Mother treat him like a prince. Or used to," she added. "I heard Father questioning the henchmen who brought me here. No, they told him, Escobar had not returned to Domberk."

"So he—this Escobar—so he did come here with your father to invade Dun Caltor?"

The shadow man who had burst out of Brock Domberk's room behind the throne, I was thinking. The one who had run away.

The one who, Albaric had said, resembled Father.

"I suppose so," Marissa answered me, "but I don't know for sure. When Mother and I returned home from Dun Narven, Father and Escobar and the men-at-arms were gone without a word for us. Mother," she added with satisfaction, "was annoyed."

"Lady Marissa." It is of great credit to the king that, having found his voice, he constrained it to be courteous. "This Escobar, what is he like? Describe him for me."

"He is thewed like a warrior and far taller than my father." Marissa faced my sire quite unafraid, despite the shadow and strain in the king's face. "Ageless and strong, like a stone, with grizzled helm-cut hair and his face beneath its beard all weathered and crisscrossed with scars, yet he stands like a lance and carries his head high, as if. . . ." Her lips parted but spoke not, and her brown eyes widened and gazed at King Bardaric and through him and far beyond, brown like forest pools with a kind of mist over them and secrets swimming in their leaf-shadowed waters.

Motionless, she remained gazing thus for moments, and as if there were a trance on Father and Mother and me also, none of us moved.

Marissa took breath, and her voice issued forth like an echo out of a Delphic cavern. "As if he were a prince. Sire, he is kin to you."

The king lunged up from his chair, shattering the spell, or trance, or timeless time; I know not what to call it. As if a strong wind had struck her, Marissa wavered in her chair, blinking up at him, only a girl again.

"What did you say?" Father demanded of her, looking grim as death.

But she tilted her head back to answer him eye to eye. "Escobar is kin to you."

"Who told you so?"

"No one." She drew a deep, quivering breath and turned her head away. "Sometimes I just know things."

A pause. Marissa was frightened now, I sensed, but not of the king.

He said quietly enough, "Then tell me, young seeress, where is Escobar now?"

Without looking up, she shook her head.

"Can you find out?"

Marissa's shoulders flinched. "Bard," interposed Mother quietly, "have mercy."

"Bah!" he said explosively, then strode off in a way that told me he meant to take care of the matter himself.

"What is happening?" Marissa whispered, looking from Mother to me. "What have I done?"

"You have done no harm and all good," I told her, greatly hoping this was not a lie and wishing I did not feel so weak and useless. Doubtless, Father was summoning his men-at-arms to ride out with him in search of Escobar, dangerous claimant to be King of Calidon, and I wished I could ride with them—even though it seemed to me most unlikely that they would find him. "He missed his chance at the throne, for whatever reason," I added, thinking aloud, "then fled, and all sense says he should be far from here by now."

"Greatly I hope so," said my mother.

"Queen Evalin, Prince Aric," Marissa addressed us almost in plea, "I have been kept ignorant. My father does not believe in knowledge for women. I have had no teachers, only tales told by firelight. How should I know *anything*?"

I leaned forward and placed my hand on hers. "Is it the first time this—this strange way of knowing things—the first time it has happened?"

"The first time it mattered!" Her voice plunged from a shout to a whisper. "This Escobar—is he truly King Bardaric's *brother*? Rival for the throne?"

I nodded.

"There could be *war*? Or—or even worse?"

"Not on your account."

Mother said, "Child, you spoke merest truth. You are but the messenger, and blameless. Take comfort." The queen arose, serene. "I know a place where always there is peace. Lady Marissa, would you care to come with me to the garden?"

Far too wrought to rest, I would not be left behind, although Mother insisted on wrapping me head to toe in a vast plaid blanket. She and I sat under a pavilion garlanded by climbing roses, and at first Marissa stayed with us, but soon the beauty of the place did its magic; Marissa forgot the shadow of Escobar, got up, and flitted hither and yon, exploring the flagstone paths laid down like a mosaic in many subtle colors of slate, exclaiming over the arbors, the foxgloves, the hollyhocks, the fragrances as she sniffed the myriad roses. Watching her, Mother smiled; no courtly compliments could have pleased her more that Marissa's transparent delight.

"Marissa," I asked her after she rejoined us, "Does Dun Domberk not have a garden like this?"

"No. We grow cabbages under our fruit trees."

I laughed. She minded not in the least. Seating herself beside me on the same bench, she asked with a bold fling of her head, "Aric, Father said this was your idea, to have me come here as a hostage for his release. Is that true?"

Trying not to laugh again, I retorted, "If he said it, then why would it not be true?"

"Because my father is a frequent and mendacious liar," she

replied in a matter-of-fact tone, and then in quite a different tone, "Oh!"

The "Oh!" was because she saw Albaric coming in through the garden gate, cradling his harp in one arm as if it were a baby.

Although he wore the plainest tunic and leggings in our collective wardrobe, and no sword, once again, Marissa whispered, "Oh!" As she had seen him truly while we were dancing at Dun Narven, so she saw him now. Darting up from her seat, she ran to meet him, stopping at a respectful distance to curtsy low.

"My Lady Marissa!" he protested. "I should bow to you."

"Fiddlesticks. Oh!" she cried as her head came up and she saw his scar. "Albaric, what has happened to your face? Someone hurt you!"

"It is nothing."

"It is terrible! Who could do such a thing to you?"

Rather than tell her it had been a Domberk, he answered only with a gentle look as he stepped forward to escort her toward Mother and me. "Queen Evalin." He bowed his head to her. "I thought I should find you here."

"And you brought your harp because all is tumult elsewhere?"

"Yes, with quantities of men sallying forth to search the uplands for Escobar, or scour the valleys, or question the villagers about him." Albaric shrugged, and I sensed what he was thinking but would not say: the king would not welcome him among the searchers.

I spoke for him. "You and Bluefire could have found him in short order if he's out there."

He nodded, and his glance lingered on me, assessing whether I felt stronger and would soon be well.

Again, I answered aloud. "I want nothing more than your music."

Marissa clapped her hands. "Yes, Albaric, will you please play for us?"

He perched on the pavilion railing, and Marissa settled herself beside me with a bounce. Albaric smiled at her, but then his gaze shifted far away. As if on its own, his hand drew a bell-like harmony from the strings of his harp. It sang along with him:

> In the west sea-eagles lament
> Salt their calls as the tears of men.
> On black legs as long as life
> The ghost-gray crane stalks in the fen.
>
> In the night the owl awaits,
> Profound and still. From its den
> The wolf sings skyward. Echoes answer.
> Dayspring answers in the east when
>
> From the world tree wings the sun
> High sky chariot soaring bright
> And from the sea arises One
> The One True King in a crown of light
> When wind and water, day and night
> Owl and eagle, moon and sun
> Out of the deep shall bring the One
> White mystery shall ring the One.

Even after he had finished, the song seemed to echo in the air, to remain, mysterious, like a legend.

"Oh," sighed Marissa. "What does it mean?"

"I do not know. It was in a book Aric gave me."

She said, "I have heard that the hands of the One True King have the power of healing."

"It might well be about Arthur," Mother said, "the great southern king of whom it is said he will rise again."

"Or it might be about the White King," Marissa added.

"The White King!" I blurted in such a heightened tone that everyone stared at me. But I did not care to say that I had seen him in my fever dreams, riding a great blue horse with a white tail and mane and a wise white face, and that I remembered him with longing. Awkwardly, I explained, "Lord Kiffin mentioned him to me, but I do not understand who he is."

Eagerly, Marissa leaned toward me. "My grandmother told me he was the One True King in the Great Time before time, when it was always summer and Calidon was a green and fertile place of peace, a place where no dragon-ships raided and no one needed to wear a sword. But once upon a time ended, and mortal time began when the White King's best friend, the companion he most trusted, betrayed him and killed him to take the throne. The traitor's name was Winter, and since his foul deed, the land has fallen prey to storm and cold, and all the Kings of Calidon have been Winter Kings, usurpers—oh!" Her hand flew to cover her mouth. "Please forgive me."

Mother smiled, albeit a bit sadly. "Never fear when you speak truth, Marissa. Yes, my husband is a usurper."

"But everyone says King Bardaric is the best ruler of Calidon in ages and ages!"

Mother's smile widened. "This, also, is true." Then she had mercy on Marissa by asking, "Is there more to your tale?"

"Only that the White King will come again someday, to make Calidon a paradise, a place of utter peace where no one need go hungry, no outlaws roam, and no raiders from the Craglands ever dare venture. Like King Arthur, he has not died; he is made of legend."

Made of legend. Did she remember the song? Much moved by that and the tale of the White King, I blurted, "You tell a marvelous story, Marissa."

She blushed, then shrugged, then said in a quelled voice, "My father says 'White King' is only a mistake for 'Viking,' making a fairy tale of how our ancestors in longboats came to Calidon."

"Your father is a frequent and mendacious liar," I responded, "or so I have been told."

That made her laugh, and then Albaric charmed us with harp and song some more, and so we passed the morning pleasantly. But when we left the garden and returned to the castle keep, the serving-folk seemed too silent and the shadows too stony, too still, waiting for word of Escobar.

I returned to my bed, exhausted by my slight exertions, and got up again only at nightfall when I heard many riders clopping into the courtyard. One look at my Sire's scowl as he strode into the great hall told me there was no good news. His mood was plain to see, as black as his tunic and tabard. I would not have troubled him with my presence, but he caught sight of me and gestured imperiously: come here. I followed him into the small room behind the throne, where he stood glaring at the humble bed once more piled with oddments.

"Tell me," he demanded without looking at me.

I obeyed as best I could. "Domberk slept there, and it would seem one other, for when Albaric and I broke in, another man burst out and ran. I saw just a dark shape with a hood, but for a moment I thought it was you." A white lie; he would have discounted anything Albaric had thought. "That was impossible, of course, and with our attention all on Domberk, we let the hooded man go." I dared a question. "Father, did you and your brothers resemble one another?"

"We were as alike in appearance as we differed in all other ways." He said it slowly, as if he had to force the words out through clenched teeth, but at last he turned to face me. "That was Domberk's game, then, that so emboldened him. He hid up his sleeve a fair title to the throne: his pet wolf, Escobar. The pompous fool, he thought Escobar would take the throne and let him live?"

I attempted no answer, my focus mostly on remaining upright, for I was not yet strong.

Wrestling in thought, Father did not notice. "But if Escobar was here," he demanded, "why did he not kill me and claim the throne? What prevented him?"

"The ring?" I hazarded.

"Bah!" This summed up his opinion of the ring.

"Yet it would seem there has been a falling out between Lord Brock and his pet wolf, Sire, for Escobar has not returned to Domberk."

His face all in furrows from the strain of the day, he glared at me, daring me to speak on.

So, to prove myself his son, I did. "One of them wanted you dead in the dungeon, and the other disagreed."

"Bah! Horsefeathers. In no way can you know this." The

king turned his back on me, dismissing me with a gesture, and I was glad enough to go.

CHAPTER THE
TWENTY-EIGHTH

THE NEXT DAY, and the next after that, men-at-arms and guardsmen and royal retainers rode forth in quest for Escobar or any news of him, but they found nothing. But within a few more days, the matter of Escobar hung in abeyance, for more pressing concerns demanded the king's attention: it had not rained since before Garth came home, and such drought was frightening, unheard of in Calidon, where one could count on foul weather if nothing else. For the first time in my life, crops were failing, and if supplies of some sort were not laid by, there would be starvation this winter. But the fishing was poor and even the woodlands stingy of nuts; there was no mast for swine to fatten on. Indeed, I felt an inkling that the very soil and soul of Calidon must have gone wrong somehow. But Father made it abundantly clear that his problems were no concern of mine. I was to devote myself to getting well.

Thus it followed that, in the days that followed, I spent most of my time with Marissa. And as Albaric had no particular duties except to take care of Bluefire, he also spent much time with me, finding ways to help me regain my strength. Quoits, for instance. A game I had not bothered with since I was a boy, but now we all played, sometimes even Mother joining us as we tried to toss the leathern rings onto the pegs. With pleasure, I saw how the queen came down from her tower more than ever before and smiled often on the girl who slept on a cot at the foot of her bed. When quoits paled, the four of us tried archery, and Mother showed herself to be master of bow and arrow, to my surprise. But I should not have been surprised. My stupidity again; I kept forgetting my parents had not always been my parents. Mother had been the daughter of the chieftain of an old-fashioned clan; evidently, her education had included some of the warrior arts. Her father had forced her to wed King Ardath supposedly for the sake of alliance, but Ardath had taken opportunity to slaughter her entire family at the nuptial feast.

I kept these thoughts to myself so as not to mar her pleasure in the archery. "This way, Marissa." Mother guided the girl in drawing the light bow I had found for her, one I had used as a boy, and both exulted when Marissa finally hit the popinjay.

Other times, we would gather flowers—not in the walled garden, but up in the meadows, venturing a little farther each day to strengthen me. One day, as I walked beside my mother, Marissa ran far ahead of us to investigate a distant patch of pink. We both gazed at the darting butterfly figure she made in the meadow, her braids flying out from under the brimmed bonnet she wore to protect her from the sun, her yellow dress fluttering like wings. "With her braids and that absurd headgear, she looks like a little girl," I remarked, "but be not deceived. She's no child."

"Your father and I knew that from the moment she marched herself into the keep—"

"All by herself?"

"Yes. The Domberk men-at-arms waited outside. Marissa came in and faced your father and me with neither fear nor enmity, reciting the words that gave herself in exchange for her father's freedom. But when we had the guards bring Domberk up from the dungeon, he barely acknowledged his child. He was interested only in trading insults with your father, and in so doing, he insulted his daughter, saying the treaty would be broken if she did not remain a virgin until wedlock."

"That dirty-minded troll!"

"Yes. Small wonder she wanted only to know where Prince Aric was."

"Really!" I was surprised; I had assumed she would ask first for Albaric.

"Yes, and it is a good thing she insisted on seeing you when she did; am I right?"

"Very much so. She saved my life."

"But, my Son, how? I still do not understand what was wrong with you."

It took me a moment to gather the words, but by now I was able to explain it, and I could speak of it because Albaric was not with us; he had stayed behind to exercise Bluefire. I told Mother softly, "I had lost heart. Father stared deadly arrows at Albaric, and Albaric defied Father for my sake, and I felt certain that the moment I arose from my sickbed, it would all start again, worse than ever."

Mother sighed and put her hand upon my arm as Marissa came running back toward us, her hands full of pink curlytop and her eyes full of her special gift, a brave joy.

Mother murmured, "Aric, you know, your father still stares arrows at Albaric."

"I know. But I think even Father is diverted somewhat by our bright-eyed guest. And Albaric feels her regard; it cheers him."

"You do not mind that she all but worships Albaric?"

"I all but worship Albaric myself. How could I mind?"

"But you seem to—"

"Love her? Yes."

Then my words hung in the air like the echo of a song, for we could converse no more as Marissa arrived with her usual bounce, giving the flowers to Mother, who accepted them as if they were made of gold. But I made no attempt, then or anywhere, to hide my love for Marissa—a quiet love, like a white coracle afloat on a still blue lake, waiting. I made no attempt, either, to steal any more kisses from her. I felt she had given that single one at some cost to herself, that her feelings for me ran unspoken but strong, much as mine did for her, and that this time, a period of blue and golden days like beads on a string, was our gift to each other.

Always, Marissa spoke with equal courteous candor to me, to Mother, to Father, and to Albaric; she gave attention and smiles to us all; but when her gaze caught on Albaric, her heart-shaped face transformed, foreshadowing the passionately lovely woman she would become.

We saw little of Father. As I grew stronger, I reported to him again, most days. Usually, he waved me away "to play," but sometimes I stayed with him for a few hours and saw how strangely his kingdom was failing, felled by no visible enemy. The land of Calidon itself seemed stricken. Hunting parties sent out for meat returned empty-handed. Unless something changed soon, this winter there would be naught but carrots to feed peasants, cattle, and castle. Father spoke little, smiled less, and he wore black, black, black. Yet as far as I could see, his temperament remained steady, like a heavy barge on a river that flowed slow but deep. I sensed that beneath his calm surface lurked trouble even worse than drought and the specter of Escobar combined, but I did not know his thoughts.

Only once, he said to me, "You do not mind that Marissa is ensorcelled by Albaric?"

"She's smitten with him, Father, as any girl with eyes would be. I assure you no sorcery is involved."

"So you do not mind that she follows him about like a bleating lamb?"

Unfair, for Marissa never bleated, nor did she accompany Albaric, unless he was with me. But I did not argue the point. "I have no claim on her heart, Father." Merest truth, no matter how I loved her.

"Well, I mind," said Father grimly, "for your sake." And although he did not say it, I knew he was thinking once again that he would like to rid Dun Caltor of Albaric. "Aric, sometimes I wonder," he burst out, "have you no pride? No mettle?"

That stung. But I took care not to show it. "No jealousy?" I parried. "No dark suspicions of treachery?"

"Bah! Remember Calidon's precious White King, how his best friend turned against him."

It startled me that Father knew the tale and guessed how greatly it moved me. "He was a legend, Father."

"But I am not."

Obliquely he referred to his father, his brothers, his mettle that had won him the throne, and I dared not speak. He had killed a kinsman, and this one thing I had never been able to understand about him, the chasm between us that I had never been able to cross, once more gapped between us, parting us so far that we could not talk.

Fervidly I wished he would wear any color other than black.

That night, in my chamber, with the bed canopy closed around us and the manservants dozing on their pallets, I whispered to Albaric, "My brother, I fear our Sire aspires to go down in legend as the Black King."

This was my poor attempt at a jest, for I hated to tell Albaric old news, harsh and hopeless, when I knew how his life had brightened since Marissa's arrival.

Albaric stiffened. "What do you mean?"

I sighed. "I sense he may yet do something dire and desperate."

"Why do you say so?"

I spoke very softly. "Because he made it plain to me today that he thinks Marissa favors you, and he resents it for my sake, he says, even though I have no claim on her. And as I refuse to cross swords with you, he may take it upon himself—"

Albaric groaned and turned his face to the bolster. "Bloody hell," he muttered.

I kept silence.

"I can no longer hope that things will ever change between me and the king," Albaric whispered after a while. "But perhaps if you could tell Lady Marissa to cease her attentions—"

"But you deserve every moment of adoration Marissa gives you."

"No, I do not, my brother, for I cannot return it!"

"Shhh. Keep your voice down."

He did so, murmuring, "Even if she wanted me—that way, which she does not—nothing could come of it. Mortal lovemaking is beyond me."

"No getting rambunctious for you?"

"No such inclination."

This did not surprise me, knowing him as I did; his were the passions of spirit, not of body. He wore flesh lightly, like a mask.

He said, "I can never give her the love she deserves. Moreover, she is meant for you!"

"According to whom?"

"Fate! I feel it!" He lowered his voice. "Ask the ring."

"It would make more sense to ask Marissa."

"She isn't ready! Right now, she cherishes both of us, don't you see? As innocently as if we were a brace of gazehounds, she makes pets of us, and if it were not for the king's jealousy, it would not matter, would it, Aric?"

I touched his hand. "No. It does not matter."

"But it does matter, for she is yours. Ask the ring."

"The ring," I retorted in a whisper, "does not speak Erse." Nevertheless, I drew the thing out. We both studied its circle of wispy light, pure lamb white pulsing like a heart. Once more, it seemed to swirl, toward Albaric, then me, then Albaric, then back again.

Deciding what I must do, I slipped it off its leash and onto the finger nearest my heart.

"My brother!" whispered Albaric, aghast. "Take it off!"

"Not until morning. It is trying to tell us something," I explained, "but we cannot understand. Perhaps it can better tell me in my dreams."

"But what if it—seduces you? Takes you in thrall?"

"No Queen of Elfland has commanded it to do so." Only my eyes admitted that I shared his unease. "Yet, in case I'm wrong—you still have your mother's hair, do you not?"

"Yes, but. . . ." I felt his horror and answered the question he could not ask.

"Should it get the better of me, wrest it off, if you love me. At the point of the sword, if you must. But my will is to remove it myself."

"You swear that you mean to remove it in the morning?"

"I swear by all the troth between us, my brother."

CHAPTER THE
TWENTY-NINTH

WHAT I LEARNED, if it had been told to me in plain Erse by anyone, even Mother, even Albaric, would have frightened me senseless—yet it made utter sense as revealed in the images, the symbol-language of dreams. It exhausted me in mind, heart, and soul, but afterward I slept deeply and in peace.

I awoke late to find Albaric dressed but anxiously watching over me. Without comment, I got up, slipped the ring from my finger, and tethered it once more on the leather thong around my neck.

"Are you all right?" Albaric asked, despite the plain evidence of his eyes that I was. "You trembled in your sleep and panted like—like a woman in childbirth."

"Albaric, you've never even *seen* a woman in childbirth."

"But what was happening? What did you see?"

I shook my head, gave him a wry smile, and reached for clothing. "I'm hungry."

The way he rolled his eyes reminded me of Father. "All's well, then, if you're hungry."

So I ate, and for the next few days, I never missed a meal,

playing at the stick and ball with Marissa, sparring with Albaric to regain my strength as a swordsman, gathering hedge myrtle for Mother, all the time letting my mind encompass what the ring had shown me, eddying in the circles of it, until the right day dawned.

The fairest of days. A sea breeze had swept the sky so clean that in the east at dayspring, the very earliest dawn, it gleamed pellucid white. "Albaric." I woke him. "We are riding out to the meadows, you and I and Marissa, quickly, before anyone can say us nay. Get dressed; I will go to send a maidservant for her while I pack us something to eat."

"What! You will wait before eating your breakfast?"

But already I was out of the chamber door, hurrying about my self-appointed tasks.

Before either Father or Mother was up, I was ordering the gatekeepers to let us out, I on Valor with a cloth-wrapped pack fastened behind the saddle, Albaric on Bluefire without saddle or any other harness, and Marissa on her gentle white Cherub with her brown hair flowing, rippling and shining like a brown river, down her back. It was the first time I had seen her without braids—there had been no time to plait them, I suppose—and she quite nearly took my breath away, for I saw not a girl but a damsel, a maiden, a royal beauty riding a steed like a throne, for a fringe of Domberk green decked Cherub's reins, and across the front of his saddle hung a drapery of Domberk tartan that swept down, nearly dragging on the ground, to cover Marissa's stirrups and feet.

"A modesty defender?" I teased her, and her answering smile rivaled the sunrise; it lighted my world for me.

"This thing?" She tugged at her pony's drapery and rolled her eyes. "It is a dustcatcher."

Indeed, due to the drought, we kicked up dust aplenty on the road through the village between the fields and hedges, even though Albaric and I restrained our big horses to keep pace with Marissa's little ambling palfrey. But once we reached pastureland, Albaric called, "Free!" and let Bluefire gallop in a wide circle. Marissa cried, "Oh! I have *never* been allowed to gallop!"

"It's a marvel they've let you ride."

"My mother and father? They let me ride for a joke because I begged. They said go ahead and break my neck, for with so many girls, what would one the less matter? Still, they wouldn't let me ride like *that*." She gazed at Albaric skimming the hilltops on Bluefire.

A palfrey, a woman's horse, had different gaits than a man's; it ambled but did not trot. "Do you think Cherub knows how to gallop?"

"I am about to find out." She leaned forward, applying her heels to the pony's flanks. "Cherub! Run!"

Tucking his chin and arching his neck, he lifted at once into a lovely, lilting canter.

"Watch for rocks and holes!" I called, trotting alongside.

"I am not a dolt and this is not a gallop. Cherub!"

The white palfrey reached with his head and lengthened his stride to shoot forward. Marissa's hat blew off and her loose hair flew like a pennant, an oriflamme, a falcon's backswept wings. Letting her go, I stopped to retrieve the hat, a bonny brimmed thing the hue of a shy violet. Amazing, how my heart swelled just because I held her wee soft hat in one hand.

I rode Valor straight up the pastureland and beyond, to explore the meadows where some brave wildflowers yet bloomed. Marissa slowed Cherub to walk beside me, patting and praising him. Albaric slowed Bluefire for a moment to join us. "Where are we going?"

"Right there, I think." I pointed toward a massive, spreading oak offering much shade and soft mossy seats between its wide roots.

Once beneath its overhanging boughs, I set the pack on the dry ground, stripped Valor of his trappings, and let him go graze on what was left of the yellowing grass. "If we give Cherub freedom of the meadow," I asked Marissa, "do you think he will stray too far?"

"My angel steed! Never," she said indignantly, only to add, "but if he does, Bluefire can find him."

We all laughed, pulling the draperies and saddle off Cherub and turning him loose. Then we gathered under the oak. I untied the cloth bundle I had brought, spreading it out to reveal much what one might expect of me: cheese, apples, oat scones, hard-boiled eggs, milk in a flask. With good appetite, we began to eat, but after a single scone and a hunk of cheese, I stopped. Comfortable on a seat of moss, with his back against the great oak, Albaric studied me.

"What are we here for really, Aric?" he asked.

I took a deep breath. "You know a few nights ago, I requested counsel of the ring."

"The ring?" Marissa's gaze forsook Albaric for me.

"This ring." I pulled it out from under my tunic, a glowing white circle that made Marissa gasp—but she did not pull away.

Indeed, she leaned toward it. "Whence came that?" she whispered. "It is fey!" Without waiting for an answer, she cried, "That should be Albaric's, not yours, Aric!"

It was as I had hoped and trusted; she was undismayed

by strangeness. With a quizzical tilt of my head, I asked her, "Albaric's ring? Why?"

"Because his name starts with Alba, which means white, and it is white, and fey like him!"

Albaric sucked breath as if he had been struck, dropping his bread on the ground.

"She saw you truly the first time she laid eyes on you, my brother," I told him, "and may I point out that she has always befriended you?"

"Your *brother*?" Marissa cried.

Albaric spoke to me only with his eyes.

"It is needful that she should know everything," I answered him, "every single detail."

"The ring told you so?"

"It showed me so."

"May I see it more closely? May I hold it?" Marissa asked, rather timidly for her.

"You must not put it on, or even let the tip of your finger slip into it. There is no telling what might happen if you did."

"I can quite believe that."

"Very well." I gave the ring into her hands without further hesitation. "Now, my brother." Moving to sit closer to him, I leaned against the tree. "Shall you tell her about it, all of it, right from the beginning, or shall I?"

"Whence came this ring?" asked Marissa again, holding it up between thumb and forefinger but nearly dropping it in astonishment. "It's changing colors!"

Indeed, it had turned into a lovely sort of circular rainbow, with the light shining through it, limpid.

"It likes you," Albaric and I said in unison. "But beware," I added. "It is a trickster."

"How so?"

So with that start, piecemeal for the next few hours, while chits and pipits and sparrows held their own conferences amid the oak boughs overhead, we both by turns told her the story of the Queen of Elfland and King Bardaric, the ring of power, how Albaric had come to Dun Caltor, and most of what had befallen him since. She listened with attention that never once faltered, draping her hair over one shoulder and watching both our faces, speaking little unless she needed to question us, putting the tale together like torn fragments of parchment. With the fun gone out of her candid brown eyes for a while, a hungry intelligence showed through. That, and sometimes emotion. Once she reached out to touch Albaric's hand, saying, "My parents do not love me, either." And once she turned to me. "I adore your mother, Aric. And she says your father used to be much the way you are now."

"Really?" I asked in genuine perplexity. "What did she mean by that?"

"That he was kind, and gallant, and brave, and great of heart."

I lowered my eyes and did not tell her my father had almost cut my head off in a rage. That, and the way I had wept afterward, was a tacit secret between Albaric and me. But otherwise, I cannot think of anything we kept from her.

On towards the end, as the silences began to lengthen while we tried to think of more to tell, she said in a low voice resonant with emotion, "You are my heroes, both of you."

"We are honored," Albaric replied. As for me, I was dumb-struck, and she saw it.

"I look more often on you, Albaric, because you are mysterious, melancholy, and passing fair." she said, but her eyes were on me. "But you, Aric—if only I could have had a father or brother like you. . . ."

"Say no more." Dew was forming in her brown eyes as fair as those of a roe deer. I took her hand in both of mine, but I looked at Albaric. "We have said enough."

"And for what reason?" He spoke sharply, for I had made his heart heavy with the weight of his memories. "Could you explain, please?

"Only in one way. Marissa, would you give the ring back to me?"

She placed it in the palm of my hand, and as I held it, at once it turned opaque shining white again. "Now, Albaric." I handed it to him. Still snow white, and somehow without moving, it seemed to whirl, eddy, spin. Then it edged toward me in the palm of his hand. Albaric took the hint and returned it. Yet even as I held it, its pure white agitation increased.

"My brother?" I prompted.

"Some dire event is at hand," he said, low.

I nodded. "Something is going to happen, and it is likely to include Marissa."

Gravely, she agreed. "The king is kind to me, but I see just the same that his mood, like the drought on his kingdom, worsens with every passing day."

"He tries to be kind to me also." Distress stretched Albaric's voice. "Why is he seething like a stock-pot of shame and rage beneath?"

Looking off into the distance, Marissa slowly said, "He is king. He wishes to be a good king. He knows that the throne should be Escobar's and he hates the knowledge, for everything he does that is less than royal shames him. He covets the throne and sees treachery everywhere. He resents the sun for outshining him. He hates his own resentment. He feels great guilt, Aric, for having hurt you, and he feels certain that illness would not have attempted to claim your life had anyone else given you the wound."

My jaw dropped. "Marissa, who told you? Surely not Mother?"

She heard my dismay. "No, of course not your mother."

"Then who?"

"No one.

"But—how did you know?" I had forgotten that my father had once called her a young seeress.

"I just know. I hear things in shadows and silences."

"The way you knew I was fey from your first sight of me," said Albaric.

"I suppose so." She turned to him. "King Bardaric also feels qualms of guilt, Albaric, for failing to love you."

"Truly?"

"Yes. But he hates the guilt and wishes to be rid of it."

"How so?" I was the one who asked. Albaric had gone white.

Marissa answered slowly, "By any means."

A silence took hold of us, for we dared say no more. Without a word, we folded the remnants of our food within its cloth. Then with help from Albaric on Bluefire, we caught Valor and Cherub, saddled them, and started on the long ride back.

Marissa's hair streamed straight down her back and rippled like brown water. In similar wise, all around us, the dried-up meadow grasses billowed like the waves of a yellow sea, while above them a spindrift of small bright creatures with wings caught the light, swooped and darted, appearing and vanishing, spirituous. We saw their beauty and smiled at one another, yet rode silently, sunshine on our shoulders, but also fate.

CHAPTER THE
THIRTIETH

T HE VERY NEXT MORNING, although closer to noon than dawn, we rode forth again, this time with Mother, as was her wish. Of the day before, we had told her only that Marissa had galloped Cherub, but it was enough; Mother herself was smitten with a desire to ride out with us. And we were glad enough to oblige her.

Villagers cried greetings to us as we swept by, a pretty cavalcade: Albaric bareback on Bluefire, I on my golden Valor, Lady Marissa in her favorite yellow dress and hat on her white pony, and Mother on her tall, almond-colored palfrey, riding sidesaddle with her oak-green gown trailing almost to the ground.

We debated whether to turn toward the hilltops or toward the sea, because Marissa had never had a close look at that endless water; she had never seen it at all until the day she had entered Dun Caltor. But once we passed the cottages and their hedged gardens, we decided to leave the sea for another day; we turned our horses' heads toward the highland meadows so inviting for a gallop.

And gallop we did, far beyond pastureland and clear to the spreading copses where swineherds roamed and peasants gathered deadwood for their hearthfires.

"Let us cool the horses by walking them beneath the trees," I said, for these were tame forests, not wilderness where outlaws roamed. Be it on my head, this decision. But it was midday at the height of summer, the horses were not the only ones sweating, and the greenshadowed paths into the woodland looked most invitingly cool.

"Bluefire has only begun to run," Albaric objected, fun in his voice and a gladsome light in his eyes. "I'll join you a bit later, shall I?" The question was merely for form. Already feeling my assent, he and Bluefire wheeled away to skim the meadowland in a wide circle once more.

The rest of us took to the shade, letting the horses walk loose-reined, choosing the widest path, although it was not quite wide enough for three to ride abreast; Mother trailed a bit behind. Overhead, the small, fluttering leaves of ash trees whispered in a woodland breeze that ruffled our hair and cooled our faces.

"That feels heavenly," Mother said.

Marissa demanded, "How parlous long can Bluefire *run*?"

"Through day and night, if need be," I replied, remembering the desperate time he had sped Albaric and me to Caltor. Suddenly, I felt a sense of danger, but how so? That time was but a memory—

Mother started to say something. "That bonny blue steed—"

Riding ahead, I heard rather than saw: branches above us crackled like lightning, something thudded down, Mother cried out. Then what I saw, as I spun Valor around, stunned me: Mother's gentle palfrey had reared! I glimpsed Marzipan's hooves over my head, cleaving the air. The next instant, a strong hand on the reins pulled the horse down and to a halt. But it was not Mother's hand. It was the rough hand of a warrior, all knotty veins and knuckles, that had seized the reins, and my heart stopped beating for an instant, then hammered hard enough to shake me as I saw more: the man himself straddling the horse behind Mother, one brawny arm imprisoning her shoulders, his dirk threatening her throat.

Marissa gasped, "Escobar!"

Indeed, it could have been no one other than Escobar. He sat so broad-shouldered and tall that I saw him plainly past Mother, and it was like seeing my father in a dark mirror, his hair coarse and grizzled, his face much harrowed by trials or time, deeply seamed and dreadfully scarred, with fierce gray brows that shadowed his eyes so that they seemed black.

In the same breath, Marissa cried, "Escobar, do not hurt Queen Evalin!"

His mouth, straight-lipped, scarcely moved as he said in a low, thorny voice, "I have no desire to do so."

"Then why do you press a knife to her throat?" demanded a voice not nearly so deep—my own.

"To shield myself from harm." Escobar turned his shadowed gaze to me, but Mother did not look at me or at anyone. Whatever fear she felt, she did not show. She sat straight as a pikestaff and far more still, her face like deep water with a quiet surface, unfathomable.

Sword in hand—I had no memory of drawing it, but I must have done so—holding my sword low for the time being, I walked Valor a few steps toward Escobar. My face had gone white; I could feel it, but as if steadying a runaway horse, I managed to curb my heartbeat, calm my body. I knew myself to be shamefully ill-prepared for such an encounter; I wore a simple tunic, no helm, no tabard. The sword and the gold-festooned baldric on which it hung were merely for show.

But a prince must be bold. When I halted Valor, I sat nearly knee to knee with Escobar and felt all the force of his stare. Face to face, I studied him as I had studied Albaric that first night, staring into the shadowy depths of his eyes, and as I had seen honor in Albaric, so also I saw it in Escobar—not greatest honor, but something of probity. Once again I judged, decided, and took a risk.

"I move my sword only to sheathe it," I told Escobar, and then slowly, so as not to alarm him, I did so, and then I lifted my baldric over my head and flung it, sword and all, to the ground. "Your safety," I told Escobar, "is assured, at least for today. I am Aric, son of Bardaric, and my word is your shield."

But he did not loosen his grip on Mother or move his knife away from her throat. Within the moment, I knew why. If it were not for my own heart still pounding in my ears, I would have heard it sooner: hoofbeats, galloping toward us.

"Albaric," I shouted even before I could see him, "halt!"

He did so just as he rode Bluefire into view. From the corner of my eye, I saw him with drawn sword, staring, but I did not shift my gaze from Escobar.

"Albaric," I called, "sheathe your sword and lay it aside, please, for the sake of my honor. Then dismount, come here, and help Mother down." Seeing doubt startle the shadows in Escobar's eyes, I backed Valor away to let him shift his attention to Albaric.

My brother walked up and stood offering his hand to Mother as if he saw not Escobar nor his knotty clutching fists nor his dirk hovering at Mother's throat. Looking only at Mother's face, he asked in the usual manner of one assisting a woman riding sidesaddle, "Would you care to alight, Queen Evalin?"

She turned her head toward him and smiled, but Escobar tightened his grip on her. "Wait!" he barked. The hand that held the dirk began to shake.

Fear for my mother's sake gripped my throat with such an iron fist that I could barely speak. "Why?" I demanded, or tried to demand; the word came out more like a plea. "Why wait? I have given you my word."

"I must speak to the king!" Escobar's harsh voice shook like his hand.

Then Mother herself terrified me by blazing into speech, she with her life at knife's edge. "Great reeking fishheads, Escobar, what is this folly? Do you think—"

"Mother, hush," I begged, for I felt time stop, teetering on the cusp of tragedy. Lunging off Valor, I seized Marzipan's bridle so that Escobar could not take the queen and ride away. Through the roaring of my own panicked heartbeat in my ears, I heard Escobar order Mother, "Be still!" and Albaric coax, "Please, my Queen, obey him," and Mother flare, "I cannot! He is insane if he thinks he can seize me and the throne of Calidon—"

"He is not insane, nor does he want the throne," a wise young voice fluted through the commotion, silencing it at once. Mouths open but speechless, we all stared at Marissa seated on her pony as if on a white throne. "Not anymore, not since his unhappy scheme with Domberk," she declared. Her brown eyes gazed at Escobar, yet through him and far past him as her visionary voice spoke on. "That attempt sickened him, as his hard life has wearied and sickened him. He has been a mercenary and faced the hacking swords of the Cragland thugs, and he has been captured and tortured, and he has escaped and been a fugitive, starving, and he has been flogged, a galley slave in the longboats of the Norsemen, and he has been many times betrayed, not only by the love of women but by men he thought were his friends. He has been bitter, hateful, murderous, but he is not so any longer. Now he has lost any heart for feud or greed, he feels old before his time, and he wishes only to return to his childhood home." Marissa's hazy gaze sharpened to center hard on Escobar. "Brother of Bardaric," she challenged him, "do you really think that you can find peace and surcease by menacing the queen with your dirk?"

All eyes turned to Escobar then, but seemingly he saw only Marissa, and his dagger hand wavered and sagged. Mother wrenched herself away from his weakening grip and dismounted with scant grace; Albaric caught her with both hands to keep her from falling and guided her several paces away; my chest heaved with relief that she was safe.

Escobar still straddled Marzipan, but he had let go of the reins, and his hand that held the dirk hung by his side. As I watched, he threw the dirk down, sinking its blade up to its hilt in the earth near my discarded sword. Then, swinging a leg over the saddle in front of him, he dropped first to the ground, then to one knee in front of my mother. He bowed his head and kept silence.

She let go of Albaric, motioned him away from her, and stood like a sword, her face hard and hot with the high color of fury. With calm that bespoke peril, she ordered her captive, "Look at me, Escobar."

He lifted his head to face her, and through his scars, I glimpsed a man who had once been gallant.

"I ask you again, what folly possesses you?"

He spoke with calm nobility that reminded me of—of what, I could not yet bear to think. He said in a deep voice with just a hint of burr, "It is as the wise lassie has said. I no longer care for fighting, or killing, or least of all for the throne of Calidon. I have eaten, yet there is only a hollow sort of starvation in me, and I wish—I planned—I thought that if I entered Dun Caltor with you as my hostage, then King Bardaric might have mercy on me."

Watching my mother, I saw the color desert her face; she went pale, as if fraught with thoughts she could not speak.

Only now could I bear to think it: the selfless candor in Escobar's voice reminded me of the way Father was wont to speak once upon a time. Before he had changed.

I imagine Mother's thoughts were much the same, and as painful. I saw her swallow hard. Then she called to our soothsayer, "Marissa, what do you make of him?"

My young love answered promptly. "He is not the same as when I knew him in Domberk, Queen Evalin. Something has humbled him. I no longer see bloodthirst in his eyes: he has left the ways of war behind him, and now he is lost and bereft. He seeks sanctuary."

I drew a deep breath, then said what no one wanted to hear. "Escobar," I told him, trying hard to keep any bitterness out of my tone, "there is small mercy in King Bardaric of late, but great choler. Most likely, he will greet you by slaying you."

CHAPTER THE
THIRTY-FIRST

A WHILE LATER, "Young Domberk," said Escobar to Marissa, "I stood in the crowd and watched you ride into Caltor. Did your father know he was sending his enemy a seeress?"

We all sat on the mossy ground, in a circle like the five petals of a cowslip, in council. The horses, tied to branches (except Bluefire), browsed on leaves. Escobar sat across from Queen Evalin, flanked by Albaric and me, while Marissa sat next to the queen.

She told Escobar, "More likely, he thought he was sending a witch."

"The more fool he. Wise lassie, would you do something for me? I wish you would bring my dirk and give it to the queen."

Marissa looked up at Mother, questioning. She nodded, and Marissa darted up and away, braids flying, to fetch the dirk.

"If you would be so good, Queen Evalin," said Escobar,

inclining his head in a bow of sorts, "please thumb the edge of the blade."

She did so and smiled, albeit faintly. "It's barely sharp enough to cut butter."

"'Twas all for show. I dulled it because I wanted to hurt no one, not even by mischance."

Mother said with dagger edge, "You mean in case your murderous Caltor blood got the better of you?"

Escobar's face darkened, yet he bowed toward the queen. "Cutting words, but true. I doubt myself, trying no longer to be evil."

"Certainly you gave me some evil moments, Escobar."

"I am sorry, Queen Evalin," he said, meaning it; I could hear his heart in his voice. "'Twas a foolish plan."

"No bones broken, Escobar. But I tell you, as one who wishes you well: even more foolish is any plan to venture to Caltor. Make no mistake: the king will kill you."

"Even if I kneel before him and swear him my fealty?"

"He will kill you."

"But all the land sings him as a fair and merciful king!"

"Lately. . . ." Mother's firm voice faltered, and her steady gaze shied away from what she had to say; she looked at Albaric, then at me. "Lately," she said very slowly, "a dark change has come over him."

"How so?"

"A fearsome thing has come into our lives." Her gaze lingered on me, significant, as if she guessed I might hide the ring under my linen tunic.

But Escobar turned his head toward Albaric, questioning.

Albaric answered with a wry half-smile. "Had you not heard that the heir of Calidon had a twin? No? Then take heed, Escobar: my coming has made the king half mad with jealousy for the sake of the throne."

"It is true, Escobar," said Mother with saddest fervor. "I hardly know my husband anymore. Sometimes I think him insane. I tell you, he will kill you if you go near him."

He honored her warning with a moment's pause before he replied, "Yet I must risk it."

"Not if you are to live! Fishheads take it all, you must flee!

"Flee far," I agreed, "and flee now. At once." I stood up, startling into flight some silver doves that had perched on a bough overhead. "Look at me, Escobar," I said, pulling back my collar to show him the scar still raw on the side of my neck. "Father nearly cut off *my* head in a rage not long ago."

He paled so greatly that his wounds made a gray webwork on his white face. He said nothing.

I decided to send him on his way without further ado. "Have you need of food, or a horse?"

He gestured vehemently and stood up to face me, his jaw set hard. "So I should flee? And when you and the queen return to Caltor, what will you tell the king?"

I opened my mouth to speak before I quite realized my dilemma. Unsure what to say, I turned to Mother. In her eyes, I saw a realization similar to mine.

Escobar bespoke it. "You are bound by the greatest fealty of all, that of kinship, to King Bardaric. If you do not tell him you have seen me here today, you will have betrayed him. Could you live with that knowledge, Queen Evalin?"

Her face answered without words. Anything that drove a wedge between her and Father was heartbreak to her.

"Indeed," Escobar said, "having encountered me, if you fail to take me directly to the king, you are guilty of treason."

Looking at one another, we all knew he was right, confound him. But he spoke somberly, with no hint of pleasure in victory. His humility made it only just bearable, what had to happen.

I turned back to Escobar. "I will stand by you, then."

"And I," said the queen.

"But not I," said Albaric in a voice crushed flat, "for the sight of me is loathsome to the king."

Escobar looked at him curiously but said nothing. Indeed, there was little more to be said. I gave Escobar Valor to ride, assisted Mother and Marissa onto their palfries, and myself vaulted onto Bluefire behind Albaric.

As we rode silently back to Caltor, I noticed that the ferns, instead of thriving green, were curled and yellowing. and the thistles had gone hoary. Yes, it was a warm day at the height of summer, but a winter king ruled the land of Calidon.

When we reached the courtyard and dismounted, Albaric took Bluefire to the stables, grooms came for the other horses, and the rest of us mounted the steps to the keep, amid stares and whispers on Escobar's account.

We found King Bardaric where we expected to find him: sitting in his court of law hearing the petitions of his people. But instead of torc and baldric, he wore a weighty black tunic and tabard, black leggings, and heavy black boots.

Lifting her long riding skirt with one hand in order to walk, Mother led the way in, followed by Marissa, Escobar, and me. We all hoped, I think, that before the eyes of many folk, and especially in the presence of Marissa, Father might curb his temper somewhat. But Mother and I had cautioned Marissa to stay back by the door. As a guest, if not actually a hostage, she was in no position to anger the king.

As it was beneath the king's dignity to observe all who entered and exited the great oak doorway, I saw my father before he saw us coming in, and the sight of him gripped my heart with dreadful force, as if the black garb he wore also darkened the cast of his features, making him morose, older than his years, and, yes, sinister. Even his golden hair and beard seemed dulled, somber.

Then, as Mother and Escobar and I entered the group of those awaiting public audience, he saw us.

He recognized his brother at once, for his face contorted and flushed blood red; with catapult force he shot to his feet, and he bellowed forth a roar like that of a great black bear. He drew his mighty sword and brandished it. His scribes dropped their pens and bolted from the room. Even his guardsmen paled and backed away, and peasants scurried to flatten themselves against the walls.

"Escobar!" thundered the king, his rage at last taking the form of the single word.

Escobar strode forward to kneel before the throne, within striking distance of the king. Mother and I followed to stand flanking him, one on each side. The king's wild, flailing glare took us in, and fury deformed his shout. "My wife, my son! Traitors!"

"No, my Liege Lord and Husband," said Mother without raising her voice. "Nor is Escobar."

Head bravely bowed despite the threatening sword, Escobar said, "King Bardaric, I am your humble servant."

The king only bellowed a foul oath and addressed his

brother by names even more vile, swearing, "I will kill you! Tell me one reason I should not slay you here and now!"

Escobar raised his head to speak to his brother with his eyes as well as his mouth. "I spared your life."

"What! When?"

"When I came here with Domberk. When, by some arcane power, the queen prevented him from doing his worst. But no such power constrained me, so it became my task to slay you as you fretted in chains in your dungeon. At any time of day or night, I could have cut your throat, and all the devils of hell know I tried. Yet I could not do the foul deed. I coveted the throne with greed that gave me no rest. I walked the nights with my dirk in my hand, yet as I roamed the corridors of my childhood, I thought of the goodly king I had seen in battle and remembered little Bard laughing and clinging to my leg when I was a stripling, and. . . . I am a warrior, I have killed many men, but I could not bring myself to slay my brother."

The whole court of law hung silent, listening to these words. Even the king stood silent for a breath or two afterward, and his sword slowly lowered.

But he raised it again. "Yet you admit you came here to claim the throne!"

"Yes. Domberk had the force, and mine was the title. But I seek it no longer." Escobar steadily met the king's maddened eyes. "I renounce any claim—"

"Bah! Once a traitor, always a traitor. Guards! Seize him!"

My mouth felt almost too dry for speaking, but I managed. "Sire, he came before you of his own free will."

"How dare you!" The king—in that moment I could not think of him as my father—turned all of his fury on me. "You are not my son! You are a traitorous knave! Silence, or I'll have them take you to the dungeon, too!"

I felt myself shaking, partly from terror, partly from relief: the dungeon. Escobar was to live for the time being, at least.

None too gently, the guardsmen seized him by the arms, lifting him off his feet. He did not resist, nor did he cry out, or shout, or sneer, or do anything except meet my eyes, merry-go-sorry, as they carried him away.

Glowering on Mother and me, the king struck at the air with his sword as if smiting us out of his way. "Go! And I warn you both, stay far from me."

I bowed to him, still shaking, and backed away. Mother curtseyed and did likewise.

CHAPTER THE THIRTY-SECOND

AS SOON AS I DARED, afterward, with Albaric by my side for courage, I slipped by back ways down to the depths of the keep, to the dungeon. There, by torchlight as always, for no sunlight penetrated that place, I found Escobar shackled to the wall, sitting upon a pile of straw, dour but unharmed.

"Greetings, Prince Aric," said a gruff old voice I knew well—Garth's. "Greetings, Albaric." Healed of his wounds but sadly maimed by them, Garth could no longer ride horseback. He could only walk in a bent and skewed way, so he now served as Captain of Guards in the keep. I breathed somewhat more easily, finding a friend in charge of Escobar.

"Garth," I told him, inclining my head toward Escobar, "this is a kinsman of mine." As well he knew. "I would like you to keep him in the greatest comfort possible in such a place."

Replying, he matched my dry tone. "His Majesty has not ordered me otherwise, my Prince."

No torture, Garth meant, no beatings, no meals of bread and water, or not yet. I took a deep breath. "I must keep my fingers crossed, then." For I hoped that if enough time passed, I might be able to talk to my father and find his heart.

"Prince Aric," Escobar told me with a warrior's dark humor, "I have slept in far worse lodgings than these. All is well enough." More lightly, shifting his glance to my brother, he added, "Even better would be if someone would explain Albaric to me."

I felt a smile comfort my face, and Albaric went over to speak with Escobar through the bars. "I am a fetch, I am told. I think that means I have been fetched from somewhere peculiar. I am sure the guards would be happy to tell you all about my arrival."

A sweet voice, Marissa's, surprised me from behind. "Albaric is all honor," she told Escobar.

He inclined his head toward her. "No more so Prince Aric. It would seem I need not have dropped like a cutthroat from a tree."

But Marissa had already turned to me. "Aric, are you all right? You looked so pale."

"Speak sooth and say I was quaking in my boots." Smiling, I reached out for her hand; it was like holding a warm nesting dove. "But Albaric played the harp to comfort me."

"Good. Your mother sent me to see how you fare. I went with her afterward, you see, for she looked even worse than you did."

As well she might, for Mother's plight was more frightful than mine; I was the king's son and heir, but she was merely his wife.

In the days that followed, I remembered how Albaric had said "Some dire event is at hand," and I thought that it had come to pass. The king's wrath, far from abating, shadowed my brother's life and mine and Mother's like the dark wings of death. Only Marissa dared join him on the dais to eat. I took my meals in the kitchen, and Mother had hers brought to her chamber. Invisible arrows of dread pierced me for her sake and for Escobar's; if I could not find a way to placate or appease my sire, would Escobar languish the rest of his life in the dungeon, or—or worse?

The first day I hid in the mews, with the hooded hawks. That night, I slipped cake and ale to Escobar in the dungeon while Albaric stood lookout for me. But rather than thank me, Escobar chided me, "Do not risk yourself for my sake, Prince Aric. Garth sees to it that I am fed well enough."

"Has Father come to see you? At all?"

"No, not even to curse at me."

The second day, I skulked in the guardsmen's barracks. Albaric kept me company, and while the king was in court, we slipped to Mother's chamber to visit her and Marissa. There we sat like a mute and unlucky four-leaf clover with nothing to say, shadowed as we were by the king's wrath.

The next day, I thought I would dare the presence of the king, but from the corridor as I approached, I heard him shouting so hatefully that a servant fled in tears. It would have been foolhardy to go on. Sighing, hoping Father's temper might abate on the morrow, I turned back.

But the morrow was no better, and day after day, I dared not bespeak the king, until I felt as if I had lost my courage, or my father, or both. Yet the stranger on the throne was still my father, my troth to him unchanged, and—and I dared not think what might happen. The ring of power hung suspended on its thong against my chest, against my skin, over my heart, and it burned with passion, burned and burned, white hot.

"It stings like hot iron," I confided in Albaric one day after suffering the king's displeasure for perhaps a week, although it felt like much longer. My brother and I had taken refuge in Bluefire's stall.

"The ring?"

"Yes. It feels as if it is branding me, yet it leaves no mark."

"Neither does the king's ire."

"Not yet," I muttered. My brother meant only to cheer, but the words chilled me in a way I could not explain.

Straw rustled as Marissa came in, and Bluefire stepped aside with a gentle snort of greeting. "The queen is sleeping," she whispered, as I reached for her hand and kissed her pert face. "What was that about the ring?"

"It burns like coals of fire against my chest." I drew it out for her to see. She touched it, then held it in her hand.

"It feels cool as a white rose petal to me," she said, puzzled.

"And it looks as innocent as a wee white lamb," agreed Albaric, with a quirk in his voice that said he knew better. We watched the ring, as white as milk but flowing, always flowing within its circle, throbbing like a living thing, pulsing like two hearts, then one, and then two again.

"Let me put it away," I whispered, for I found it hard to bear the sight—yet no wonder, for everything in that dark time was hard to bear, and the ring burned me more fiercely the moment I tucked it back under my tunic. "Marissa, you should go back inside." She would be in danger, I thought, if found with me. "When Mother awakes, please tell her I am well."

Marissa said, "She knows better, and she is not well, not at all. Never before has King Bardaric failed her so, turning his back, unspeaking, scorning her bed. She says she cannot bear confinement for even one more day; however foolhardy, she must breathe sunlit air again. She wants us to go riding with her on the morrow if we are willing."

Given the king's mood, Mother's idea was indeed foolhardy; she had to be feeling quite desperate.

Albaric questioned me with his eyes. I nodded but said to Marissa, "When you breakfast with the king, does he speak to you? At all?"

"Yes. He is courteous." She flashed a merry smile. "I am, after all, his bonnie wee lassie."

"Then could you bonnie wee tell him that we are riding out to look upon the sea, as is your heart's desire?" The king would be mightily wroth, I thought, if we sallied forth without his knowledge, as if in defiance. Better he should be told beforehand. "But if you think it will turn him against you," I added, "speak not."

Marissa smiled up at me. "Gentle Aric, I would gladly join company in disgrace with the rest of you! Certainly I will speak to the king."

The morrow turned out to be another sunny day such as I used to think a marvel in Calidon's brief summertime. Now, it signified only more drought. At least the sunshine meant a respite from the gloom within the castle, but alas, we were a subdued company who rode forth. As if she had no heart for finery, Mother wore a simple kirtle of unbleached wool that barely covered her feet as she rode sidesaddle on Marzipan, and even Marissa in her bright tartan frock seemed downcast.

"Did it go badly with the king?" I asked her in a low voice once we had passed out of the village, beyond where any peasant might overhear.

"Not for me, no. He was all courtesy." But it was plain to be seen on her soft young face that something troubled her. Glancing at Mother and Albaric trotting ahead of us, she slowed Cherub to a walk. I reined in Valor to walk beside her, waiting with an uneasy heart for her to speak.

When the others could not hear, she whispered, "King Bardaric has decreed that tomorrow at dawn, Escobar is to be put to death. Executed," she added, "with all the honors of a nobleman." Irony fraught her musical voice almost as much as horror did. "His head on a block to be taken off by a doomster's axe."

I think I said, "Don't tell Mother," but I do not remember surely, for I might as well have been struck on the head and thrown into whirlpools and waterspouts to drown. Some dire event indeed! So direly wrong that I knew I would act, must act, tonight, to save an innocent man and thus betray my father. Betray my father! The king! I very nearly could not bear the thought of being his enemy, and outlaw, a fugitive, even with Albaric at my side, if I lived—but Marissa! Would I ever see Marissa again? If not, then how would I live?

No. It bore no more thinking of, none of it, not Father or Escobar or what to do, not now, not in daylight. Later, tonight, I would judge, decide, and act. Meanwhile, I would claim this one last day for joy.

Mentally, I thrashed my way out of a stormy ocean within me that would not let me breathe, and I turned my back on it.

My young love rode by my side on her white pony, and on the other side rode Albaric, who had no doubt sensed the tumult in me and was wondering if I needed his help. I gave him one quick touch of the hand, then turned to Marissa, smiling for her sake and at the sight of her. I told her, "Let us speak no more of it now."

Riding ahead of us, Mother turned and spoke sadly. "Even the heather is dry and dying."

"But not yet dead." We had reached the place where the shoreline cliffs lessened. "Look," I told Marissa, "above the crest of the heather, you can just catch sight of the sea."

She looked, and her eyes answered the sea, wide and shining.

A path to the sea opened, and we turned to ride down to the very spot where Albaric and I had first reached the sea that desperate night when Domberk had taken Dun Caltor. The salt-scented wind lifted our hair, and Albaric sang two lines very softly:

> *I would follow you to the end of the land.*
> *I would follow you to the coldest sea strand.*

"Oh," whispered Marissa, "is it really so sad, so foreboding? To me it seems beautiful."

"It truly is beautiful," I said.

Indeed, in sunlight, the place was all peace and loveliness. We took saddles and bridles off the horses and turned them loose to graze on the moor, and then Mother sat in the sunshine while Albaric, Marissa, and I ran down to the black gravel shore. I watched Marissa with pleasure, as if watching a lovely wild creature, a bird, a deer, while she studied the sea, approaching as close to the vast, splashing water as she dared, then running away as a wave washed in, looking back over her shoulder as a gray swell turned to white foam. Albaric laughed: I laughed and took Marissa's hand. Three in a row, we stood as close to the waves as we dared, the salt spray in our faces, the sea wind playing with our hair. A tall wave threatened to drench us, and we fled, shouting and laughing. Again and again, we played tag with the waves, and more than once, hands in hands with Marissa, Albaric and I swung her clear off her feet to save her skirt from a soaking. But we were all more or less moist, boots sodden, and breathless with mirth, when we returned to the top of the seaside slope. It gladdened my heart to see the queen smiling at us as we plopped down to rest on the heather, which still smelled sweet even after weeks of drought.

"Have you packed us something to eat, Mother?" I asked, jesting to tease another smile out of her.

She did smile, although barely, and she rolled her eyes at me.

Grazing nearby, Bluefire lifted his handsome head, looked back toward Caltor, and snorted.

I, for one, forgot about smiles. We all stood up, shaded our eyes, looked, and saw: there, all alone on Invincible, came King Bardaric riding along the top of the cliffs toward us. Plovers ran crying away before him, the black-clad king on his black charger.

Very softly, Mother said, "I rue this day that I never thought would come, when I am not gladdened by the sight of my husband."

CHAPTER THE
THIRTY-THIRD

FTER THAT, none of us spoke, for what could we say? As Father reached us, although nothing in the sky had changed, a dark cloud seemed to chill the sun. He halted Invincible and stared down at us, stony of face, stone silent.

Dangerously silent. I dared not let that silence go on, so I bowed my head and said, with courtesy that sounded false even to myself, "Greetings, Sire."

"Hah!" he barked, and I raised my eyes to see him raking all of us with his glare. "I have come to show you I am not a fool. What treachery are you plotting? A way to rescue your darling Escobar? I assume, Marissa, you have told them he is to die at dawn?"

I felt the news stun Albaric like a blow, while Mother gasped and swayed as if she might fall; I reached out to steady her.

"Hah!" The king's bark this time had a different tone. "I see that you did *not* tell them, little Lady Marissa. Come here."

She walked forward to stand at his left stirrup, gazing up at him with no fear, only wonder, in her face.

"Why not?" he asked not too harshly.

"Liege?"

"Why did you not tell them?"

"I saw no good to come of it, Your Majesty."

"You look for the good, do you?" His face still stony and unreadable, the king contemplated her for a moment—but then quite suddenly, his glare swerved to me. "You!" he shouted, pointing an imperious finger my way, beckoning.

I strode forward to stand beside Marissa, looking up at my sire. His eyes—what I saw there, I hated to call hatred, but never had I seen darker rage in him, and he bespoke me as if he loathed me.

"If you wish me ever to call you my son again," he said, spitting out the words as if he had bitten each one off with steely teeth, "you will marry this wise young lassie. Forthwith."

My jaw might well have dropped open, I felt so dumbfounded, dizzied with the strangeness of having my fondest wish granted in so ugly a way. Something felt badly wrong, but I tried to make it right. Turning to Marissa, I lowered myself to bended knee before her.

"I love you, Marissa," I told her, feeling my shy passion for her blushing in both my heart and my face. "Will you marry me?"

"Dearest Aric, of course I will."

"I know you are too young. I will not ask it of you until—"

"Forthwith!" thundered the king.

"I am not a child, Aric!" Marissa burst out at the same time. "I am more woman than you know. Please," she added impatiently, "stand up."

Doing so, I saw Mother actually smiling, while Albaric

gave me such a glad look that I felt all the warmth of his hope for my happiness, despite the shadow over everything.

King Bardaric's shadow.

He looked down on Marissa and me, his very face in shadow, his voice still harsh. "Lady Marissa, you make this decision on your own, as a woman? You will marry Prince Aric?"

"Yes. Utterly. I have dreamed of him since the first night I met him." Her hand sought mine, and mine met it swiftly.

"That cannot be true, young lady. All the world knows your passion is for Albaric." The king's voice grew a sharper edge with each word. "You cannot keep your eyes off him."

"I never speak untruth, Your Majesty. Albaric is a wonder to me, and I marvel when I see him. But what I feel for him is not the love of a woman for a man. My true love is Aric." Her hand tightened on mine.

"You would be faithful to him?"

"Completely!"

My heart should have been bursting with happiness, yet I felt a strange foreboding that my "trying to make it right" had been folly.

"False wench." The king's voice struck like a weapon, a sword.

"Bard!" Mother cried, "What are you saying!"

"I say false wench, and I say it also to you! Be still!" he thundered at her, and then, to Marissa, "You lie. But eyes do not lie. Your eyes look always to Albaric. When you wed my son, all the world will think him a cuckold, and I will not have it." His glare turned on me. "*I will not have it*, Aric."

And I stood as if turned to ice on a hot summer's day. Even my hand felt cold in Marissa's warm grip, for in my sire's glowering eyes, I saw triumph, gloating triumph, and something even worse. I did not at first recognize it, so unfamiliar in my sire: malice.

I could not speak.

The king spoke. Not even loudly, and not even turning his head to look at—at his son, his other son! The king ordered, "Albaric, go away."

"Albaric," I whispered, for I could not live without him. "Albaric!" I cried, my eyes searching for him, frantic, as if he might already be gone. But not far from me, he stood, white-faced, staggered by the battle-ax force of the king's decree. Our eyes met.

"My brother," I babbled to him like a child, "I have been befooled, tricked, trapped." For now I was pledged to stay and wed Marissa; I could no longer go with Albaric in exile.

"Silence," the king ordered, still enthroned on his high horse above us. "Albaric, heed my command. Go away. At once."

"No! Slay me!" Albaric strode forward. With his head high, his eyes wild, he stood at the king's right hand. Father turned toward him with a sneer of distaste, his hand strayed toward the pommel of his sword, and Albaric challenged, "Draw that great heavy sword of yours and smite my head off. Do it!"

I could not help him; I could only back away, taking Marissa with me, out of danger.

With perilous patience, Father told Albaric, "Just go. I care not where."

"There is nowhere for me to go! My mother cares naught for me, nor does my—my father. I have no family, no country, no liege lord, no clan, no friends but the ones you would part me from."

"Take heed and go," said the king in a dreadful tone as flat as the cold sea's far horizon. "Obey me now, or there will be more than one head cut off at dawn tomorrow."

Albaric faced him feral and stricken, like a deer with an arrow in its heart, for a moment longer, then turned to me. Speechless myself, I reached out to comfort him, hold him, stop him, keep him somehow—but my fingers just touched him as he whirled and ran past me, dashing straight toward the sea, down the slope, and across the narrow strand into the endless water.

I felt, inwardly, the force of his will to die, and it staggered me like a blow, so that for a moment I could not move or breathe. Then, with a gasp, I ran after him. Father cursed and roared at me to stop, but nothing could have stopped me from trying to save Albaric. Already he had reached the breakers and let them take him when I plunged into the waves.

The sea is a cruel thing; its vast water pretends clarity yet will not show what it has swallowed. Too frantic even to shout, scanning wildly, I thought I would die also in the sea, for my heart would break. But then a golden glint caught my eye, a shining circle uncoiling on the surface—Queen Theena's hair! I lunged toward it, saw fair flaxen hair floating nearby—Albaric's!—and seized it. I yanked his head out of the water—sputtering, trying to pull away from me, he yet lived! Despite his struggles, I hauled him up by his shoulders and stood him on his feet in the waist-deep water, one arm wrapped around him tightly, pressing him to my chest. The mere fact that he still lived, that he was not yet lost to me, gave me strength to keep my footing as the breakers washed over us. I tried to reach for the Queen of Elfland's red-golden hair swimming into the waves, but I felt Albaric shake his head.

"Let it go," he muttered.

Then I knew utterly that he had let go of his life.

"Death's dark strand," he murmured as if he had heard me thinking. "Not for you, Aric. You must not follow me."

"My brother," I told him, "there is another way."

"No."

"Yes, there is. The ring showed me."

At the mention of the ring he lifted his head, ceased resistance, and took the slight weight of his body onto his own feet.

"In a dream," I explained, "that one night I wore it to sleep." I reached under my tunic and drew out the ring—that circle of light still gleaming white—and impatiently I snapped the thong that held it.

Both of us stared at the white ring I held in my fingers.

"I am to put it on you," I told my brother softly, "which is nearly as desperate as drowning, for I truly do not know what it will do."

"But it will do something."

"Yes. Let us get out of this confounded smother." Together, we made our way back to the shallower water, knee deep when the waves washed in. On the nearby moorland, I saw, the king had dismounted from his charger and was flailing his arms and shouting at me. Keeping their distance from him, my mother and Marissa clutched each other and watched, their faces two white ovals that neither moved nor spoke.

I gave the three of them only one brief glance, then faced Albaric, and I am sure he knew the salt water washing down my face came not from the sea, for I could not bear the thought of being without him. But even worse would be prolonging the pain of his despair. In my dream, I had seen him flying away, a white bird, or swimming away, a silver fish, free and happy. He would not miss his mortal body; he wore it lightly—an Elf, or even a half-Elf, can be many things. But I would miss the touch of his hand for the rest of my life.

"We know the ring is a trickster," I told him—the thing pulsed like a white heart as I held it—"but this is what I will tell it: that I wish it to take you someplace where you are no oddling but where you *belong*, where you are assured of peace and joy, where you are well loved." I looked to him for assent.

He nodded, unable to speak.

I bespoke my formal command to the ring, then hugged him close, my beloved brother, my Albaric—we hugged each other one last time as I placed the ring on his finger—and even as I embraced him, it took charge of him.

And something took charge of the sea, whether the ring, fate, or some power even greater, for at that moment it sent up a wave like a white fountain to drench us and hide us.

To those watching from shore, I supposed it looked for a moment as if my brother had disappeared, gone in a great splash of light such as the one that took the horse he had ridden into Dun Caltor that first night—but as the wave receded, it was he and I both who threw back my head, raised my arms, and cried forth a wordless shout of surpassing joy to sea and sky. I knew where Albaric had gone. As if I had hugged him into myself, as if the salt water of the sea had washed him into my skin, I had felt my second self dislimn to come in where he truly belonged.

Into me.

And now that we shared one mortal body, I felt his ecstasy redoubling mine. He lived in me and he was me, cherished as I cherished my soul, loved by me and all who loved me. His heart and mine, now one. His mind and mine, now more than ever one. His soul and mine, now ineluctably one. His music, now mine. His scars, his sorrows and angers and betrayals now mine, even as my happiness was his. His ring, the white ring of power, on my finger as I turned toward shore, where my family stood stunned and staring.

CHAPTER THE THIRTY-FOURTH

AVING SHARED ALBARIC'S HEART nearly from the moment we met, I felt not very different; I felt like much the same Aric, albeit overjoyed that Albaric had not died, after all, but lived on in me. Overjoyed that my mortal body so willingly provided him sanctuary.

But I suppose I looked rather different.

As I strode out of the sea, only my brave Marissa ran to meet me with just such a bounce of joy as was her wont—but when I clasped her in my arms, I felt her trembling. "My love," I exclaimed, "what's wrong?"

But she stopped shaking nearly the moment I touched her. "Great silly gudgeons!" Smiling, she tilted her face like a flower to look up at me. "Nothing's wrong, beloved; all's better than right! Aric, *you are the One!*"

Too dumbfounded to speak, I gazed back at her.

"Lackwit," she told me with tender exasperation, "You come from the sea, with a white cloak trailing from your shoulders, and all your clothing is dry and white, your tunic pure white lamb's wool, and white fire encircles your head in a crown!"

Incredulous, I put up a hand to feel my own head—dry hair, finer than before—and my face, where there ran a trace of a scar from my cheekbone to my chin. "Do I look like my brother?" I asked Marissa.

"You look like yourself and him and more, like the prince you truly have always been, my Aric." With sudden passion, she hugged me hard, pressing herself to my chest.

Embracing her, stroking her hair, glancing past her, I met my mother's wide-eyed gaze, and I smiled. "We were mistaken," I told her. "I was not a marvel, to be so transparent like glass. I was merely incomplete."

"Oh," she breathed, nodding, yet she did not seem to understand; indeed, she looked as if she might faint. Letting go of Marissa, I stepped toward Mother and reached out to steady her. But as my fingers closed on her arm, strength returned to her, and she stood tall, once more Calidon's stately Queen Evalin with gray eyes that gazed upon me with tender wisdom.

"Truly spoken, Aric." Gravely mischievous, she tousled my hair as if I were a child, although she had to reach up to do so. "Look, my hand is not burned," she teased. "Crown of flame, fishheads. That's just white glamour."

"The ring's not," I said, for I felt fire on my finger. The ring blazed golden, then orange, then forged-iron red, no longer content. Very well; it had served Albaric in the best possible way. Now it wished to go, so I pulled it off.

"Give it here," rasped a deep voice close at hand.

Instead, I turned, and with all the strength of an arm that had flung many stones, I hurled it far out to sea.

"What the bloody blue blazes?" Father bellowed. "You dare to disobey me? You! The fetch that has stolen my son? Prepare to die!" Raising his sword, he lunged at me.

"Aric!" Marissa screamed.

"Bard, no!" cried my mother. "It's Aric, and he's not yet strong!"

Indeed, I had seldom lifted a sword since before my illness. But Father was gone beyond hearing Mother call his name, far gone beyond hearing the words she spoke. I saw my death in his hooded eyes, and as he struck, I reacted the only way I could, blocking his sword with my shield arm—he sliced it to the bone—while I drew my own weapon. He stood uphill of me and bore down on me with all the weight of his black-clad rage. And despite everything he had done, I myself could not muster rage of my own to help fend him off, for I knew him to be a madman, and I pitied him. But my sword arm proved swift and strong to parry his blows. All of Albaric's skill had increased mine, and all of Albaric's strength, although it had never been great, had joined with mine to give me a warrior's fair chance.

Mother and Marissa cried out only once; after that, I felt their silence at my back, taut as harp strings and begging the fates that I would neither kill nor be killed. Stroke by stroke and clash by clash and step by cunning step, without hurting him—although myself taking a few more blows—I drove my opponent back up the slope to level ground, where I let him attack me—King Bardaric, my father, how had he become such a figure of pathos, a mockery of his former self? Bellowing, snarling, and raining sweat, he came at me with not much more wit than an animal. I was able to hold him off and let him circle me and circle me and wear himself out until he became hoarse, then silent, barely able to move for panting. Finally, his sword sagged, point to the ground, and he leaned upon it, staring at me, no longer with hatred but with what was almost worse, a bleak and hopeless despair.

And no recognition at all. My father did not know me either as Albaric or as Aric.

Indeed, for weeks he had not known me truly. But this no longer hurt me. Somehow all the pain had turned on him instead, so that he suffered dreadful agony of spirit. Something had broken in him, or he had given up, and in him I saw a shadow too deep for any mortal help, sadder than ashes, murkier than sludge. As if he were a warrior dying after battle of no visible wound, doomed without hope. As if his fetch stood there.

I would not add to his misery; I would not order him to yield. Instead, "Put the sword away," I told him.

Perversely, he turned and hurled it toward the sea, but so spent was he that it merely tumbled, clattering, down the rocks to the gravel shore.

I slid my own sword back into its scabbard. Blood dripped from my wounds; I ignored it. Standing to confront him as was my right—the victor, by law I could have killed him—I demanded, "Look at me, King Bardaric. Speak truth. Why are you so unhappy?"

"Once more I must murder my brother!" he cried as if the true words were torn from him by some force in me.

"Why so?"

"He has come back to take my throne!"

"He has told you he wants it not."

"But I cannot trust or believe! I do not deserve—"

"You have been the most deserving of kings."

266

He stamped his booted foot in a sort of thwarted frenzy. "Words and words and words, the ashes of a dead fire!"

"Your fire is not dead, Sire."

"Bah! You are young! Young and glorious! I am old and grotesque and weary unto death!"

"Then rest. Your throne is safe. What else so deeply troubles you?"

"I cannot live—if I was ever—unfaithful to my Evalin!"

"You were not. Never." Despite my conqueror's advantage, I felt my voice softening. "What else, Father? Out with it. What else has made you wretched?"

"Jealousy. My son, his heart stolen—by a wyrd—"

"Not so. My candle's flame now burns twice as bright."

"I should love—visitant so fair—yet I am all horror and hatred and fear—"

From some distance behind me, Marissa's soft voice called, "The hands of the One are the hands of a healer."

I would not have thought to attempt it otherwise. Although I knew what had become of Albaric and rejoiced for him, I did not yet understand what the ring had been trying to show him and me for weeks, swirling two as one and one as two, white and white. Nor did I yet comprehend all that had happened to boyish, peaceable Prince Aric. But despite the crazed glare of my father's eyes, I walked up to him, lifted my hands, and placed them gently on each side of his head, nestling my fingers into his harsh hair wet with sweat.

His haunted shadow-blue eyes glared at mine as if he would strike me, but I faced him and willed myself past the anger, looking into him, seeking the inner man, finding at first only glimpses of scars worse than Escobar's, of courtly cruelty suffered with a smile, of silken shackles and velvet chains—

glamour's dungeon. Elfland! For the first time, I sensed how it must have unmanned the king to be captured without a blow and imprisoned by fragrant, invisible bars. His mind could not remember, but his soul could not forget that timeless time, and I saw—I heard his soul cry out—dreadful, horrible, I wanted to flee, but *I, Albaric son of Bardaric, must be strong.* The foreverness of Otherwhere had been—still was, to the king—an instrument of torture, a golden rack upon which his selfhood had been torn, dismembered, thinned to tatters. His spirit was broken world without end, and I, a stripling prince, almost a lost child in that world, I had to help somehow. Terribly weak in that place, with all my small strength, I reached out to touch his tortured soul, if only to comfort. . . .

I felt an indescribable pain such as nothing I had ever experienced before, agony I could not bear for long, could not withstand at all but had to for—for just a breath more, one more gasping grasp—

I could stand it no longer. I blinked and thought I had failed, and my heart could have broken.

But when I opened my eyes, it seemed I had held out just long enough. I saw my father again, in Calidon and in truth.

There we two stood, on a headland above the sea. Blinking, I looked into the king's eyes and they had cleared, theirs the cerulean blue of springs of living water; my father wept. The king wept. Lunging forward, King Bardaric pulled me into his arms. "Albaric!" he cried. "Albaric, my son, my son!"

Warm in his embrace, Albaric felt such joy—*I* felt such joy—that I thought my heart would burst, and I laid my head on his shoulder not only with love but with need, feeling as weak as a baby. Indeed, it would seem that, swaying in his strong arms, I fainted.

Some few moments later, I found myself lying on sweet-smelling heather with my head pillowed on Marissa's lap—somehow I knew it was Marissa—and I felt so comforted, lazy, content that I did not move or open my eyes but listened to my family talking.

"Are you sure he will be all right?" My father, with more heart in his voice than I had heard for many a day.

"Of course he will be all right." Mother sounded happy enough to sing. "He's strong as the cliffs of Caltor. Look at him."

"He has Aric's features yet finer somehow. More royal." Father sounded glad yet bewildered.

"The scar only makes him more handsome," said Marissa, as I felt her soft touch on my face.

"He is a swordsman beyond compare."

"You taught him," said Mother with warmest pride.

"He has all of Aric's honest strength yet a grace, a light—"

"His white fire nimbus, you saw it?" Marissa's eager voice.

"No."

"That's a pity. It's gone now."

"I mean a different kind of light. Within, not on his skin. I can't explain—"

"There is poetry in him now," Mother said serenely. I could feel her deftly binding the worst cut on my arm. "And, I hope, music."

"How could I not have loved Albaric from the moment he saved my life?"

"Bard," said my mother with greatest affection, "everything

always looks different afterwards. Do not blame yourself; let the past go. My heart fills, overflows, with joy to have you back."

"Everything that happened was fated," Marissa said. "Necessary. Not your fault."

"You think so, young seeress?"

"I know so."

There was a long, resonant silence, during which I decided it was time for me to stop being a sluggard. I opened my eyes.

"Aric!" Marissa exclaimed. "He's awake."

"Albaric!" cried my father, his voice choked with emotion. Seeing him, hazily I wondered why he was bare-chested; later, I realized he had given his black tunic to be ripped into bandaging, to bind my shield arm and put it in a sling.

"Father." I put out my hand to him where he knelt on the moorland by my side. He took it, and I felt his fingers trembling.

He swallowed hard. "My son redoubled," he said with difficulty, "I have been—wrongheaded—"

"Sire," I interrupted, "never mind all that, please. Just tell me no one will die in the morning."

"Great blue blazes, no!" Letting go of me, he leapt to his feet. "I must go back at once to free Escobar!"

"No need, Bard," Mother said placidly, pointing back along the sea cliffs toward Dun Caltor. "Look. He is coming to you."

CHAPTER THE
THIRTY-FIFTH

ATHER TURNED TO SEE. Wishing to do likewise, I forsook Marissa's lap and tried to stand up but succeeded only in floundering to my knees, then sinking to a seat with my back against a pile of saddles. Still, from there, I could see horsemen approaching at a gallop, and the foremost rider, tall, broad-shouldered, and nobly upright on his steed, even at the distance looked like Father's twin.

"Escobar!" the king shouted in a very different way than the week before. "Escobar! My brother! Well come!"

Within a moment, the horsemen moiled to a halt before us, dismounting, and the first one was indeed Escobar, and Father opened his arms to him, and they embraced.

How it warmed my heart that my father had a brother!

Trying not to smile too widely, I looked elsewhere, lest I embarrass them, and there, among other guardsmen, I saw Garth! I stared at him with greatest wonder, for he stood straight as a lance, no longer maimed but doughty and hale, waiting to report to his king.

Escobar and the king gazed at each other, my father

smiling, his brother quizzical. "Look around you, Bard," said Escobar. "Why is it springtime again? What fey thing has come to pass?"

Startled, I noticed how merrily the breeze blew the scent of rain and blue violets my way. The drought was gone as if it had never been; I sat in honey-sweet heather shining with dew.

Garth could wait no longer to tell the king, "My liege, the lock shattered and the dungeon door swung open, the shackles fell to bits—"

But the guards were all talking at once, to Mother or Father or each other.

"Dun Caltor shook, the keep shook to its roots!"

"Garth reared up and stood strong as a bullock—"

"The stones rattled atop the sea cliffs."

"—but too dumbstruck to bellow."

"Green and thriving, all the land within that moment turned green again."

"King Bardaric, what has happened?" Escobar insisted, removing his cloak and placing it around father's brawny, bare shoulders.

"I'm King Bardaric no more," Father told him with the warmest of regard. "The throne is yours by birthright."

Escobar shook his head as if bothered by a wasp. "I've told you, I don't want your confounded throne."

"Nevertheless, you are the king."

"Balderdash. I'm glad enough to be out of that blasted dungeon. I take it from your welcome that I am pardoned?"

"You are free with no need for any pardon. It is high time we Caltors forsook the family tradition of killing one another."

"Bah. For the matter of that, what sort of king would I make when I hadn't even the guts to slay you?"

"A goodly king."

"I'm cranky and weary and old, Bard. Have mercy."

Yes, mercy had returned to King Bardaric. Greatly moved to see my father himself again, I sat watching, with Marissa by my side as if she had never left it; I found we were holding hands. She asked, "Aric, my love, how do you feel?"

I lifted her hand to my lips and kissed it. "Happy as a wee puppy, and nearly as feeble."

"Oh, no! Is it a wee *white* puppy you are?"

"Bah!" I smiled at her, knowing with uncanny certainty that *she* knew my strength would return. "Tweaking my beard, already, Mischief Marissa?"

"What beard?" But even as she said it, her merry eyes widened and sobered. "No need."

"What? Why?"

"Even without your white fire crown, they recognize you, my love."

I heard her soft voice clearly, for the hubbub had quieted, and with an odd, fated feeling I saw that people were staring at me. One after another, they had caught sight of me and ceased talking, until all was silence except for sea birds calling, the soughing of the breeze, and the thrum of the sea. My mother gazed at me with fondest pride, and even Father and Escobar had turned to study me.

"We have been a pair of fools, Bard," said Escobar to my father with gruff good humor yet a kind of awe. "We're neither of us King of Calidon. Right under our noses, seated on a throne of heather, behold the White King."

"The White King has returned!" someone exclaimed, and then other voices joined in as if strummed like a harp. "The White King!"

"The One True King!"

"The One has come back to Calidon!"

"The White King from the sea!"

Escobar came and kneeled in front of me so that his head would not rise above mine; I hoped that was the only reason. Father did the same.

"My liege," ventured Escobar, "how did this wonder come to pass?"

I shook my head. "Later. Right now I feel weak as buttermilk, mine Uncle." He ducked his head to hide his smile when I called him that.

"Albaric, my son. . . ." Father sought my eyes with his. "Is it well if I call you that?"

My heart swelled; I felt tears mist my eyes. "It is well. It is wondrous!"

"Then Albaric, White King, what is your command? Will you now take the throne?"

"No, not yet." Still holding Marissa's hand for strength, still half in a daze from all that had happened, yet I knew some things quite surely. "I wish you to reign for the rest of your days, please, King Bardaric; the people of Caltor love you." Because I was now the White King, I knew my words settled the matter. My mind could encompass my new self, made of legend, only a little, but that little I shared. "What I think I should do is ride throughout Calidon with my bride"—turning to Marissa, I consulted her with my eyes and found troth in hers—"spreading peace to the reaches of the kingdom and doing what good I can." There would be quarrels to end, outlaws to befriend, many kinds of healing. . . . "Prince Escobar, I would be honored if you would advise me."

He bowed his head. "The honor is mine."

Close at hand, Mother cried out, "Look! Look at the sky!"

I took one glance, then said to Father and Escobar, "Help me up," and with their support, I stood between them, surprised to find myself a bit taller than either. We all gazed up at the blue—more deeply and truly blue than I had ever seen it, the sky of my kingdom, with white, white clouds blowing in the high wind—but they formed the mane and forelock around the head of a great blue horse that looked down on us, regarding us with wise violet eyes.

Bluefire! I alerted my steed, the earthbound one, with my mind.

And I heard him bugle a neigh of greeting to his sire in the sky.

ABOUT THE AUTHOR

Nancy Springer is the bestselling and award-winning author of more than fifty novels, beginning with the Books of Isle fantasy series (*The White Hart, The Silver Sun, The Sable Moon*). She writes in a plethora of genres, including mysteries (the Enola Holmes series), magic realism, contemporary young adult, and children's fiction. Springer has also published hundreds of short stories and poems. Her work has been included in school curricula and reprinted in textbooks.

Springer was born in Montclair, New Jersey, and has been a full-time professional fiction writer for more than four decades. She began writing immediately after her graduation in 1970 from Gettysburg College, although teaching classes, attending conferences, and raising her son, Jonathan, and her daughter, Nora, slowed her down a bit at times.

In 1986, Springer's fantasy short story "The Boy Who Plaited Manes" was a finalist for the Nebula, Hugo, and World Fantasy awards. By that time she had also started writing in other genres. In 1994, Springer received the James

Tiptree Jr. Award for the gender-bending novel, *Larque on the Wing*; in 1995, she won the Edgar Allan Poe Award for her young adult mystery, *Toughing It*; and in 1996, she received an Edgar Award for children's literature for *Looking for Jamie Bridger*. But Springer never completely left fantasy behind her. Her Arthurian novel *I Am Mordred* won a Carolyn W. Field award in 1997, and its sister volume, *I Am Morgan le Fay*, was nominated for a Printz award in 2002.

After living most of her life in Pennsylvania, in 2007 Springer moved to an isolated area of the Florida Panhandle, where, despite being "retired," she wrote *The Oddling Prince* as a deliberate return to her beginnings as a writer. She has come to consider writing not so much a career as a calling. In a recent interview, Springer said, "Writing fiction has always, for me, been an alchemy of turning pain into poetry, ugliness into beauty. It has been a kind of redemption."